ORCHESTRATOR

Paul K. Pattengale

iUniverse, Inc.
New York   Bloomington

Copyright © 2010 by Paul K. Pattengale

All rights reserved. No part of this book may be used or reproduced by any means, graphic, electronic, or mechanical, including photocopying, recording, taping or by any information storage retrieval system without the written permission of the publisher except in the case of brief quotations embodied in critical articles and reviews.

All characters appearing in this work are fictitious. Any resemblance to real persons, living or dead, is purely coincidental.

iUniverse books may be ordered through booksellers or by contacting:

iUniverse
1663 Liberty Drive
Bloomington, IN 47403
www.iuniverse.com
1-800-Authors (1-800-288-4677)

Because of the dynamic nature of the Internet, any Web addresses or links contained in this book may have changed since publication and may no longer be valid. The views expressed in this work are solely those of the author and do not necessarily reflect the views of the publisher, and the publisher hereby disclaims any responsibility for them.

ISBN: 978-1-4401-7756-9 (sc)
ISBN: 978-1-4401-7757-6 (hc)
ISBN: 978-1-4401-8398-0 (ebook)

Printed in the United States of America

iUniverse rev. date: 02/03/2010

For Michael Crichton

and

Jason Fleiss

ACKNOWLEDGEMENTS

I would like to thank my wife, Elizabeth, for inspiration and patience; my three exceptional sons, Nicholas, Kenneth, and Brendan, for help with plot consistency, artistic design, and photography; my Los Feliz/Pasadena writers group, Mike Farquhar, Melina Price, Larry Kronish, Emily Adelsohn, Rudd Brown, Fran Yariv, Mary Marca, Darcy Hawes, Shelley Duffy, the late Bob Rodgers, and last, but not least, the late Mark McCloskey, for constructive comments and advice; Rick Beardsley, Richard Brewer, Beth Lieberman, Nina Wiener, Brooke Warner, and the late Dorris Halsey for critical reading of the manuscript; and finally, Tess Gerritsen and Michael Palmer, who showed me the way, and who gave generously of their time at the SEAK workshop on Cape Cod.

CHAPTER—1

The condition of the body was shocking. Dr. Jonathan Drake was accustomed to seeing dead people, but nothing like the deformed corpse lying in front of him on the autopsy table. He moved in closer. The skin was thickened and scaly, rendering the subject's physical features unrecognizable, and its oily smell evoked a sour taste in his mouth. Worst of all, it belonged to a nine-year-old boy.

He pulled the instrument tray toward him, cranked up the overhead light, and put on his mask and gloves. As he prepared to cut into the upper chest, he noticed something discolored in the hollows above both collarbones—the areas were dark blue, triangular, ribbed, and the size of a quarter. He cut into them with the scalpel and found that they were spongy in consistency and seemed to curl downward into the upper regions of the chest cavity. If these structures connected with the chest, he would have to confirm by a direct examination from the inside out.

He sliced through the cartilaginous junction of the ribs, exposing the thoracic cavities. The upper surfaces of both lungs were directly attached to these strange, triangular columns of tissue. He stared at the structures in disbelief. He had never seen a case like this.

Fifteen minutes later, he was still bent over the autopsy table, tugging at the thickened skin with a pair of forceps. It was hot, the smell was bad, and he was struggling.

The boy had come in with a bizarre diagnosis of icthyosis, a rare dermatological disease characterized by marked thickening of the outer skin layers, its name derived from its resemblance to a fish's scales. Icthyosis was rare enough, but the strange fleshy structures that connected the lungs to the outer surface of the body were beyond explanation. And why were the boy's back and chest muscles so large for his age?

Drake was relieved when Dr. Abraham Lowenstein, the attending pediatric pathologist, ambled through the doors. The tall, gaunt physician was a distinguished man in his early seventies with impeccable credentials and an international reputation.

"You look confused, Jon. I thought you'd be further along by now," he said, his eyes bright and inquisitive.

"I'm stuck. I don't know what these are." He gestured toward one of the discolored spongy structures above the boy's clavicle.

His eagle-like profile accentuated by the high-intensity overhead light, Lowenstein donned his mask and gloves and then lifted one of the structures with a pair of forceps. As he pulled on it, its connections with both the skin and the lung tissue became even more pronounced.

"Well, it's not a congenital pharyngeal pouch abnormality. I've never seen anything like it," Lowenstein said, letting go of the tissue. "Any other surprises?"

Suddenly, an entourage of interns and residents poured through the side door of the autopsy suite like frustrated theatergoers in search of a performance.

"Do you have anything on this kid yet?" asked an animated pediatric intern. "The chief resident's breathing down our necks."

Orchestrator   3

"It looks like he's turning into a fish," another said. He covered his nose with one hand to stifle the smell.

"When he came into the ER, his skin was so thick we couldn't even get an IV started," a resident said.

"What have you found so far?" another resident asked.

"Not much yet. Tell Dr. Cunningham I'll know more in a few hours," Jon answered.

He could have told them more, but he really didn't want them hanging around. A series of loud beeps sounded, and all of them fumbled for their pagers.

"We've got to go—there's a code red on 3 East," their leader announced, looking up from his display.

Jon watched the pack of white-clad house staff migrate through the morgue exit, the stainless steel doors slamming shut behind them. Dr. Lowenstein let out a sigh.

"What do you say we have a better look at the lungs?" Jon said.

Lowenstein nodded.

Jon picked up a scalpel and made a deep incision at the junction of the skin-lung connecting structure, exposing a series of large nodules. *Cancer!*

"Jesus." Jon pointed at the corrugated, mottled masses with the edge of the scalpel. This case had just got a lot more interesting.

"They're originating from the connecting structure," said Lowenstein. "What about the other side?"

Jon cut into the upper surface of the opposite lung and revealed a similar array of tumors.

"Same story over here," he said, amazed.

"This is a special case, Jon. I shudder to think what this child might have been exposed to."

"We don't have much to go on. A charity group called the Flying Samaritans airlifted him from a remote area of Baja California. The admitting diagnosis was shortness of breath."

"That is most unusual," Lowenstein said. "What's our plan?"

4   *Paul K. Pattengale*

"I'll take all the relevant sections. We might be able to make more sense out of it under the microscope," Jon said.

"Good idea." Lowenstein looked at his watch. "I've got to run to a medical staff meeting. If you can think of anything else, do it."

After Lowenstein had gone, Jon cut the necessary microscopic sections of the skin-lung connecting structures and saved some extra pieces for his research lab. After sectioning the rest of the internal organs and finishing the remainder of the autopsy, he removed his gloves and took a series of digital photographs, which included both the body's exterior and interior.

Nothing else could be accomplished at the autopsy table, so Jon went to the sink and cleaned up. The act of performing a postmortem aroused mixed feelings. Although the dissection of dead bodies was viscerally unsettling and spiritually distasteful, autopsy pathology presented him with an opportunity to understand how a particular disease affected the human condition. It also activated his scientific mind, inspiring him to push experiments in his research lab to the edge, the results of which would be eventually applied to the diagnosis, treatment, and prevention of disease in the future. Bench to Bedside, the process was called.

Multiple cancers and tissue malformations in a nine-year-old with icthyosis—it was outrageous and demanded a scientific explanation. He sat down at the steel desk and dictated the case. While he was arranging his notes, the phone rang.

"Autopsy room, Dr. Drake here."

"Dr. Drake, this is the charge nurse on 4 West. Dr. Cunningham wants to know when he can go over the autopsy findings with you."

"Give me another thirty minutes." He checked his watch. "Tell him around seven-thirty."

Jon hated being pressured to come up with a final diagnosis, especially with an unusual case. It only reinforced his dislike of aggressive, egotistical clinicians who expected the rest of the world to do their bidding on short notice, if not yesterday.

Thirty minutes later, Roger Cunningham and another man with a stethoscope draped over his shoulders appeared in the doorway. Jon's heart started racing as he stared at the taller, bearded man.

"Elliot? Is that you?"

"You know Dr. Adams?" Cunningham asked.

"Jon and I are old high school buds," the man answered. "I know it's been a long time. Don't look like you've just seen a ghost."

"I feel like I have," Jon said. "What are you doing here?"

"I've been volunteering for the Flying Sams from my pediatric practice in the Valley. Roger and I saw Jose in Baja at the Santa Inez clinic, and I was part of the airlift to L.A. I had to find out what happened. It was so sudden and tragic," Adams said, a pained look on his face.

"Sorry to break up your reunion, gents, but I've got a dead kid to explain," Cunningham said.

"That makes two of us," Jon said, walking over to the computer console. He pressed a key, and the Provisional Anatomic Diagnosis came up on the screen.

He recounted what he had in his notes and showed them a digital photographic image of the dissected skin-lung connecting structure, and of the cut surface of the lung.

"The cancers are huge, and they're connected to those weird structures, aren't they? Is there anything in the medical literature on this?" Cunningham asked.

"Not that I'm aware of. I'm still going to run a literature search, and Lowenstein said he would rush the permanent micros. They should be back tomorrow. In the meantime, I'm preparing a frozen section from the connecting structure. I'm also going to analyze its DNA."

Jon pointed at the vial of tissue on a bed of dry ice.

"I still don't know why I didn't spot those structures on

his skin when I examined him," Cunningham said, nervously shifting his shoulders.

"They were probably flesh-colored and inconspicuous before the boy died," Jon said.

"That would explain it then," Cunningham said, looking relieved. "Anything else?"

"Yeah, as a matter of fact, the kid's upper back and chest muscles were enlarged. I was starting to wonder if he had been working out."

"You mean like lifting weights?" Elliot asked.

"I know, it's preposterous, a nine-year-old indigent kid from Mexico getting buffed out. There's got to be some other explanation. Here's what they looked like."

Jon brought up an enhanced computer image that showed a side-by-side composite of the boy's prominent chest and back musculature.

"You're right, this kid definitely has hypertrophy of both the scapular and pectoral muscles," Cunningham said. He paused and then walked back and forth shaking his index finger. "And now that you mention it, I remember somebody on the Medevac Unit remarking that the upper muscle groups on his chest and back were way big." When he stopped pacing, his pager sounded.

"Well, gentlemen, I have another emergency on the ward. Elliot, stay in touch," Cunningham said, then turned in Jon's direction. "And Dr. Drake, I'd like to have a look at the permanent micros with you and Dr. Lowenstein."

"Not a problem."

"Later then," Cunningham said, hurrying out of the autopsy suite.

Jon took a deep breath and looked at Elliot.

"A bit intense, wouldn't you say?"

"He's a pain in the ass, but he means well."

Jon remained silent as he looked his old friend up and down. "I still can't believe it's you," he said.

"It's been a long time, Jon. The last time I saw you was at your dad's funeral. I have been keeping up with your career moves, though. Mom told me that you left biotech for an academic pathology residency."

"How did she know that?"

"She still stays in touch with your mom, believe it or not."

Jon didn't respond.

"I'm on call tonight, and I've got to hit the road." As Elliot turned toward the door, a technician dressed in a white coat walked in.

"Here's the frozen section you requested, Dr. Drake," he said, handing him a stained glass slide.

Minutes later, Jon and Elliot were looking into a two-headed microscope at the far end of the morgue.

"I took this section from the skin-lung connecting structure because it looked like the cancers were arising from it." He moved the slide around and focused the microscope. "My hunch was right: the tumors are growing out of the structure and are extending into the lung tissue."

"What kind of tumor is it?" Elliot asked.

"That's the amazing part," Jon replied, moving the slide from side to side. "It's a mosaic of miniature embryonic organs with malignant transformation occurring in each of them."

"Embryonic organs, multiple cancers? Be more specific, Jon, I'm not a pathologist."

"Okay, here's fetal pancreatic tissue with pancreatic cell cancer," Jon said, highlighting the cells with an illuminated arrow. "And fetal adrenal tissue with adrenal cell cancer, and fetal bone marrow with white blood cell leukemia, and on and on it goes—fetal kidney, fetal liver, and ..." He pushed back from the microscope, took a deep breath, and wiped a thin line of sweat from his forehead. Looking back into the scope, he said, "What's more startling is that these fetal organs and their cancers are originating from this line of stem cells in the connecting structure."

It was Elliot's turn to position the arrow. "These guys, right?" he asked, pointing to a tight row of dark blue cells.

Jon nodded enthusiastically. "And they're morphing into full-blown cancers right before our eyes! If I had only gotten some tissue while the boy was still alive, I would have had a decent shot at pinpointing what caused the stem cells to form the tumors."

"I completely forgot." Elliot hit his forehead lightly with his palm. "The boy has a younger brother with thick skin. Maybe he's got the same condition. Both boys were seen at the clinic."

"A younger brother—*alive*? We have to find him!"

"We?"

"When are you going back to Baja?"

"This weekend."

"I'm going with you. I've got a couple of days off. We can catch up on old times."

"Okay, then, it's a deal. We can always use more doctors."

Jon smiled.

"Give me a call and I'll set you up with one of our pilots. We're flying out of Van Nuys on Saturday morning," he said, handing him a business card.

After Elliot left, Jon changed back into his street clothes and tracked down the morgue attendant at the other end of the basement, where he was playing cards with some of the other employees.

"Hey, Doc. You done with the body?" He glanced up from his hand.

"It's ready to be sewn up, Thompson. And if Dr. Lowenstein comes back later, tell him I left the organs in the fridge. He may want to examine them."

Five minutes later he was making his way to the parking garage. While crossing Sunset Boulevard, the palm trees waving in the wind, he obsessed on the white blood cell cancer he had just seen in the dead child. His father had died from leukemia. More ominous than that, his own family was genetically predisposed, and he could be next. It was this cancer that Jon had vowed to cure in his lifetime. He had to find the dead boy's younger brother. He had to go to Baja.

CHAPTER—2

Jon drove up the long, concrete-walled driveway to his home in the San Raphael area of Pasadena. After parking his BMW 745i in the rear carriage house, he pulled his briefcase from the back seat, and made his way through an obstacle course of strewn bicycles, skateboards, and water pistols abandoned earlier that day by his nephews. He wished that he had been there to play with them. Christ! But there was never enough time—he had to make some.

As Jon unlocked the back door, the sound of distant wind chimes brought tidings of the Santa Anas. *Dry devil winds.* He wondered how many arsonists were poised to strike, and how high the hospital census would be driven with the acute respiratory admissions they triggered.

He pushed open the door and greeted Chelsea, his chocolate Lab. His sinuses tightened. He hoped he had left the humidifier on in the bedroom.

Heading for the refrigerator and resisting a strong urge to open a can of malt liquor, he eyed a brief note posted on its door. He put down his briefcase, took a swig of bottled water, and read his sister's neat handwriting.

Sorry Mark and Paul made such a mess. Had to rush off to soccer practice and then home to meet Bob and the contractor. This remodel is taking forever! We're spending the night at our place, not sure about tomorrow night. Will clean up tomorrow. I brought Chelsea down from the upper yard and fed her. The boys want you to take them to the zoo. I'll call you later.

Love ya, Cathleen

He tossed the note onto the kitchen table, finished the bottle of water, and walked down the long, partially lit hallway. Elliot had fallen hard for his sister in high school. What would her thoughts be now?

God, it had actually been thirteen years since they had last seen him. Jon had talked to Elliot on the phone a couple of times after Dad's funeral and had received the perfunctory Christmas cards from Elliot's family, but they had never reconnected after Benjamin Drake's death in June of their senior year at La Canada High School. Elliot's father had been unexpectedly transferred, and he and his family had moved out of L.A. early that summer. Elliot went off to college on the East Coast and then medical school on the Caribbean island of Grenada. Jon had lost track of him after that.

Jon's memories were interrupted by a staccato beeping from his computer. He quickly rounded the corner, entered the mahogany-lined study, with Chelsea close behind, and saw that the literature search he had requested earlier in the day from the National Library of Medicine was ready for viewing. He scrolled through the search, pausing on the key points:

Icthyosis: a group of inherited skin disorders in which the skin is excessively oily and covered by an accumulation of fishlike scales.

He enlarged the inset photo of a representative pediatric

patient and then clicked onto the 3-D option. He found the center of rotation and dragged the mouse through the x-, y-, and z-axes, systematically viewing the virtual body of the disfigured, thick-skinned child in all three dimensions. He then searched for the subtype that appeared to best fit with Jose Gonzalez's condition at death.

Icthyosis simplex: a skin disease of early childhood, which often affects members of the same family.

This might explain the surviving younger brother in Baja having a similar condition, but it certainly didn't explain the bizarre skin-lung connections or the multiple cancers. Furthermore, there were no publications documenting skin-lung congenital anomalies and/or lung tumors in patients with simple icthyosis. What kind of kid was this?

He heard coyotes baying in the distance. Were they coming down from the San Gabriel foothills? The dog raised its ears and growled.

"Chill, girl," he said, stroking her head until she stopped and lay down on the floor next to him.

Two malt liquors later, he was in bed staring at the ceiling. He heard them again and jolted up, looking from left to right across the full circumference of the bay window. Was there a full moon tonight? A slow scan of the Los Angeles skyline from southeast to southwest unveiled Orion's Belt sparkling in the southern sky over the shimmering city lights. Seeing that there was no full moon, and attributing the coyotes to the Santa Ana winds, he calmed his dog, lay back down, and tried to fall asleep.

Soon his thoughts again drifted back to his father. Did he really want to catch up with Elliot on old times? He didn't really want to relive the pain of his father's death. His life, as well as his mother's and sister's, had never been the same. He wanted to cry but couldn't. He finally dozed off at midnight, thinking about the last time he had seen his dad alive.

It was his high school graduation. His father had just completed another exhausting round of chemotherapy, and despite his weakened condition he had somehow managed to make it to the school auditorium. Jon could still see him sitting there in his three-piece suit next to his mother in the audience.

When he and Elliot returned to the house later that night after dropping off their dates, several emergency vehicles were parked on the street and in the driveway. The coroner's van was the one Jon remembered the most.

§

At two A.M. the phone rang. Jon woke up in a sweat, his heart pounding in his throat. He picked up the receiver from the night table and managed a brisk hello.

"Jon. It's Abe Lowenstein. There's been a security breach here at the morgue. They tried to get the boy's body."

"Who's they?"

"Two guys in black suits showed up with a hearse and tried to claim the body. The release papers didn't match, and the morgue clerk called security in time to scare them off."

"Is anything missing?" Jon asked.

"I don't think so," Lowenstein answered.

"I'm worried about the morgue freezer," Jon said. "The abnormal tissues are there in a plastic vial. We were going to extract DNA from them in the morning."

"Looks okay to me from where I'm standing, Jon. The lock's in place and the attendant says they left in a hurry."

"Good."

"Jon, something else."

"What's that?" he asked, standing up and walking away from the bed.

"I kept thinking about the autopsy. I went back and retrieved some of the extra lung tissue from the chest cavity before the body was brought back to the morgue compartment."

"Why?"

"The lungs looked boggy and heavy."

"Because of the tumors?"

"No, the lungs had very little air left in them. The pieces that I saved didn't float in water or in the chemical fixative. Instead, they sank to the bottom."

"They sank?"

Jon moved the receiver to his other ear and sat back down on the bed. He was wide awake.

"Affirmative. So I extracted some tissue fluid and ran it through the chemistry analyzer. It had a very high mineral-salt content. I started to wonder if the boy had drowned in the ocean. Where did you say he was from?"

"That's odd. He was airlifted from the Santa Inez clinic. It's supposed to be in a remote mountainous area in central Baja, nowhere near the ocean. I'll confirm that for you. I'm scheduled to go there this weekend to look for his younger brother. He might have the same condition."

"That's exciting, Jon. Wish I were going with you. This kid really has me going. Just remember, if we suspect Jose was drowned, we have to report it to the county coroner."

"Dr. Lowenstein, I ran a literature search on icthyosis, and there were no reported cases associated with either skin-lung structural abnormalities or lung tumors." Chelsea had jumped up on the bed, and he began to stroke her.

"Doesn't surprise me a bit. I've never seen anything quite like it. There's something crazy going on with these kids, and somebody else besides us is definitely interested. I'll speak to you in the a.m. I've got a presentation to prepare for the big pediatric path meeting in Boston next week. In fact, with your permission, I would like to discuss this case with my Harvard colleagues."

"Do it," Jon answered.

"I will," Lowenstein said. "Good night then." He hung up.

Jon wondered how a man of Abraham Lowenstein's age could

still stay excited about morbidity and mortality—especially at this hour of the morning.

He lay back down, unable to think about anything but Jose's deformed body and the aberrant stem cells that formed his cancers. He shivered, and for the first time, felt scared. Had the boy drowned, or worse yet, been drowned? What had really happened to the poor kid? He had to know.

CHAPTER—3

The next morning, after parking in the doctor's garage, Jon went directly to the tenth floor of the Research Tower. When the elevator doors opened, he narrowly missed bumping into his research technician, Diane Peterson, a lean, green-eyed redhead in her late twenties. She was attempting to get into the same elevator, but quickly pulled him aside into the open hallway, allowing the elevator doors to close behind them.

"We need to talk," she said. "Abe Lowenstein brought over some frozen autopsy tissue earlier this morning and has been calling me every fifteen minutes. He keeps jabbering about special DNA studies. Says the fresh tissues he saved were useless. What's going on?"

"Diane, we did this crazy autopsy yesterday afternoon, and if that wasn't enough, two men tried to break into the morgue last night. They were after the boy's body. Is everything okay up here?"

"As far as I can tell," she said.

"What does he mean by useless? What happened to the fresh autopsy tissues?" Jon asked.

"He didn't say."

16

Orchestrator   17

"Where's the frozen tissue?"

"In our Revco," she said.

"We better have a look at it," Jon said.

They rounded the corner, went halfway down the hall, and entered the common equipment room where the Revco freezers were kept. Jon disengaged the rotary slip lock with a ninety-degree upward motion, and the large, heavy door creaked open, exposing a tier of Styrofoam panels that puffed condensed moisture like cigarette smoke. He opened the top panel.

"There it is," she said, pointing to the vial in the middle.

He carefully picked up a plastic container, which was neatly marked on the outside with indelible ink: *Gonzalez, Jose. Skin-Lung Connecting Structure, Right Side. Autopsy #99-33.* He unscrewed the top of the container, and they peered into the foggy interior. Jon blew the vapor aside and studied the vial's contents.

"It looks just like it did last night. I wonder what he's worried about."

"Haven't a clue. What do you want us to do with the specimen?" she asked.

"Start with a DNA screen on the stem cells."

"Then what?"

"I'll check in with you later after I've talked to Lowenstein. Sorry to run off, but I'm late for morning conference."

He walked out the hallway door and headed for the elevator.

"Jon, one more thing, a Dr. David Kreeger called several times, sent a letter, and said you hadn't answered his e-mails. Something about needing your transgenic leukemia mice. He sounded like a bigwig."

"Affirmative, he's the CEO of Pathgene, International. If he calls back, tell him he can't have them until after my paper is published. I'll try and remember to contact him. Remind me."

§

The morning had come and gone before Jon had a chance to track down Abe Lowenstein about the Gonzalez autopsy. After the departmental secretary had told him that the old professor was in court testifying on the plaintiff's behalf in a disputed case of sudden infant death syndrome, Jon went to his hospital office and began preparing his talk for the Cancer Biology Consortium. He was scheduled to present his research findings the following week to a select, sequestered audience of academic, business, and entrepreneurial types at a hotel downtown.

His seminal work with transgenic mice could now be clinically applied to early diagnoses and better treatments for certain human white blood cell cancers. But despite these advances, he was still miles away from understanding and curing the drug-resistant, refractory leukemia that had killed his father.

He refocused on the Gonzalez autopsy, its unusual tissues, and the excessive number of stem cells. If only he had gotten access to them before the boy died—*living stem cells* would have given him a fighting chance to pinpoint the precise molecular events that had triggered the formation of the boy's leukemia. Once causality was established, a cure would be feasible and within reach. Maybe the stem cell DNA from the autopsy would reveal something. Maybe he would get another chance with Jose's younger brother. But he had to find him alive!

§

At one P.M. David Fox, a fellow pathology resident, popped his head into the office.

"Ready to do lunch, Professor?" he asked. "It looks like you're working way too hard. In fact, I know you are. You've missed our last two softball games." He drew up his arms and mocked a swing. "We could have used your bat against radiology. What's been happening?"

Before he could answer, Jon spotted the frayed backside of a plaid sport coat whisk across the hallway.

Orchestrator 19

"That was Dr. Lowenstein, wasn't it?" Jon asked.

"I think so. I saw him earlier this morning motoring around like the Roadrunner. I've never seen the old guy so animated. What did you guys turn up on that kid yesterday?"

"I'm about to find out," Jon said starting for the hallway.

Fox followed, sticking his head out into the corridor, and then chasing him for a few steps.

"Jon, the next game is a week from Saturday at three. Bring a date—it's coed this time."

"I'll try but I'm super busy, Dave," Jon yelled back as he ran after Lowenstein. He finally caught up with him at the far end of the hallway near the entrance to the autopsy room.

"Dr. Lowenstein, I've been looking for you all morning."

"Sorry, I was stuck in court. Come with me, young man."

Jon followed Lowenstein through the double steel doors of the autopsy suite. When they reached the metal cutting table, he could feel his sinuses burning as the acrid smell of tissue fixatives permeated the air around them.

Lowenstein grabbed a bottle of formaldehyde and swirled the tissue in the bottom of the glass jar.

"Remember what I told you on the phone last night about the lung tissue?"

"You said it was heavy, had a high mineral salt content, and didn't float in the fixative."

"That's right," he said, setting the jar down and heading for the refrigerator. "I wanted to run some more tests, but it got to be too late. So I saved some of the fresh tissue and put it in the fridge thinking that I could work on it this morning before court."

He opened the door of the autopsy room refrigerator and carefully took out a cold, cloth-covered metal pan, placing it on the table and peeling off the covering.

"This is the way I found it."

A decomposing, liquid amalgam of tissue glowed with a reddish-orange hue from the pan. While Lowenstein put on a pair of rubber gloves and opened a tin of surgical instruments,

Jon gasped at a stench so putrid that he tried to hold his breath while choking back the urge to vomit.

"It looks like rotten fruit," Jon said, gulping his saliva.

"It's almost pure liquid," Lowenstein said, probing the fluid remains of the tissue with a pair of steel forceps. "And what's even more amazing is that it happened in the cold at four degrees centigrade. I've seen tissue decomposition in my time, but never so fast, and not with this consistency and color. This, combined with the suspicion of drowning, definitely makes it a coroner's case. We need to transfer the body as soon as possible."

Lowenstein took off the gloves and carefully cleaned the lenses of his glasses with his handkerchief. He took a deep breath.

"Dr. Lowenstein, what about the body? Do you think ...?" Abe looked startled.

"I was in such a rush, it completely slipped my mind. I didn't even ..."

Not missing a beat, they left the autopsy room and walked through another pair of adjoining steel doors, which opened into the large morgue suite. They found two attendants sitting on a steel gurney at the far end of the room. One was strumming an acoustic guitar to loud music emanating from a stereo boom box; the other was sitting sideways playing solitaire. Jon recognized the card player as the autopsy assistant who had helped him the night before. He looked up at them and turned the volume down on the sound system.

"Hey, Doc, what's doing? You need some help?" he asked.

"Yes, Thompson. Dr. Lowenstein and I want to have a look at the body we autopsied last night. What's the locator number?"

The attendant picked up a clipboard and scanned the paper.

"Station 3B, follow me," he said, pointing at the steel tier on the far right and walking toward it.

Drake and Lowenstein approached the expansive wall of steel compartments and watched while the attendant opened the door and pushed the trigger-release mechanism on the body tray. It shot outward and slammed into its full stop position, displaying the brightly colored, putrid remains of Jose Gonzalez's body quivering from the impact like an oversized Jell-O mold. The other attendant, his eyes wide and bulging, tentatively joined them.

"Chill out, Hawkins, and get a hold of yourself. It's not going to bite you," Thompson said. "The docs and I did a regular autopsy on this poor boy yesterday, and he sure didn't go into cold storage looking like this."

"What are we doin' with the remains?" Hawkins said holding his nose.

Jon and the two attendants looked to Lowenstein for the answer.

"Scrape up what you can and put it in a plastic body bag," he said. "Fill out a report, and transfer the remains to the coroner's office. I'll call him and explain the situation. Abner Woods is an old friend of mine."

"Okay, Doc," Hawkins said.

"Did anyone try to claim the body this morning?" Jon asked.

"No, Doc Drake, not so far. Not much left to claim anymore, is there," he answered as both doctors left the morgue through the autopsy suite.

"Jon, I've got to go, but I'll catch up with you later. Meet me in my office at five and we'll have a look at the micro slides."

After Lowenstein had left the autopsy room, Jon heard music playing. He moved closer to the morgue entrance, pushed one of the doors open, and heard someone humming loudly to "Knockin' On Heaven's Door." He let the steel door slam shut and walked away.

§

Two hours later, Jon's head was still spinning. He had made some progress on his cancer biology presentation but found himself distracted by the day's events. He had also learned that

Lowenstein had personally escorted the boy's decomposed corpse to the coroner's office. He checked his watch and hoped that the old professor would be back by five P.M. to review the autopsy slides.

Feeling antsy, he decided to do the five-minute walk from the hospital across a grassy quadrangle to the Research Tower to see if Diane had some preliminary results on the stem cell DNA. When he got there, he saw his graduate student, Chris, looking up at him from the bench top surrounded by reagent bottles. He held a rack of test tubes in one hand and a pipette in the other. "Dr. Drake," he finally managed.

"Quit staring, it's really me. How are you?" Jon asked.

"Sorry, Dr. Drake, I didn't expect to see you. You've been so busy lately." He put down the test tube rack. "I'm doing okay though. I've been thinking of calling a committee meeting to see if I'm ready for my oral qualifying exam. What do you think?"

"If you think you're ready, go for it," Jon said, looking around the lab, distracted. "Where's Diane?"

"I think she's in your office inputting data into the computer."

Jon walked into the office, where Diane was hunched over the keyboard. He sat down next to her.

"You startled me. I thought you were going to call me first."

"Sorry, I couldn't stay away. Have you got anything yet on the autopsy tissue?" he asked.

"I did one round of extraction on the amplified stem cell DNA and ran it through the analyzer. It was a little degraded, but I think we have enough for a good analysis. I'm transferring the data from the disc to the hard drive," she said, punching in a series of commands.

"Here comes the first run," Jon said, studying the monitor. "Chris, come in here."

Chris joined them at the computer as Jon read the results out loud.

"Run Date: Tuesday, 12/10, Specimen 99-33. Stem Cell

DNA Physical Characteristics: High Z-DNA Percentage with a complete absence of methyl groups. End of Run."

"Man, that DNA's supercharged. Humans aren't supposed to have that profile," Chris said, moving in closer for a better look. "Can it give us the actual percentages?"

"Supercharged DNA?" Diane asked, skeptically. "I need an update."

"Let's see if I can reconfigure it," Jon said, giving the computer a series of commands. "Here it is. Z-DNA, ninety-five percent of Total. Methyl groups, zero percent of Total. It's hard to believe, isn't it?" He looked at Chris. "Take it away. You're the student. Make it simple and to the point. Give us an update. Pretend it's an exam question."

"Okay, here goes. DNA exists as a double helix that's coiled in a right-handed configuration. Though not normally found in nature, DNA can theoretically exist in a series of left-handed turns called Z-DNA. Unlike right-handed DNA, Z-DNA, though double-stranded, is loose and not as tightly coiled, and some have postulated that this relaxed state renders the genetic material more accessible to the cell for rapid increases in both cell number and function."

"And the lack of DNA methylation?" Jon asked.

"That completely astounds me," he said. "Methyl groups are associated with DNA inactivity. If you take all the methyl groups away and couple it with the Z-DNA configuration, the stem cell DNA is wild and crazy."

"So by supercharged, you really mean super-fast," Diane said.

"Exactly!" Chris answered.

"Super-fast DNA," Jon mumbled. *Had they discovered an entirely new species of DNA?*

His cell phone rang twice. Jon hesitated, looking at the caller ID. It was his sister's phone number.

"Hello."

"I hope I'm not bothering you."

"No worries, Cath. What's happening?" he asked trying to contain his excitement.

"When the boys and I were at your house yesterday, an obnoxious courier from a biotech company called Pathgene tried to deliver an envelope to the front door. Since he was such a jerk, I refused to sign for it. I told him you weren't home."

"What did he do?"

"He grumbled and left in a hurry. They'll probably try you at work."

"They already have. Their CEO wants some of my mice. I'll deal with it. Sorry for the hassle."

"No problem. Jon, something else, Paul and Mark want to know when you guys are going to the zoo. They said you promised to take them to see the koalas."

"Tell me about it. Paul has been texting me nonstop."

"I told his father not to buy him a cell phone. A ten-year-old, can you believe it? Next thing you know, his eight-year-old brother will have one."

"The technology works for me. I feel more connected to them."

"That's a nice spin," she said, her voice softening.

He hesitated. "It's going to be hard to fit them in this weekend." He told her about his encounter with Elliot, promising that they would all try to get together for a reunion after the Baja trip.

She laughed. "I'm not so sure I want to, Jon. It's been a long time, if you know what I mean."

He paused. "Hey, Cath, how about between Christmas and New Year's? I could take off a day then and go with the boys."

"Sure, we're around. This remodel is like an albatross. We're not going anywhere. Paul and Mark would love to spend a day with their uncle. Sounds like a plan. Let us know what day works for you."

§

Abe Lowenstein removed the plastic dust cover, turned on the sub stage light source, and placed the first glass slide labeled *Lung* on his four-headed microscope.

"Are you both in focus?"

"I am now," Jon answered after twisting the eyepieces on his side of the scope.

"Shoot," Roger Cunningham said.

"Then let's go where the action is," Lowenstein said, navigating the slide onto the stage of the multibarreled scope. "Hello there, I think we have a cause of death. This explains why the lung tissue was heavy and sank to the bottom of the fixative."

Jon watched as Abe deftly maneuvered through the lung tissue under high power and stopped on a representative area.

"Here's the telltale sign."

He positioned the arrow in the center of the slide.

"Look at all this fluid between the air sacs. I'm sure it's the salty liquid I measured on the chemical analyzer last night. Enough to asphyxiate anyone, especially a child."

"Also explains his abnormal blood gases," said Cunningham.

"Wait a minute," Jon interrupted. "If this boy aspirated water through his mouth and into his lungs, wouldn't we expect to see the fluid *inside* the air sacs and not *between* them?"

"Yes, if it were a conventional drowning. But nothing about this case is conventional, gentlemen. This unfortunate lad suffocated from the inside out, so to speak," Lowenstein said.

"But then how did the fluid get there?" Jon asked.

"Look at these tubules surrounding the air sacs. They have the same bubbly fluid in them. And these small tubes come together and form medium-sized tubes." He removed the slide and replaced it with another labeled *Skin-lung connecting structure*. "And the medium ones anastomose and form one large tube that opens onto the surface of the skin, right here," Lowenstein said, pointing with the arrow.

"So, what you're telling us is that water entered the lungs

from the skin through these channels in the skin-lung connecting structures," Jon said.

Lowenstein paused and looked at him.

"I think that's what I'm saying, Jon. And it also looks like the tubules grew down into the lungs from the boy's skin. I've never seen anything like this before."

He took out his handkerchief and wiped his forehead.

"And the multiple tumors?" Cunningham asked.

"Dr. Drake will address that," Lowenstein answered, placing another slide on the microscope's stage.

"The permanent micros confirm what Dr. Adams and I saw on the frozen section. The cancers are originating from the same line of stem cells that are forming the tubes and tubules of the connecting structure. They're located up and down the whole length of it."

"Look at all those stem cells!" Cunningham exclaimed.

Jon moved the slide up and down and back and forth on the stage, finally settling into a specific area.

"It's startling because the cancers resemble embryo tissues," he said. "Look, the stem cells are trying to form fetal organs, but instead they're transforming into sheets of cancer cells—like these leukemia cells arising from fetal bone marrow," he said, moving the pointer from cell to cell.

"And these findings fit with the DNA workup," Jon continued. "Our biochemical analysis showed that the predominant DNA species in the dividing stem cells was left-handed and that it was undermethylated. We dubbed it 'super-fast' because its theoretical structure predicts rapid cellular increases in growth and proliferation."

"Theoretical structure?" Cunningham asked.

"Well?" Jon hesitated. "Theoretical, because, to the best of my knowledge, that species of DNA has *never* been described in human beings."

CHAPTER—4

"Delta Charlie 306, this is Van Nuys tower. Cleared for takeoff on runway three-niner right."

"Roger that, this is Delta Charlie 306."

Jon watched as the pilot positioned the Cessna 172 on the open runway and inched the throttle to the full-power position. It was his first time in a small plane, and as it rolled down the runway, Jon's heart pounded. The pilot pulled back on the yoke and guided the small aircraft off the ground into the early morning mist of the south San Fernando Valley. Jon could feel his entire body pulsating with adrenaline as the Cessna continued its ascent through the light clouds, finally attaining a west-to-east cruising altitude of 6,500 feet. His sense of exhilaration was heightened even further by the wide-angle sweeping vistas of the Los Angeles basin.

"On a clear day, you can see all the way to Palm Springs," said the pilot, a graying man in his fifties named Don Buckingham.

"Is everybody comfortable?" he asked, looking back at Jon and Elliot, who were in the rear, and then to Yolanda Esquivel, the Santa Inez nursing coordinator, who was in the copilot's seat.

They all nodded.

"We should be clearing customs in Mexicali in about an hour, so sit back, relax and enjoy."

Jon took a deep breath, leaned back in his seat, and took in the view. Elliot, who seemed fidgety, spoke first.

"I haven't been able to stop thinking about what you said to me at breakfast—you know, the abnormal cancerous tissues, the funny DNA, the decomposed body." He rocked in his seat some more. "What's your take?"

Jon paused and took another deep breath before speaking.

"I think the skin-lung connecting tissues were derived from stem cell implants."

Elliot looked horrified.

"You mean he was part of a deliberate, cold-blooded experiment."

Jon nodded back. "It took a while for it to sink him, but it finally hit me."

"So, someone custom-designed them, then deliberately grafted them onto the boy's skin, and from there, they grew down and connected with the air sacs in his lungs," Elliot said, sitting up straight. "Why would anyone do that? And even if someone wanted to, who could have generated such a sophisticated genetic program? That kind of technology doesn't exist!"

"I know it's outrageous, and I don't have an easy answer, Elliot, but I do know that the tissues were bizarre, and the DNA was different."

"You said it was left-handed, undermethylated, and super-fast, right?"

Jon nodded again.

"So maybe this wild, super-fast DNA caused the skin implants to grow downward into the lungs, and on the way down, the DNA pushed the cells to reproduce so fast that they produced multiple cancers." He pulled nervously at his seat belt. "And, maybe for closers, the DNA raced the cells so hard and fast that it eventually exhausted itself, and the whole body turned to mush—even in the cold." He leaned forward, almost out of breath. "How's that for a mad scenario?"

"I couldn't have explained it any better," Jon said.

As Elliot slumped back into the seat, Jon stared into the distance contemplating their new theory. Elliot's knowledge of molecular biology was impressive. Jon had learned from him earlier that he had spent four years doing research in a gene therapy lab at U.C. San Francisco after completing his pediatric residency.

"Thanks for letting me come along, Elliot. I sure needed a break. I was burning out on work," he said, stretching in place.

"Same here. Every kid in the Valley has the flu."

A few minutes later, Elliot nodded off. As the Cessna droned toward the Mexican border, Jon took the opportunity to relax and chat with Yolanda.

"Dr. Adams looks pretty wiped out. Is he okay?" she asked.

"I think he's been working too hard," Jon replied, thinking that Elliot looked pale.

They talked about the history of the Flying Samaritans and its lofty mission to provide free health care to indigent Mexicans south of the border. Before long, Don lowered the right wing and started his descent.

"Mexicali tower, this is Delta Charlie 306. I'm ten miles out. Request instructions for landing."

"Delta Charlie 306, call me back two miles from final," the voice said with a Mexican accent.

Jon's ears popped as the plane descended in the direction of the Mexicali airport. When the altimeter dropped below 2,000 feet, the small aircraft began to bounce in the strong wind. He looked down to see the Mexican-American border flanked on either side by rolled barbed wire fences, which paralleled a central irrigation ditch. Don made a final pass of the control tower and landed the Cessna onto the main runway.

After a brief pit stop and a show of passports, they were back in the air. Yolanda stayed in front with Don, who was all smiles as he explained the instrument panel to her.

Elliot, who looked refreshed from his nap, was wide awake now.

"Jon, I've been meaning to tell you this for a while. You look fabulous. You're tall and strong," he said, reaching out and clasping Jon's upper arm. "And you lost your glasses. I never knew you had blue eyes. What gives?"

"It's been a long time, hasn't it?"

"Thirteen years since our high school graduation, to be exact," Elliot said.

"Okay. For starters, laser eye surgery cured my nearsightedness. I lucked out and had a big growth spurt in college, then did some serious weight training after that. I don't have a lot of time to go to the gym now, but I've got a set of weights at home. I try and keep up with my program, but it's a struggle."

"It's all about maintaining a balance, isn't it?" Elliot said.

"That's what my sister tells me. She says that I need to spend more time with my nephews and less time at work."

Elliot paused and reflected for several moments.

"I always had a crush on Cathleen, you know. That's why I hung out with you." He laughed and pushed at Jon's shoulder with the palm of his hand. "Just kidding, bro."

"It's just like the old days, huh? You always gave me a rough time, didn't you?" Jon responded with a mock punch to Elliot's jaw.

He pretended to dodge Jon's fist. "You were short, studious, good-natured, and fun to tease. What more can I say? You're my friend, my long-lost best buddy. But why didn't you call me after I left L.A.?"

"Why didn't you call me?" Jon countered.

"I don't have a good explanation. I guess I just flaked out."

"Same here," Jon said.

"I don't buy it," Elliot said. "You had to face your father's death, grow up in a hurry, and, from what I heard, had to support your mom and younger sister. That must have been a major league distraction."

"Agreed, it was all a big blur."

Elliot paused for a moment.

"So, how's your sister doing now?"

"She's doing great. She and her husband are both struggling lawyers, and they have two young boys. They don't live too far from me."

"And you, Jon. No wife, no kids?"

"Not yet."

"Me, neither."

He saw a look of longing flicker briefly across Elliot's face. A medical career had been as all-consuming for Elliot as it had proved to be for him.

"So, Jon, I heard about how you worked your way through college, got a full ride to U.C.L.A. Med, earned a Ph.D. in molecular bio on the side, launched your own biotech company ..."

"Whoa, slow down. You're going to give me a swelled head."

"I'm not done. And during that time you supported your mom and sis. You're a legend."

"Me, a legend?" Jon said, pointing to himself and looking surprised.

"At least you are to my mom."

They both laughed.

"Still, it had to have been tough on all of you," Elliot added.

"You've got that one right, it was terrible. All of Dad's life-insurance policies had suicide exclusions, and on top of that, he had made a bunch of bad investments. We even had to sell the beach house. We were pretty broke. Mom still hasn't gotten over it." Jon felt his jaw tighten.

He glanced at Elliot whose eyes were wide.

"Suicide! I never knew that! I thought it was a complication of the chemo."

"That what we let most folks think, but it was a sleeping pill overdose. He just couldn't take it anymore," he said, his back stiffening.

"I won't tell a soul, Jon. Thanks for sharing this with me. How difficult it must have been for you."

Elliot reached over and squeezed his shoulder.

"I'm still haunted by it," Jon said, his voice cracking. "Mom was so freaked out, she moved back to St. Louis to be near her sisters."

They sat silently for several minutes, looking at the desert scenery below.

"Why did you choose pathology? It sounds like you were doing fine in Biotech."

"Dad's leukemia had a huge effect on me. I wanted to understand it better: how it starts, how it spreads, what it looks like, how it kills, how to slow it down, how to cure it. Pathology embodies *all* of those concepts."

"Sounds like a passion," Elliot remarked.

"More like a fixation," Jon said, deciding not to disclose his own preoccupation and fear of cancer. He turned and looked away. "That's why the Gonzalez autopsy was so enlightening. I could actually see the leukemia forming from that line of stem cells. It was happening so fast."

"It wasn't only leukemia," Elliot said, trying to reestablish eye contact with Jon.

"Exactly, it was a smorgasbord of different cancers. If only I could have gotten some fresh tissue from Jose before he died, I would have had a shot at understanding what caused them. Transgenic mice are great, but they're limited." He looked back at Elliot.

"I see your point. Maybe we'll have a better chance with his brother."

"We have to find him. What's our plan?" Jon asked.

"The local rancher knows most of the people who visit the clinic. We'll start with him, and also have a look at the boys' charts."

"Sounds promising," Jon said, settling back into his seat.

Five minutes later, to the left of the plane, he saw the azure blue of the Sea of Cortez, which stood in sharp contrast to the washed-out brown of the Baja desert. Ahead in the distance was an inland range of large, arid auburn mountains. The plane maintained its cruising altitude of 8,000 feet, and forty-five minutes later had crossed the mountain chain. On the other side was a barren, rock-strewn plateau dotted with mesas. As the plane began its descent, he could see that the mesas were about 1,000 to 2,000 feet in height, with their brownish-black, flattened tops approximating the size of several football fields.

"There it is," Don Buckingham yelled, as he lowered his wing flaps and put down the landing gear.

Jon could now make out the end of a graveled runway, whose color blended into the desert floor. The bright orange windsock was clearly visible when the Cessna made its final approach and landed upwind.

As the plane taxied to a stop, Jon wondered how young Jose Gonzalez had come to misfortune in such a remote place as this.

§

The *Clinica Familia* was bustling with activity. By the time they had unloaded their gear from the plane and brought it the short distance to the clinic, there was a long line of families waiting for their chance to see a doctor. The first plane was joined by three more planeloads of American clinic volunteers, whom Jon later learned were a preplanned mix of pilots, translators, and health-allied professionals. While Elliot retrieved the boy's medical records, Yolanda visited the adjoining buildings to find the local rancher.

Jon was assigned to one of the medical examining rooms and given a Spanish translator. He saw a multitude of routine sore throats and runny noses before an older, dark-skinned man with aquiline features and deep creases in his face was escorted into the examining room by Elliot and Yolanda. The man removed his sombrero to reveal numerous red bumps on his face and neck. Elliot, who was holding two manila folders, came closer.

"Jose and Ricardo Gonzalez were here three weekends ago, and, according to the clinic records, were accompanied by this old Indian," he said. "The report says that both of them had thick skin and prominent upper body musculature. This is the lead we're looking for!"

"How did you find him?" Jon asked.

"He found us. He's got a skin problem, and he seems a little spaced," Elliot said.

"*Como se llama?*" Yolanda asked.

"*Ximicheya,*" he answered in a singsong pitch.

After several more minutes of conversation, she relayed the relevant details to Jon and Elliot.

"He's a Oaxacan Indian. His name means *estrella brilliante* in Spanish."

"And in English?" Jon asked.

"Brightest star in the sky."

"Awesome name. What brought him here?" Jon asked.

"*Cual es su problema?*" Yolanda asked, kindly.

He stripped off his red, gold, and green hand-woven shirt exposing a bronzed torso dotted with an array of raised, red lesions each about the size of a dime.

"Jesus, there must be a hundred of them," Jon said, as the man began to tell Yolanda his story.

"From what I can gather, he's a local shaman. He speaks Spanish with a strong Oaxacan inflection—I'm having trouble understanding him."

"Ask him what happened," Elliot said, examining the raised red wheals.

"He says he awoke at dawn and went to his sacred place to pray. He heard buzzing sounds, and suddenly a swarm of flying insects stung him on his face and body."

"He must have been praying without his shirt. There are

no bites below his waist. There aren't any stingers either, so I'm betting they were wasps," Elliot said.

As he was placing his stethoscope on the shaman's chest, a nurse with bright red stains splattered on her uniform burst into the room.

"Dr. Adams, I've got a kid vomiting blood in Room 4. Please come with me," she said.

"Here, Jon," he said, handing over the stethoscope. "See if you hear any wheezing. I'm thinking he may be having an allergic reaction."

After Elliot and the nurse left, Jon saw a look of panic come over the Indian's face. He had suddenly turned pale and was having trouble breathing.

Listening to his chest with the stethoscope, Jon heard the telltale whistling sounds resonating through the Indian's narrowed airways. His breathing was labored, and his lips were blue.

"He's wheezing, all right," he said, looking at Yolanda. "And I don't like his color."

Jon grabbed a blood pressure cuff off the examining table, placed it on the Indian's right arm, and took a reading.

"It's sixty over forty. He's going into shock and needs a shot of epinephrine," Jon said, looking around the examining room.

Without delay, Yolanda pulled the emergency syringe from its taped position on the wall and handed it to Jon. He removed the needle cover, plunged the needle deep into the Indian's thigh, and pushed the clear liquid into the belly of the muscle.

Twenty minutes later, the patient was breathing comfortably, with an IV in his right arm. Jon, Yolanda, and Elliot gathered around the makeshift hospital bed in a semicircle. The old Indian muttered some words.

"He says you saved his life. He wants to know what he can do for you," Yolanda said.

The Indian smiled and gestured toward Jon.

"First ask him if it's okay to call him Bright Star. Tell him it's gringo talk," Jon said.

"He says it's okay," Yolanda said.

"Then tell Bright Star to keep getting better. That's what he can do for me."

Bright Star reached and grasped Jon's right arm with his leathery hand.

"*Gratias,*" he said, tugging at Jon's sleeve.

"*No problema,*" Jon answered, gripping the Indian's arm. "Give him some more time to recover. We'll ask him about the boys a little later. He doesn't handle stress very well, plus I could use a break. I'll be back in about thirty." He headed for the door, smiling at Bright Star as he exited.

"Okay, later," Elliot said.

Jon walked out of the examining room and eased through the crowded waiting room. He paused, then crouched down and greeted several of the local children with a broad smile. One of them, a boy with dark, inquisitive eyes, wearing a Mickey Mouse sweatshirt, reached out and gently touched Jon's cheek. Moved by the boy's spontaneity and warmth, Jon pulled out his cell phone, cued up several pictures of his nephews, and showed them to the youngster.

"*Sus ninos,*" the boy said, pointing at Paul and Mark.

Jon nodded and smiled, basking in the short-lived joy of having his own children. Even if he had wanted to correct him, he didn't know the Spanish word for nephews. Jon waved to the boy as he pushed open the front door of the clinic. Once outside, he strolled past a string of old pickup trucks and a cadre of stray dogs. He took in the fresh air and checked his watch. It would be dark in a couple of hours. Even though the sun was low in the clear sky of this early December evening, the air was warm and embracing. In the distance on all sides, rock formations of varying sizes and shapes were visible, and multiple species of cactus dotted the Sonoran desert landscape. He had a clear view of the airstrip with its three parked airplanes, and on the opposite side of the clinic building was a cluster of single-story ranch-type dwellings. He refocused on the clinic and wondered about the events leading up to the Indian's asthma attack. Would Bright Star be able to help them find the younger brother?

Feeling revitalized, he returned to the clinic and found Elliot and Yolanda talking to Bright Star, who was sitting up in bed. His voice had an eerie quality, which alternated rhythmically from a high to a low pitch.

"He says the boys were orphans and he was their caretaker. He feels terrible about Jose," Elliot said.

"*Was* their caretaker? Where is the younger brother?" Jon said.

"*Donde es Ricardo?*" Yolanda asked.

Bright Star stuttered for a moment and broke eye contact with Yolanda.

"Hold the questions! We're rattling him, and he's stressing again," Jon said.

Elliot quickly positioned the blood-pressure cuff on his arm. Simultaneously, Jon put the diaphragm of the stethoscope on Bright Star's right lower chest.

"His blood pressure is low," Elliot said.

"And he's wheezing again," Jon added. "Push some more epi."

Bright Star's vital signs took an hour or so to return to normal. The decision was made to keep him overnight in the clinic for observation. They would have to save their questions for the morning. The clinic closed at five-thirty P.M., and Jon made the arrangements for a physician's assistant to remain behind and stay with Bright Star. He would spell the PA later that evening.

The staff was housed in the dwellings next to the clinic. Jon walked over to the modest-sized room he was sharing with Elliot and Don. When he entered, he noticed his roommates were dressing for a local fiesta hosted by the Mexican community.

"Geez, Jon, you gotta do better than that. It looks like you just walked out of an REI catalog. We're going to a fiesta, not a Sierra Club event," Elliot joked.

"That's who I am," he said, looking down at his hiking boots and khaki pants while unzipping his North Face parka. "Hiking and backpacking keep me sane."

"I can relate. Flying does it for me," Don added.

"Where do you shower around here?" Jon asked. He moved closer to the mirror, which hung over the old oak bureau, and ran his hands through his light brown hair. After all he had been through the past few days, he was definitely in the mood for a party.

"There's one in the central area between the ranch houses. Hope there's some hot water left," Don answered. He whistled as he doused his hands with cologne, rubbing it on both sides of his face and then on his arms. "Take a right turn out the front door and go straight about fifty yards. You can't miss it."

Jon stuffed a washcloth in his toiletries case, threw a towel over his shoulder, and headed outside. It was getting dark, but he was aided by the giant yellow globe of a rising full moon suspended above the desert floor. He could make out the small corral in the distance whose perimeter was rimmed with strings of brightly colored Christmas lights. He approached the structure.

The wooden door of the shower stall resembled the entrance to an old Western saloon. Two brightly lit oil lanterns adorned both sides of the shower entryway. He thought he could hear a soft feminine voice singing. Glistening water droplets danced off the exposed calves and bare feet of the shower's lone occupant. Her right leg was decorated with a gold anklet, which reflected the lantern lights and glimmered from below. Above the door, the stainless steel showerhead sent vertical streams of water onto a crown of blonde hair. Jon stopped in his tracks and let out a small cough.

"I'll be out in a minute," the voice said.

"No problem, I can wait," he answered.

He heard the valve turn and saw the water stream slow to an occasional drop. The door swung open, and out stepped a shapely woman in her early thirties, wrapped tight in a striped pink-and-white bath towel. He hadn't seen her at the clinic earlier.

"Hi, I'm Mona Larsen. I'm a translator for the Flying Samaritans. Sorry I can't shake your hand," she said clutching the towel tightly.

"I'm Jonathan Drake, one of the clinic doctors."

"See you at the party," she said, wiggling her bare feet into a pair of leather sandals. She looked at Jon, smiled, and headed for the cluster of ranch houses. As she walked off into the night, he could see her wet hair reflecting the bright moonlight.

CHAPTER—5

Jon arrived at the courtyard thirty minutes later to find the clinic volunteers gathered in small groups, talking, drinking and hovering over a well-laden table of local fare. A loud mariachi band played by the central fountain. He recognized Yolanda, who took it upon herself to introduce Jon to several of the clinic personnel.

"Jon, this is Bill O'Neill. When he's not flying his plane, he's working for the Department of Water and Power in Los Angeles. And this is Sylvia Rosen, a social worker from Santa Monica, and Elizabeth Bennington, a physical therapist from L.A."

"Don't let me interrupt," Jon replied, shaking hands and making eye contact with each of them.

"You're not. Bill's been telling us that the Mexican Federales have been looking for drug traffic in this area," the social worker said.

"Pretty arid climate to grow dope, wouldn't you say?" the physical therapist said.

"They're not looking for growers, they're looking for layover sites and hidden airstrips," Bill replied.

After several more introductions, Yolanda led Jon over to

40

Elliot, who was talking to an attractive young woman wearing a white-flowered luau dress.

"You know Elliot, of course," Yolanda said. "And this is one of our new translators, Mona Larsen from San Diego."

Jon had wondered what she would look like in clothes. He wasn't disappointed. Red lipstick highlighted a generous mouth and accentuated the deep blue of her eyes, while a long pair of pierced turquoise earrings dangled in the gentle wave of her shoulder-length blonde hair.

"Dr. Drake and I met earlier," she said, winking at him and extending her hand.

Jon circulated some more, meeting the rest of the staff and engaging a number of them in conversation. Later, he came upon Elliot, margarita in hand, still chatting with Mona.

"Hey, Jon. Great news. Mona and I were discussing our patient. What a coincidence! She knows Oaxacan dialects and is going to help us translate tomorrow morning."

"Thanks, Mona," Jon said. "We need all the help we can get."

"No problem, I'm there," she said, lifting her glass in agreement. "I'm going to grab some food before the line gets too long. I'm starving."

"Man, she's a babe and then some," Elliot said, watching Mona making her way to the buffet table.

"No argument here. I'm heading over to the clinic. I want to keep an eye on Bright Star."

"You want some help?"

"You're having way too much fun. I can handle it. I brought some work with me. I'm putting together a big presentation for Monday."

Ten minutes later, Jon entered the clinic building carrying a paper plate piled high with tacos, enchiladas, rice, and beans. A leather briefcase was slung over one shoulder and a day pack over the other. A physician assistant, an athletic-looking man in his mid-twenties, was sitting in the waiting room paging through a *Sports Illustrated* swimsuit issue.

"Dr. Drake, I'd say you're mighty hungry. Let me give you a hand," he said, putting down the magazine, taking the plate of food, and setting it on the desk.

"How's our patient doing, Robert?"

"He's good, blood pressure stable, lungs clear, resting comfortably."

"Great, I can take it from here. Go and enjoy the party."

After finishing his meal, Jon retrieved several pillows and a blanket from a cabinet and put them on the old sofa in the waiting room. Soon he was working from the makeshift bed with a PC perched on his lap and a view down the hallway to the shaman's room. Several hours and a Power Point presentation later, he dozed off.

His dream started with the weekend trip to the beach house in Santa Barbara, where he and his mother discovered that his father hadn't returned from his ritual walk on the Montecito beach. Something had happened, something bad—he had blacked out. Not long after the incident, a diagnostic MRI and a spinal tap had shown that Dad's leukemia had spread to his brain. In the throes of the dream, Jon began to sweat and tried to call out his father's name but couldn't get the words out. He awoke in the middle of the night and sat up on the sofa—then went to check on Bright Star.

The old man's bed was empty. The IV was unattached and hanging at the bedside. A nearby window was ajar. He looked outside and saw someone moving in the faint moonlight. After returning to the waiting room, he grabbed a jacket and a flashlight, stuffed an emergency first-aid kit in his day pack, and headed out the front door.

Once outside, he let his eyes adapt to the dark, then slowly walked in the direction of the moving figure. As he got closer, he could make out Bright Star's serape and heard him uttering a soft, low-pitched hum. Determined to intercept him, Jon switched on the flashlight and moved swiftly toward him. A person dressed in black was blocking his way. He tried to point the light at the intruder, but the person grabbed his wrist, pushing it aside.

"Back off. Don't interfere!" a female voice barked.

Jon was taken aback and hesitated. Then he exploded.

"*You* back off. That's my patient you're messing with. He pulled out his IV and left the clinic. He has an unstable medical condition. He needs me." Jon pushed against her, trying to regain control of the flashlight.

"I need him. He's a narcotic suspect," the person in black said, flashing an official photo ID, which read U.S. Drug Enforcement Agency in capital letters. As he scanned the woman's name below the picture, she relaxed her grip on his arm, allowing the flashlight to illuminate her face.

"Mona! It's you?" What the hell's going on here?" he asked, looking into her blue eyes. Strands of her blonde hair peeked out from underneath the black baseball cap.

"Look, Jon. Your patient is implicated big time in a Baja drug ring and he's going to lead me to his buddies. You're going to stay put. This is official government business."

"Nothing doing, he's not well. I don't care what he's done."

"Keep it down, don't blow my cover."

"I'll do whatever I have to do. He needs a doctor."

"Have it your way then, but you're coming with me. And don't fuck things up. I don't want to lose him. Let's go. He's headed east up that dry wash. Stay close to me and keep quiet," she said, pointing to the left and moving quickly in Bright Star's direction. Even though the full moon was low in the western sky, it was bright enough to light their way.

Jon matched Mona's pace, and as his eyes adjusted to the moonlight, he could see Bright Star walking thirty to forty yards in front of them. As they got nearer, he could hear his rhythmic chant.

"We don't want to get too close. I think he's in a trance, and I

44   *Paul K. Pattengale*

don't want to break it," she said, moving quietly and deliberately like a prowling feline.

Jon had to work to keep up with her. It was clear to him that she had the moves and the temperament of a seasoned professional and he had to trust her, at least for now. What choice did he have, he asked himself, looking back at the setting moon and checking his watch. Jesus, it was five-thirty A.M., and the night air was cold. He zipped up his jacket, but the wind still stung his face.

The dry wash had taken several large serpentine turns, and the ranch and clinic were no longer in sight. In the distance, they could see that it narrowed and entered a ravine, which was lined on either side by rocks and desert cactus. Mona stopped and turned to look at Jon. A kaleidoscopic display of red and green moved across the convex surfaces of her dilated, jet-black pupils. He jerked his head back for a view of the sky and saw a fast-moving, silent object with alternating red and green lights.

"What kind of aircraft is that?" Jon whispered.

"I don't know. I'm still trying to figure out how high it is. It's not DEA, that much I know."

They both watched as the object continued east at a high speed until it disappeared behind a distant mesa.

Jon could still hear Bright Star's haunting incantations, and strained to see him through the darkness.

"He stopped. We'll wait here," Mona whispered.

They crouched together on a rock in the middle of the wash, and he felt the warmth of her body.

When the faint orange glow of dawn was visible on the horizon, Bright Star was on the move again. Saguaro cacti flanked the rocky entrance to the ravine like giant sentinels with outstretched arms. Never looking back, the old Indian slowly made his way uphill through the narrow wash in the direction of a higher rocky plateau. A trickle of water was evident in the middle of the wash.

The ravine made several convoluted turns before the wash ended abruptly in a citadel of brown sandstone. Only twenty

Orchestrator   45

yards ahead of them, Bright Star's chanting had now changed in tone to a higher pitch as he scrambled up the rock face, soon disappearing from view. They both ran to the place where the old Indian had been standing. Only his footprints remained.

"Let's get a move on," Mona said.

Without thinking or looking down, Jon followed and scurried up the brown rock escarpment behind Mona until it began leveling off onto a plateau. As they ascended higher, palm tree fronds were now visible, and as they moved closer to the edge, he could see that the trees were surrounding a sunken circular pool of water about thirty yards in diameter. Their trunks cast long, angular shadows across the water's surface in the early morning light.

"There he is, between those two trees," she said.

"This must be the sacred place he was talking about when we examined him back at the clinic," Jon said. His eyes took a minute to adjust. Had Jose Gonzalez met his demise here, he wondered?

"I'm going down to get a closer look. I want to hear what he's saying."

Before Jon could react, Mona had already begun to make her way down the steep rock embankment. When he caught up with her, she was stooped beneath a rock overhang about ten yards behind Bright Star, who was sitting at the water's edge. To their right, a small stream meandered into the pool from under the rock ledge. Beyond that a dirt path followed the stream for a short distance and then disappeared to the left. Jon removed his day pack, took out a small plastic test tube with a blue screw top, and sampled the water in the stream.

He moved close to Mona, excited.

"I'm going to check out the composition of this fluid and see if it matches the chemical profile from the L.A. autopsy."

"Autopsy?" Mona asked.

"The boy I autopsied may have drowned here. I'll fill you in later. I'm going to see where the path goes. I'll be careful."

Before she could stop him, he headed down the dirt path to where it continued under the overhang and emerged into an open area with several wooden buildings. Jon strained to see if there were any signs of activity but saw none except for a bevy of wasps buzzing around. He decided to explore further and neared the largest of the three buildings. The front door was locked, so he circled the structure and tried without success to make out what was inside through the thick dust on the windowpanes. He moved on to scope out the second building, which turned out to be similar to the first. The third, the smallest of the three, wasn't a building really but a storehouse with an array of inactive generators. There seemed to be no one on site.

He returned to Mona and sat beside her.

"Sssh, what did you find?" she whispered.

"Some abandoned buildings, rusting generators, and a lot of dust."

Bright Star sat shirtless with his elbows on the knees of his crossed legs and his arms extended, palms facing upward. As Jon listened to him, he couldn't help but fixate on the multiple discolorations on his upper body.

"What's he saying?"

"He's praying to the earth spirits and asking them to intervene and stop the evil on the boys with the thick skin," she said, mimicking his robotic tones. "I don't get it. What evil?"

Before Jon could answer, he heard a low-level but distinct buzzing sound behind them. He turned around but saw nothing.

"Mona, do you hear that?"

"I hear it, but what is it?"

"There were some wasps back there, but ..." Within seconds, the buzzing became more intense. They watched the swarm emerge from the rock crevice behind them.

"They're crazed," Mona said, fear registering in her voice for the first time since Jon had met her.

He pulled her arm and ducked down low to avoid the frenzied

insects flying past them. The swarm viciously attacked Bright Star's head and exposed upper body. The old Indian screamed and began to flail. Within seconds, he fell over.

"I've got to help him," Jon yelled, trying to extract the emergency first aid kit from his day pack. While moving toward Bright Star, he felt several sharp flashes of pain on his neck. Wincing, he brushed the attacking wasps off the top of his jacket. When he finally reached him, the shaman lay lifeless on the ground, covered with wasps.

Mona had followed close behind Jon and stood over the body. "You really are nuts, aren't you," she screamed. "We're outta here, there's nothing you can do for him. He's not breathing, he's gone. He's dead!" She grabbed Jon's right arm and pulled him away. They hustled down the dirt path toward the small compound; in the early morning light, Jon now saw that there were wasps gathered under the wooden eaves of the structures.

"What are they attracted to?" Jon said, rubbing his neck.

"I don't know, but we're not going to stand here and find out," Mona said, steering them toward the front door of the larger building.

"It's locked," Jon said.

"Not for long," she said, rearing back and kicking the door with her foot. After another unsuccessful attempt, she picked up a rock, hurled it through the door's window, reached in, and unlocked it from the inside. She opened the door and ran in with Jon close behind.

"You okay?" she asked.

"I've got a few bites on my neck. Otherwise, just shaken up," he answered, trying to catch his breath.

"Jesus, what died in here?" she said, holding her nose.

She took out her flashlight and rapidly scanned the dimly lit room, which contained several bench tops and a series of alcoves that housed equipment of varying sizes and shapes.

"Slow down," Jon said, trying to identify a metal object resembling an antiquated washing machine.

She illuminated the alcove again, and Jon walked closer to inspect the machine in more detail.

"It's an old-model refrigerated centrifuge," he said. "And a water bath, and a ..."

She followed with the high-beam flashlight as he walked back into the main part of the room and entered a larger alcove.

"It's an upright Revco freezer. Mona, this is some kind of makeshift research lab."

"But it's not cold," she said, touching the front of the freezer.

"The place looks abandoned. You can't run a lab without electricity, and from the looks of it, the generators haven't been used in a while," he answered.

"What's a research lab doing in the middle of nowhere?" Mona asked.

"Good question. I've got a hunch. I want to see what's in this thawed-out freezer. Shine the light this way."

She reluctantly steered the light toward his hands while he unlatched the slip lock and swung the heavy metal door open. In the inner compartment, pushed to one side, was a small, decomposed body colored with a reddish-orange hue. A putrid stench emanated from the freezer.

"Great, it's the Saturday matinee monster. That does it, I'm calling for help," Mona said.

She lifted her sweatshirt over her face, pulled out a two-way radio from her belt, and walked toward the front door where the air was fresher. Seeing that several wasps had entered through the broken window, she attempted to cover the break with a piece of cardboard. Meanwhile, Jon had retrieved a camera from his day pack and was prepping to document the lab's interior.

"I'm going to shoot up this roll. Wait till I tell you about this kid's brother," he said, advancing the film.

"How can you tell it's a kid? And what about his brother?"

"If you can believe it, his older brother ended up the same way. I did his autopsy in L.A., and it became a coroner's case. That's why Elliot and I came to Baja, to locate his younger brother, and I think we may have found him. Bright Star was our link—he was their caretaker."

"So what was the old Indian praying for?" she asked, excitedly.

"To stop the evil experiments that occurred in this makeshift lab," Jon said, as he began shooting a panorama of photos from left to right, the successive strobe-like flashes giving the lab an eerie look. After finishing the roll of film, he returned to the front room where Mona was still trying to make radio contact with her colleagues.

"Shit, he's not answering! Where is he when I need him?"

She flipped the frequency dial back and forth, and shook the radio.

"I think I hear an airplane," Jon said, listening at the front door. "But it's hard to be sure with all that buzzing."

Mona leaned against the door and listened.

"I hear it too. I'm sending up the flare," she said pulling it from her day pack. "Move back."

She opened the front door, aimed the flare gun upward, and shot it. The flare hissed and smoked as it arced above the compound approximately fifty yards in the air, its wake scattering some of the wasps and its smoke trail appearing to calm the rest. Thirty seconds later, the radio crackled.

"This is Spider One, I can see your flare but I can't see you. Do you copy, Rover?"

"I copy, Spider One, can you read me? This is Rover. Where have you been? I've got Dr. Jonathan Drake with me and we're in a wooden building near the water hole. Our suspect needs medical help. Can you pick us up?" Mona asked.

"Sorry for the blackout, my radio's been twitchy. But roger, can do Rover. It's a go. There's a plateau about fifty yards to the south. I'll be there, pronto."

"Roger, Spider One, this is Rover. Give me a few minutes

to get to you. Keep your motor running. We've got a bunch of angry wasps down here. Do you copy?"

"Roger, I'm on my way."

"There he is," she said, spotting him through the window.

Jon looked in the direction of the chopping noise and saw a black helicopter flying toward them. The pilot made a pass over the buildings and landed on the plateau to their right. Mona and Jon darted from the dwelling and ran toward the waiting aircraft. The idling rotor's windy downdraft blew dust in their eyes but also kept the wasps at bay. Jon couldn't wait to jump in the back seat.

"Get your belts on, we're blowing this place," the pilot said, lifting the chopper off the ground.

"There's your suspect," the pilot said to his colleague in the copilot's seat.

From their position, Jon could see Bright Star's motionless body. A dark cloud of wasps still swarmed around him.

"You're talking about *my* patient. We can't leave him here," Jon yelled.

"Sorry, Doc, we're not equipped. I've called for a Medevac unit. They're on their way, and we're gone," the pilot said pulling back on the joystick.

CHAPTER—6

As the helicopter gained altitude, the pilot glanced over his shoulder. Jon was stuffing the camera in his pack.

"Been doing some sightseeing Doc?"

"Very funny, Larry," Mona said. "So where are we headed?"

"You better check it out with the boss. He sounded a little miffed that you let the doc go along for the ride. Worse than that, our prime suspect is history."

She glared at him as he straightened the bill of his *USS Nebraska* hat and smacked his bubble gum.

"Jesus, what does he expect? Dr. Drake insisted on going with me and almost blew my cover. I had no choice, I had to take him. Stringfellow can't fault me for that."

"I'd calm down if I were you, Mona. You're only going to make it worse. You're in enough hot water already."

"Butt out, Larry. I can handle myself."

She grabbed for the radio headset.

"This is going to be ugly," the pilot moaned to Jon.

After several minutes of heated conversation, Mona took off the headset and returned it to its place on the instrument panel. She looked back at Jon, obviously pissed.

51

"He's going to drop us off on the main road about a half mile from the clinic. We'll walk the rest of the way, or maybe hitch a ride," she yelled.

"Spider One to Home Base, waiting for instructions," the pilot said.

"Home Base to Spider One, Agent Larsen will instruct you," the voice said.

"Roger, Spider One out."

She glared at him again.

"Just double-checking. Take it easy. Don't take it personally." He lifted up his arms in surrender. "Look, ma, no hands."

"Fuck off, Larry. Put us down on the main road near that sign. The dirt road to the clinic forks off to the right about fifty yards from it."

"Whatever you say, ma'am."

He maneuvered the chopper as directed and touched down onto the asphalt surface.

"*Vamanos*, you guys. Grab your stuff, Doc. See ya 'round, Mona-san."

Mona hopped out onto the pavement, and Jon quickly followed. Ducking the swinging blade, they ran to the gravel shoulder and watched Larry lift the chopper off the highway.

"Asshole," Mona yelled, gesturing upward with her middle finger.

As Jon hoisted his pack onto his back and started walking toward the sign, the horror of all he had just witnessed finally struck him. He quickly turned to the side and vomited his guts out. While he continued to wretch with the dry heaves, Mona came closer and touched him.

"Jon, let's get off this gravel shoulder," she said, rubbing his back, and guiding him toward the clinic sign, which was on a patch of sand. "Like I said before, don't blame yourself for what happened. You gave it your best shot."

When they got to the sign, Jon had stopped heaving and was able to take off his pack. With Mona's help he sat down and propped himself against the sign. She pulled out his canteen from his pack and offered him a sip of water.

"Are you okay, now?"

Jon nodded and took a couple more sips of water.

"Doing much better, thanks." He took a deep breath and exhaled slowly. "What's next?"

"It's all a big bloody mess," she said, sitting down next to him. "And I'm going to get a big ration of shit for it, unless I can come up with a pretty good explanation of what happened back there." She sat down next to him and took the water bottle. "So what's with the dead brothers, Jon? Fill me in. Maybe we can figure this out together."

Jon took a few more deep breaths, paused, and collected his thoughts.

"Okay. I autopsied a boy in L.A. last week, who had been airlifted out of here by the Flying Samaritans. Elliot and I came here to find his younger brother. Both boys had been seen with Bright Star, and the boy I posted had a bizarre pathology. The morning after the autopsy, his body decomposed into an orange gelatinous mass and looked like the body we saw in the fridge."

"How can you be sure it's his younger brother?" she asked.

"I can't definitively prove it, but the body breakdown and the color were similar, and I could still see that the skin, or what was left of it, showed signs of icthyosis."

"Icthy-what?" she grimaced.

"It means fish-like, thick skin. It's an extremely rare genetic disorder."

"Okay, so let's assume that these two kids are who you say there were. So what do these poor messed-up boys have to do with drug traffic? Look what I found in one of the cabinets near the body," she said, taking out an assortment of drug paraphernalia from her pack—several needles and syringes as well as a plastic bag of white powder.

"It's either heroin or cocaine. I'll confirm it when I get back to San Diego. Did the older boy have evidence of drugs?"

"We sent the body to the coroner's. I'll know more when I get back to L.A.," Jon said.

"I want to know the results. Remind me to give you my contact numbers."

Suddenly, a gray pickup truck emerged at the crest of the blacktopped highway. Mona stepped onto the pavement and waved at the oncoming vehicle. It slowed to a stop. The driver was a young Mexican man wearing a dark brown cowboy hat. Seated next to him in the cab was a woman holding a baby wrapped in a red blanket. A boy and a tan dog sat in the truck's bed.

"*A donde vayan? A la clinica?*" she asked the cab's occupants.

"*Si,*" the young woman answered with a tinge of worry in her voice.

"She says her baby's been sick, and she's going to the medical clinic. I told her you were a doctor. They want to give us a ride, and there's room in back."

"*Muchisimas gracias,*" she said to the couple.

Jon and Mona jumped in and settled down with the boy and his very friendly dog in the truck's bed. The driver made a sharp right turn onto the narrow dirt road, and Jon found himself rolling from one side to the other, first into Mona and then into the dog. As hard as he tried, he just couldn't maintain his serious composure any longer. Welcoming the comic relief, he finally broke into laughter as he tried to dodge the dog's busy tongue. Mona and the boy laughed even harder.

"Sorry for dragging you into this mess. You probably got much more than you bargained for, huh," she said, yawning and stretching her hands up.

"Especially from this vicious dog," he said, trying to fend off the affectionate beast.

Before she could answer, the boy called to the dog. "*Ven, Fido,*" he said, prompting another burst of laughter from Mona.

"Abraham Lincoln had a dog named Fido," Jon said, still trying hard to be serious.

Orchestrator 55

This time they laughed together as the boy tried to distract the dog.

"Amazing trivia, Jon, I'm impressed."

He grinned as the dog jumped in between them and the truck sped down the desolate desert road in the soft morning light.

§

When the truck pulled up to the medical clinic, they escorted the couple inside. The baby had a middle-ear infection. Jon gave the necessary antibiotics and sent them on their way. They waved to the boy and the dog and then walked behind the main building in the direction of the airstrip.

"We'll need to talk in a few days, Jon. I'm going to clean up and check in with my boss. If I don't see you again before you take off, here's my card. I've got voicemail at work—just leave me a message and I'll call you back. I promise. And take it easy," she said.

She handed him the business card.

"What about Bright Star? What will they do with him?" Jon asked. He felt a slight twinge of nausea.

"He'll be flown to Ensenada. If there's an autopsy, I'll fill you in later. Call me." She touched his shoulder and lingered for a moment before pulling away. "One more thing, don't tell anybody about this."

Jon watched Mona walk toward the far ranch building. It was seven-thirty A.M. He headed back to his bungalow.

Don Buckingham came out of the front entrance as he arrived.

"Jon, you must be an early riser. You've been gone for a while."

"I couldn't sleep so I took a walk. Nice morning. Hey, is Elliot up yet?"

"Looks like he's just starting to stir. I'll bet he's got a pretty good headache. Too many margaritas last night."

56   *Paul K. Pattengale*

Buckingham grinned and so did Jon.

"By the way, I've had a slight change in plans," he added. "I'm leaving for L.A. right after lunch. Does that work for you?"

"Shouldn't be a problem," Jon said.

"Great, try to have your luggage up by the plane before you eat. Should have an exact time later," he said.

"You just let me know when," Jon answered, as Buckingham yanked on the bill of his cap and sauntered away.

Jon thought about Mona's request and wondered if he could really trust her. After all, he had known her for only twelve hours. He paced for several minutes outside the bungalow pondering the circumstances some more, and finally deciding to take some common sense precautions and tell Elliot what had happened.

§

Elliot was getting dressed when Jon entered their quarters. "Jon, where have you been? Boy, you look like I feel."

"It was an eventful night, a lot happened." He sat on a wooden stool and recounted the events to Elliot, who listened carefully from the edge of his bed.

"Have you told anyone else?"

"No, and I don't plan to," Jon answered.

"So, you're pretty sure the body was Jose's younger brother?"

"Damn sure, and I'm super-bummed—I was hoping to find him alive. I have it right here."

He took his camera out of the backpack and began to rewind the film.

"You don't use digital?" Elliot asked.

"I'm old-fashioned, okay?"

"Don't freak, just asking. By the way, Don's leaving right after lunch. Did he tell you?"

"Yeah, he just told me, no problem. I'll be able to catch up on some sleep."

"I've got a whole bunch of sick kids to see, so I'm going back on a later flight. Let me bring the film back for you. It sounds like the DEA might be interested in it."

"Agreed," Jon said.

He handed the used roll to Elliot, replaced it with a new one, and then proceeded to shoot the entire roll with the camera aimed at the far wall.

"I'll drop it by your office tomorrow," he said.

Elliot put the roll in his pocket just as the bungalow door opened and Don Buckingham walked in.

"There's a bunch of families waiting to see a doctor at the clinic, I told them someone would be along in a few minutes."

"I'm just about ready," Elliot said, reaching down and tying his shoes. He picked up his stethoscope and medical bag from the bedside table. "See you later Jon. Travel safe."

§

The rest of the morning was hectic but uneventful. After a lukewarm shower, Jon returned to the clinic where he saw a variety of patients with maladies ranging from the common cold to acute appendicitis. He looked for Mona but was told that she had returned to the States on an earlier flight.

At one-thirty, Jon and Yolanda met on the gravel airstrip and boarded Buckingham's Cessna. Once airborne, he told them that they were returning to California by way of Tijuana and that they would clear U.S. customs at Brown Field, thirty miles south of San Diego. Exhausted, Jon barely glanced at the desert scenery below before drifting into sleep.

The flight was smooth and he slept soundly, but awoke with a start when the single engine Cessna touched down on the runway. After refueling, they took off and flew the short distance to Brown Field on the U.S. side of the border. As the plane taxied off the runway onto the apron, a customs agent with a clipboard waved them in his direction.

"Looks like someone's taking an interest in us," Buckingham

said, taxiing closer to the steel hangar and cutting the engine. They climbed out of the plane. A man in a khaki brown uniform approached them with the stern look of authority written on his face.

"Identification, please. Bringing back any plants, fruits, vegetables, or large sums of money?"

"No," each of them said in succession as he checked their passports.

He looked into the rear window of the Cessna. "Take out your luggage and stand by it, please," the agent said.

"Do what he says," Don grumbled. "The sooner we get it out, the sooner we get outta here."

The agent squatted down and proceeded to unzip and rummage through each bag.

"Dr. Drake, would you please come with me," he said.

"I don't understand," Jon said.

"Follow me, please, and bring the rest of your personal belongings."

Jon reluctantly complied, and carrying his luggage and day pack, followed the agent to a nearby office adjacent to the tarmac.

"How long will this take?" he asked, trying to contain his frustration.

"You're being held for questioning. I can't tell you for how long. It's up to my commanding officer. You'll have to ask him," the man answered.

Jon immediately dropped his bag and glared at the man.

"I'm a doctor returning from a medical clinic. You're holding up my flight!"

In the meantime, Don had caught up with them. Jon looked back at him.

"I'm being detained and held for questioning. I don't know how long it will take and I'm not getting any answers."

Don looked at his watch.

"Not sure I can wait. But, tell you what, I'll get on the horn and have someone pick you up in a few hours. There are at least two planes that still have to cross the border. I'll find someone. Hang in there."

"I'll try, but it's not going to be easy," Jon said, picking up his bag and looking impatiently at the agent. He tried to get a grip on his stress level, which wasn't helped by his lack of sleep and the loss of Bright Star.

Twenty minutes later Jon sat in a chair facing two burly government officials. One stood, the other sat.

"Dr. Drake, what was the purpose of your trip to Baja?"

"I told you! I was providing medical care to indigent Mexicans."

"A pathologist? I thought pathologists didn't see patients."

"This pathologist sees patients. I completed a clinical medicine internship."

"Then what were you doing in an abandoned lab facility?"

"We were escaping a swarm of wasps, the same ones that killed my patient!" he said, gesturing with his right hand.

"Your patient was a drug dealer."

"Are you saying that he deserved to die?"

"I'm saying he was drug dealer and you were aiding and abetting him. Is that clear?"

"And I'm saying he was sick and he was *my* patient. Don't you have any soul, man? Am I making myself clear?!" Jon said, leaning forward toward the man, who instinctively moved in the opposite direction. The man who was standing moved closer to Jon and stood behind him.

"Dr. Drake, please control your outbursts," the seated man said.

"I'll do whatever it takes to care for my patients," Jon yelled, standing up. Instantly, he felt a blow to the back of his head with a blunt object. He crumpled to the floor.

§

60   *Paul K. Pattengale*

Jon found himself dazed and alone in a small office sitting in an antique swivel chair, his day pack and green carry-on perched in front of him on a wooden desktop. The blinds were open. It was dark outside.

He checked his watch. It was eight o'clock. Had it been five hours since he had deplaned at Brown Field? Was it even the same day? That was the last thing he remembered. He felt the painful bump on the back of his head and noticed that his tongue and jaw were sore.

A door opened, and a heavy, wide-jawed uniformed man in his mid-forties strutted into the room.

"Dr. Drake, Colonel Robert Stringfellow, U.S. Drug Enforcement Agency. We've confiscated your film and must advise you that you're not at liberty to discuss what you've seen with anyone. If you don't comply, you'll be charged with possession of narcotics," he said, his jaw tightly clenched.

"But ..."

"And if you get any other cockamamie ideas about unfair treatment, we'll press charges and you'll find your ass in the slammer."

He held up a plastic bag of white crystalline powder in his right hand.

"Possession of heroin is a felony, Dr. Drake."

Jon was so astonished he was speechless.

"If you have nothing more to say, you're free to go."

In a daze, he collected his personal belongings and soon found himself speaking with a bored, matronly secretary who was smoking in a small anteroom.

"The last plane from Mexico came through here about three hours ago. There are no more flights after dark," she said.

"Then where can I stay around here?" Jon asked, checking that his money and credit cards were still in his wallet.

"You're about twenty-five miles southeast of San Diego. You can call a cab. There's a phone out in the breezeway next to the parking lot," she said, handing him a smudged business card from the Acme Cab Company.

He opened the screen door and stepped outside into the cool night air. It was foggy, and the pay phone was barely visible at the far end of the building. Somewhat reinvigorated by the prospect of getting the hell out of there, he walked toward it and checked his pockets for loose change. A pair of headlights emerged from the fog as he picked up the receiver, and a white, late-model Miata with smoked glass windows pulled up alongside him. The driver's window and trunk opened at the same time.

"Jon, no questions, just throw your stuff in back. Let's go," Mona said.

He did what he was told and climbed into the car.

CHAPTER—7

Jon grimaced when the force generated by the car's rapid acceleration pushed him back into the bucket seat. Mona shifted into a higher gear and glanced at him.

"Don't look so happy to see me," she said.

He rubbed the back of his head.

She reached over and touched him.

"What went wrong back there? What happened? I got back early and went off duty. I thought they were just going to take the film, not interrogate you like a POW!"

"They worked me over pretty good," he said, rubbing the lump on the back of his head.

"Christ, I should've held on to the camera. Larry had a hair up his ass about it. And Stringfellow's crazy to beat up on a prominent doctor."

"Prominent?"

"Jesus, you are out of it! I saw your security check."

He paused.

"Oh," he said, trying to crack a smile.

"Oh," she mocked. "Jesus, it sounded pretty kick-ass to me. They must have hit you pretty hard. You're acting goofy." She looked at him with great compassion, like no woman had looked at him for a long time, perhaps ever before.

He looked back at her, but his neck was sore, and he felt nauseated. He leaned against the headrest and closed his eyes. His eyelids felt heavy, and the droning of the car's engine dominated his senses. His thoughts began to blend like melted wax, but he could still hear Mona's voice in the background.

"Try and relax, my place is a good forty-five minutes from here," she said.

Her hand brushed his cheek as he slumped back into the leather seat.

§

He awoke in a dimly lit room, a cool sea breeze against the side of his face. He sat up on the white-quilted queen-size bed. A white lace curtain danced in the wind above the engraved wood headboard, and an assortment of multicolored stuffed animals—including a grinning Jiminy Cricket and a silly looking sea gull wearing a sailor's hat—peered at him from the top of the dresser. He tried to sit up but his head spun and he felt like vomiting. He laid back down and felt better.

Next to the bed was an antique wooden nightstand with a goose-necked tensor lamp. He reached over and turned on the switch, illuminating the green silk cover of a solitary book entitled *The Poetry of Jim Morrison*. He opened it at the bookmark, which read "City Lights Bookstore, North Beach, San Francisco."

"He was a great poet," Mona said, appearing in the doorway. She was wearing a loose-fitting beige jogging suit. She sat down next to him at the end of the bed.

"After I dragged you in from the car, you slept a couple of hours. Your color looks better. How are you feeling?"

She leaned over and looked into his eyes.

"Much better, but I'm still a little nauseous."

"That entitles you to a Larsen home remedy. Meet me in the living room in five minutes."

The surrounding menagerie of stuffed animals seemed to nod in agreement as she stood up and left the room.

She had been so close that her body smell lingered. Why was she so concerned about him? Not long ago, she was kicking in doors and swearing, and now, she was a sweet, sensitive young woman with stuffed animals and an appreciation for poetry. It was too much to fathom. What was her agenda? It didn't matter right now. Her energy excited him, and he already felt better.

He heard the phone ring in the other room. It stopped after one ring and was followed by a crescendo-decrescendo whistling sound. No longer feeling light-headed, he slowly stood up, walked to the open door, and peered into the living room. Mona was talking on a cell phone and sitting cross-legged in a cushioned lavender chair. She ended her conversation, put the phone down, and stood up.

"Tea's just about ready. Come on in and sit. I'll bring it to you," she said, pointing to the chair she was sitting in.

He entered the living room feeling her hospitality and warmth but had to keep reminding himself that hours earlier she had been wearing stealth black and sporting a government ID. His struggle was worsened by his latest calculation, which put her somewhere between a movie star and a supermodel in the body of an athlete. He felt paralyzed and wondered if this was how a female black widow attracted its male victims. He sat in the chair, and she handed him a cup of steaming tea in a *Howdy Doody Show* mug.

"It's jasmine tea with a teaspoon and a half of organic honey and a squirt of lemon. My Montana grandmother gave it to my sisters and me when we had an upset stomach. It's her little organic secret."

She took a long sip and sat down in the chair next to him.

"Jon, we need to talk about the Gonzalez brothers."

He gazed through the steam at the brim of the cup and felt a surge of courage welling up in him.

"Mona, *we* need to talk. Your hospitality is awesome, but I just got my ass handed to me by your peer group. Why should I trust you? Why are you helping me?"

It was his turn to take a sip as Howdy Doody's freckled face grinned back at him from the cup's outer surface, and the liquid warmed his innards.

"You don't waste any time getting right to the point, do you? I respect that, so I'm going to level with you from the gitgo."

She squared her shoulders and sat up straight.

"I thought I was investigating a Latin American drug connection, a routine bust-seizure kind of scenario, but after stumbling onto that kid's decomposed body and hearing the old Indian talking about evil experiments, it's clear to me that something way bigger is going on. What's more confusing is that my boss got real twitchy and paranoid when I reported the details, almost like I uncovered something he didn't want me to know about."

"My being with you didn't help," Jon said.

"He was super-pissed about that, and it looks like the bastards took it out on you."

"What's he covering up then?" Jon asked.

"I don't know. I'm not privy to his inner circle; in fact, Stringfellow sees me as a threat."

"A threat?"

"Believe it or not, I'm the only woman field agent in his macho boy's club, and I've come this close to filing sexual harassment charges."

She held out her right hand and closely approximated her index finger and thumb.

"Sounds terrible. Why do you stick around, then?" Jon asked, remembering that the helicopter pilot had been derogatory when addressing her.

"That's precisely the point. I want to get to the bottom of this case, solve it, get a promotion, and transfer out of the San Diego district."

"Even by going around Stringfellow?"

"If it plays out that way and his lecherous ass gets fired, I don't have a problem with it. In fact, bring it on. I hate his fucking guts!" she said, her whole body quivering.

Struck by both her candor and intensity, Jon sipped the tea and looked at her, contemplating the plausibility of her story, his head slightly cocked.

"Okay, I'm in. Calm down. Don't blow a gasket."

She smiled.

"Thanks for understanding, Jon. It means a lot to me. Now, are you sure you're up for this? How are you feeling?"

"I'm doing fine. Grandma's recipe's got a pretty good kick to it." He held up the mug like he was making a toast.

They both laughed.

"So what do you want to know about the boys?" he asked.

"Give me some more detail on the older boy's autopsy. You called it 'bizarre,' didn't you?" She grabbed a notepad and pen from the coffee table. "And keep it simple; remember, I'm just a country girl."

"Yeah, right," he answered, then dove into a description of the thick skin, the enlarged upper body muscles, the abnormal skin-lung tissues, the stem cells, the multiple cancers, and, finally, the different species of DNA that was found in the remains of Jose Gonzalez.

"That's totally off-the-wall. You mean those abnormal tissues looked foreign enough to have come from somewhere else— almost like a transplant." Her eyes were wide as she looked from Jon to her notepad and back again. "So, it was some kind of medical experiment."

"Pretty good for a country girl, I'd say."

"You think so? I took a few bio courses in college."

"I think so," he emphasized, making eye contact.

"But why in Baja?" she asked.

Orchestrator 67

"The kind of experiment we're talking about here is so outrageous that it would be hard to pull off in the States. How about a no-questions-asked, just-give-me-the-hush-money, south-of-the-border, out-of-the-way scenario?"

"Okay, but what about the white powder I found in the lab. It turned out to be cocaine on chemical analysis. What do you say to that?"

"Maybe coincidence, maybe a red herring, maybe related to the experiment. I'll check with the L.A. coroner to see if they found it in the boy's body. What did your boss say about the cocaine?"

"He played it up as evidence that Bright Star was in on the drug trafficking, and downplayed the body in the freezer. In fact, he didn't want to talk about it."

"Did you file a report?"

"Yeah, but who knows what he's going to do with it. I don't trust him. He's hiding something, and I'm going to find out what it is."

"I wouldn't cross him. He was pretty scary, at least from where I was sitting. And I think he's going to be really pissed when he finds out that the roll of film he removed from my camera isn't what he thinks it is."

"Where's the roll that you shot in the lab?"

"In L.A., I sent it back with someone else," he said, cautious enough not to risk Elliot's neck for the moment, and not wanting to tell her that he had told someone else about their adventure. "I replaced it with a new roll and shot it up in my room."

"Oh boy, he's gonna be boiling."

"Will he come after me?" Jon asked.

"Hard to say. Make an extra set of prints and hide them. If they show up, play dumb and give him the other set of prints and the negatives."

Jon put his cup down on the glass table.

"Jon, there's something else you should know. Elliot's security check wasn't as clean as yours."

"How's that?"

"He was arrested a bunch of times for civil disobedience. He belongs to a group called Physicians for Social Consciousness. It's primarily a left-wing anti-nuclear group. I don't think it's a bad rap, but I thought you should know."

"I've heard of them. I haven't seen Elliot since senior year in high school, so I haven't kept track of his politics. Thanks for the info, I'll keep it in mind," he said, wondering if he made the right decision in giving the film to Elliot.

"Something else, and you're not going to like this. Bright Star was DOA in Ensenada. I don't even know if there was an autopsy. Stringfellow was vague on the details. I'm wondering if he was part of the experiment too. Wasps aren't supposed to attack humans like that."

Before Jon could react, the cell phone rang in her lap. She flipped it open and didn't bother with a greeting. "I'll be there in thirty minutes," she said speaking into the receiver.

She placed the phone in her jacket pocket.

"We're working on another project. I'm gonna have to leave you here."

"When will you be back?"

"Not until tomorrow afternoon. I'm working on a local sting operation on a party boat in the Mission Bay harbor. You can crash here tonight, if you want."

"I need to be back in L.A. tomorrow. I'm supposed to give a talk at a downtown conference in the afternoon."

"You need a good night's sleep. The Solana Beach Amtrak station is just up the street. It's only three hours to L.A. I've got to get ready."

Mona walked down the hallway and into the bedroom. After several minutes, Jon heard water running. He closed his eyes and thought of Bright Star's disfigured body. Had he made a mistake in trusting her? Why had she told him about Elliot's security clearance? Tired and in need of sleep, he would have to trust her for now, and worry about the consequences later.

Orchestrator   69

Fifteen minutes later Mona appeared from her bedroom dressed in a low-cut, black party dress and spiked black heels. A red scarf was loosely wrapped around her neck. Jon tried not to stare.

"The earliest train in the morning leaves Solana Beach at six-thirty," she said, handing him a train schedule. "We need to stay in touch. I'm going to need your expertise in unraveling this."

"Let's talk soon. I should have the results on the coroner's drug screen in a few days. And my research lab is working up the kid's DNA as we speak. I should have a better idea of what went wrong with his genetic structure in the same time frame."

She scribbled a number on the schedule.

"That's the phone number here in Solana Beach. Just give me a call. I need to know. Oh, and there's an alarm clock next to the bed."

"Thanks for taking such good care of me, Mona. I'm going to miss you. We've been through a lot together," he said, standing up and kissing her on the cheek.

"C'mon Jon, you can do better than that."

She pulled him closer and kissed him hard on the lips, then she pulled back and looked deep into his eyes. "Did anyone ever tell you that you're a great guy?" she said. Then she kissed him harder and longer.

"Not quite like this," Jon said, still holding her in his arms. "Be careful, Mona."

"Will do. You too," she said, pulling away.

She walked out the front door and stood under a set of tinkling wind chimes.

"See ya around," she said, looking back at him as the wind picked up the ends of her scarf.

"Later," he answered, trying to sound as cool as possible.

She closed the door behind her, and he wondered, for a moment, if he would ever see her again.

CHAPTER—8

When Jon's train pulled into Union Station at eleven o'clock the next morning, he called the lab on his cell.

"Diane, did a Dr. Adams stop by?"

"Yeah, he dropped off a blood sample and a manila envelope about a half hour ago."

"Blood sample?"

"He said it was from an Indian that you both saw in clinic. What do you want me to do with it?"

"Hmmm, let me think about that. Keep it at room temp for now."

"I locked the envelope in the file cabinet. Want me to open it?"

"No, I'll be there in a half hour."

"Jon, you know your talk is scheduled for three o'clock this afternoon at the Bonaventure."

"I haven't forgotten," he said.

He located the taxi line and hopped into the tattered back seat of the green and white checkered cab. As the cabbie turned north onto Alameda and then onto Sunset, Jon wondered how they should go about analyzing Bright Star's blood.

As they cruised westward through the corridor of Sunset Boulevard barrios, he thought about the afternoon lecture and experienced a tinge of nervousness. The recently formed Cancer Biology Consortium was populated with medical scientists who had financial ties to the biotech community and who were passionate about translating the advances made in cancer research to the care of their patients. He, too, shared their passion and hoped he was up to the task. Such an approach could have benefited his father, whose leukemia didn't respond to conventional chemotherapy. It was therefore the aggressive, poor-outcome white-blood cell cancers that Jon had focused his research efforts on. The blare of the taxi's horn jolted him into the reality of the moment, reminding him of the headache that he'd experienced in the San Diego DEA facility twenty hours earlier. The dizziness and the dull ache behind his eyes had returned.

As the sun struggled to break through the late-morning haze, his mind shifted to Abe Lowenstein. He had tried to reach him on his cell but there was no answer. Was he back in town from the Boston pathology meeting, and had he had a chance to show the Gonzalez autopsy slides to his Harvard buddies? Was there any more news on the Gonzalez DNA? The green-and-white screeched up to the front entrance of the Research Tower. He paid the driver and got out of the cab, luggage in hand. Still feeling dizzy, he paused for a moment and then entered the building.

When Jon got off the elevator on the tenth floor, he saw Diane carrying a rack of plastic vials from the equipment room to the main lab.

A look of concern came over her face. "Are you okay?"

"I didn't get much sleep, and I've got a miserable headache."

"Sounds like you did have a good time then. I've got some Advil in my purse. Want a couple?" she asked.

"Good idea. Let me get rid of these first."

"I'll meet you in your office," she said.

A few minutes later, Diane handed over the pills, a bottle of water, and Elliot's envelope as he was placing his bags next to the desk. "I need to keep moving. I'm in the middle of an experiment," she said, on her way out the door.

"Okay, thanks." Jon didn't know if she had heard him or not—he was more interested in washing down the Advil and opening the manila envelope from Elliot. A yellow Post-it note was stuck to the roll of film, and the message written on it was short and sweet: *See you later, Elliot.* He put the film in his pants pocket and rejoined Diane in the main lab.

"What's happening with the stem cell DNA?" he asked.

"A lot."

"Let's hear it then."

"Chris and I have been working on it all weekend."

The lab phone rang.

She walked over and picked it up.

"It's for you, Jon. The chief resident is saying you have a case to present at the hospital noon conference."

"I completely forgot. Tell him I'll be right over. Man, am I spaced."

She hung up.

"No problem, we can talk about the DNA later. Chris and I aren't going anywhere."

"I'm tied up the rest of the afternoon. How about six o'clock. Does that work?"

"That definitely works. I'll tell Chris."

"Diane, two more things. Can you drop me at Van Nuys Airport later? My car's still there from the weekend trip. And I need to borrow your car to get to and from my talk downtown."

"Sure, no problems on both counts. Keys are on my desk. And the Indian's blood, Jon, what should we do with it?"

"Isolate the white cells. We'll talk later about next steps."

§

Jon sat next to the podium as the session chairman introduced him to the consortium. He was running on pure adrenaline.

Orchestrator 73

"It's unusual to have a pathology resident present his research to such a distinguished group," said Dr. William Arrowsmith, a silver-haired man in his early sixties. He gripped the lectern with both hands. "But extraordinary individuals deserve extraordinary treatment."

Jon felt the flutters starting up.

"After receiving both an M.D. and a Ph.D. from the University of California at Los Angeles, Dr. Jonathan Drake launched a successful career in the biotech industry. Fortunately, for those of us in academia, Dr. Drake has recently joined the medical school faculty at County Hospital as a pathology trainee and is an active member of their research institute. During his entire professional career, Dr. Drake has made, and continues to make, seminal contributions in the field of cancer research. He's listed in *The American Scientist* as one of the ten most promising medical scientists in the U.S. It is therefore with great pleasure that I introduce Dr. Jonathan Drake to you. The title of his lecture is 'Of Mice and Men: An Approach to Cancer Diagnosis and Therapy.'"

Jon walked to the podium to the rhythm of the audience's applause. After thanking Dr. Arrowsmith for his generous introduction, he began, first, by reviewing the history of genetically manipulated mice and then focusing on his own home-grown transgenic strains that were reproducible models of certain human cancers. When he went on to highlight a particular mouse strain that developed an aggressive leukemia at an early age, he felt both the closeness and attentiveness of his audience. He told them this strain closely mimicked poor-outcome, human white-blood-cell cancers and served as a working model for early diagnosis and effective new treatments. And when he told them he already had promising preliminary data that certain new experimental therapies were able to slow the disease in its early stages, and offered a hope for a cure, he knew they were in the palm of his hand. He finished by saying that mouse models would play a major role in human cancer therapy.

Following a thunderous round of applause, the chairman opened the floor to discussion.

After a number of stimulating questions and a string of congratulatory comments, a graying, impeccably dressed man in his early sixties wearing a loose-fitting, dark suit and walking with a slight limp approached one of the house microphones in the rear of the auditorium. He tapped on the mic with the gold head of his walking cane and cleared his throat.

"Dr. Drake, to what do you attribute your success? As you know, most of us have been unable to reproduce your experiments. We should all be so fortunate," he said.

Taken aback by the nature and tone of the man's question, Jon paused several seconds before answering.

"The human leukemia mouse is based on my own personal modifications of the gene-transfer method. The details will be available in my next paper," Jon answered.

He again tapped loudly on the microphone with his cane.

"That's quite noble of you, Dr. Drake, but that doesn't help any of us today."

The gaunt man limped away from the microphone and exited the auditorium. The room was dead quiet. Dr. Arrowsmith returned to the podium.

"If there are no more questions, thank you, again, Dr. Drake for a most stimulating talk. There will be a ten-minute break before the next presentation."

The audience applauded again and then dispersed toward the back of the room. Jon looked at Arrowsmith.

"Who was that?" he asked, his mouth open.

"Dr. David Kreeger."

"The CEO of Pathgene?"

Arrowsmith nodded.

"He looks terrible. Is he ill?" Jon asked.

"That's the rumor," Arrowsmith said. "Try not to take what he said too seriously. You're doing great work, Jonathan, and will share your findings at the appropriate time. We need people of your caliber in the field."

"Thanks, I'll try to keep it in perspective," Jon said, heading toward the exit.

CHAPTER—9

On his return trip to County Hospital Jon ruminated on the way his presentation had ended. Was David Kreeger a jealous scientist with an attitude or had he been right on the mark when he accused Jon of being selfish and unwilling to share his breakthrough discovery with others? Jon recalled the words his mother had spoken after the successful launch of his biotech company. Jon's father had been a hoarder obsessed with money and personal gain, and now she was concerned Jon was heading down the same path. Jon even had his father's icy stare, his mom had said.

He made the turn onto Cesar Chavez Boulevard. Money was important to him and had been for years ever since Dad's passing. And yes, he admitted it, he was ambitious. Ever since his Little League team had won the district championship, he had wanted to be first. It was in his blood. He could taste it. But his being the best never hurt anyone. Kreeger's complaint was ill-founded; it wouldn't harm a single cancer patient. In fact, it had the opposite effect and would benefit them. Since he had prenegotiated and shared the patent and proprietary rights with a leading drug company, the information derived from the human

76

Orchestrator 77

leukemia mouse, if positive, would result in new therapies and perhaps cures for these patients. Kreeger would have access to Jon's unique methodology in due time and would have to wait for the published paper. It was that simple.

Feeling reinvigorated, he focused his thoughts on the Gonzalez boys. He felt for the roll of film in his pocket and wondered if he should take it to medical photography. His pager sounded, and he called the number on his cell phone.

"This is Dr. Drake."

"Jon, Elliot here, time for a coffee? I've got about forty-five minutes before I have to head back to the Valley."

"Perfect. I need to be back in the lab by six. See you at five then. I'm still on the road."

Returning to the hospital, Jon proceeded to the coffee bar adjacent to the cafeteria. Elliot was standing in line. They ordered two tall cappuccinos and waited at the far end of the bar for their drinks.

"How was your flight back to L.A.?" Elliot asked.

"Okay 'til we got to Brown Field," Jon said.

"What happened?"

"We need to sit down for this," Jon said.

After getting their drinks and finding a secluded table, Jon explained to Elliot the details of his detainment and the events that followed.

"I'm totally shocked. I didn't hear a word about you being left behind at Brown Field. We cleared U.S. Customs in Calexico at around six and flew directly to Van Nuys. It sounds like you had a terrible experience," Elliot said.

"I was feeling pretty beat up and abandoned. Buckingham told me he would try to get someone from the Flying Sams to pick me up, but it never happened."

"It's hard to know whom he reached and whom he didn't. How do you know he even tried?" Elliot asked. "Maybe he's a gopher for the DEA."

"I also wondered about that. I was going to ask Mona, but I forgot," Jon said.

"Which brings us to Mona," his friend said.

Jon sipped his coffee and watched the bubbles in the foam pop and deflate—anything to avoid looking Elliot in the eye.

"I mean, can you really trust her? Don't look so sheepish. I'm only thinking about you."

Jon put down the coffee cup. "What she told me made sense. She said her job situation was bad, and from the little bit I saw, I had to agree with her. The helicopter pilot talked down to her, and her boss, whom I met face to face, is an asshole, who harasses her on a regular basis. She's desperate for a promotion and definitely wants to be transferred. Besides, she helped me out, and I owe her one."

Elliot didn't look convinced.

"You think she's using me, don't you. You can say it."

"Well even if she's using you, it's not gonna change the way you feel about her. You're already hooked."

Jon gulped down the last of his cappuccino. "You think so?" he asked.

"I know so. I can see the excitement in your eyes. And who could blame you? You're close to a quantum-leap scientific discovery and a beautiful woman just happens along and wants a piece of the action. What guy wouldn't jump for that kind of scenario? I sure would."

Jon smiled.

"I'd be careful, though. I think you're headed into some pretty rough territory."

"I've already been there," Jon said, rubbing the back of his head. "I'm having off and on headaches and my ears are ringing. I should probably see someone."

"I'll hook you up with a great neurologist," Elliot said.

"That's right, you got your Ph.D. at U.C.S.F. in ... whose lab was it?"

Orchestrator 79

"Brett Johnstone's. Not only is he a great neuroscientist, he's an outstanding clinician, and he relocated to Southern California."

"Okay, then, set me up with him," Jon said. He checked his watch. "I'm meeting with my lab people at six. There's one more thing before I run."

"What's that?" Elliot asked.

Jon took the film out of his pocket and put it on the table in front of them. "Mona said Stringfellow might come looking for it."

"Listen, let me develop a set of prints tonight. I have a makeshift darkroom at home."

"And you were giving me grief about not using a digital camera," Jon said.

Elliot laughed.

"I remember your shots of the homecoming parade in the yearbook. They were pretty good," Jon said picking up the film and handing it to Elliot. "Okay, but be careful."

"Let's get together tonight and have a look at them. I'll page you," Elliot said.

§

Jon walked into the research lab to find Diane chatting it up with Abe Lowenstein. They were standing next to a DNA sequencer the size of a clothes dryer and looking at its attached computer display.

"I've been explaining how we process and sequence DNA," she said to Jon.

"And for a pre-molecular biology, classically trained pathologist, I'm thrilled that I actually understand some of what Diane has told me. But as the poet said, 'a little knowledge is a dangerous thing.'"

"You're far too modest, Dr. Lowenstein. You understand a lot more than you give yourself credit for," she said.

"I have a good teacher," he said. The three of them were all smiles.

"Okay, then, Diane is going to give us an update on the stem cell DNA," Jon said.

"Here goes." Diane cleared her throat. She reached for a lab notebook and opened it. "The 'super-fast DNA' is living up to its reputation. Our rough estimate is that it's activating ninety percent of the boy's functional genome," she said.

"Ninety percent, that's huge. Ten percent is normal," Jon said, his heart pounding.

"There's more."

"Fire away," Jon said.

"Two species of DNA were the most prevalent, and when we sequenced them, we couldn't find matches for them in the human genome bank."

"That fits with our preliminary analysis. Keep going."

"Chris computer-searched the non-human gene banks and found that the larger piece had an eighty-percent match in *Xenopus*."

"Frog DNA! Which gene?" Jon asked.

"An early one in amphibian embryo development. It's called *sym* for symmetry."

"The plot thickens," Lowenstein said with a boyish grin.

"And the second DNA species?" Jon asked.

"It was much smaller than the first piece. We couldn't find a match for it," Diane said.

Jon looked back at Diane, saying nothing.

"My trip to the East Coast might shed some light on the subject," Lowenstein interjected.

"That's right, you took the autopsy slides to Harvard," Jon said. "What did they say?"

"Well, the Mass General pathologists had no idea what to make of them, so I took them to a Harvard comparative biology professor, Dr. Rex Townsend, who's also on the marine biology faculty at the Woods Hole Institute."

Orchestrator 81

"What was his take?"

"He said that the skin-lung connecting structures resembled the breathing apparatus found in an African species of lungfish called *Protopterus annectens.*"

"Lungfish go way back in evolution, don't they?" Jon asked.

"Three hundred and fifty million years to the Devonian period to be precise. The lungs developed in response to the extreme climatic conditions of the time," Abe said.

"Fish with lungs! Aren't fish supposed to breathe through their gills?" Diane said.

"Lungfish can go both ways. Gills in a wet climate, lungs in a dry climate. Think of them as early amphibians. Their lungs inflate through air ducts connected to their gut."

"So the lungfish's connecting ducts look like Jose's connecting ducts," Jon said.

"Almost identical. I verified it with my own eyes," Abe answered.

"Then maybe the DNAs match better with lungfish genes," Jon said.

"I'll check the database, but I don't think we'll find *Protopterus.* It's too obscure. I'll give it a try though," Diane said.

"A puzzle in need of a solution," Lowenstein commented.

Several minutes later, Diane reappeared holding a printout.

"No listings for *Protopterus,*" she said.

Just then, Chris walked into the lab.

"Chris, come over here, I want you to meet somebody," Jon said, waving him in their direction and introducing him to Dr. Lowenstein.

Chris was carrying a Styrofoam container. Jon saw that his eyes were puffy and had dark circles under them.

"Chris, Diane just told me about the two species of DNA, and Dr. Lowenstein has anatomic evidence that Jose's connecting structures look amphibian," Jon said.

"I'm not surprised, wait 'til you see this," he said, lifting the top off the box. He removed a plastic container filled with water.

After situating it on the lab bench, he picked up one of several floating objects with a pair of steel forceps and placed it in a plastic Petri dish.

"Look." He poked at the malformed, greenish-brown mass with the forceps.

"What is it?" Jon asked.

"It's supposed to be a tadpole."

"Supposed to be?" Diane asked.

"Well, when we learned that one of the cloned autopsy DNAs had amphibian characteristics, I went over to my buddy's developmental biology lab at Caltech and injected the cloned autopsy DNAs into fertilized frog eggs. Anyway, you're not gonna believe this."

"I have the evidence right here on tape," he said, producing a miniature videocassette from his shirt pocket. As he cued it up on the player, everyone swiveled around in their chairs to face it.

Too excited to be tired, Chris pointed to the pulsating cellular mass on the screen. "Here's a time-lapse of a normal fertilized frog egg going through the usual series of cell divisions."

"How did you photograph that?" Lowenstein asked, on the edge of his chair.

"High resolution magnetic resonance microscopy with a razzle-dazzle video cam and a Media-1000 editing option. My friend at Caltech let me use the equipment," he answered, while the three viewers continued to stare at the vivid three-dimensional image. "Pretty high tech, huh."

"I'd say so," Lowenstein said.

"I'm gonna fast-forward through some of this, so hold on," Chris said.

On screen, the unicellular fertilized egg progressively transformed into a robust multicellular sphere. Chris maneuvered the remote to freeze the frame and pointed to a conspicuous black spot on the near side of the hollow cellular ball.

"This is the embryo organizer. It's where the germ layers originate and where the amphibian embryo ultimately derives

Orchestrator 83

all the genetic information it needs to become a complete and whole organism."

"And originally described by the 1935 Nobel laureate Dr. Hans Spemann at the University of Freiburg," Lowenstein said, pulling an empty cherry-wood pipe from the pocket of his plaid sport coat and placing it in his mouth.

"Dr. Lowenstein's correct: this is Spemann's organizer, and it's precisely where I injected the cloned autopsy DNAs," Chris said, putting the picture back into motion.

A tiny needle-tip entered the microscopic field and pierced the dark spot on the multicellular sphere. Chris paused the frame, pressed another key, and brought up an adjacent frame showing an unmanipulated sphere.

"Before we consider the effects of injecting Spemann's organizer with the Gonzalez DNA, I'm gonna run you through amphibian development as it normally occurs."

"Fast-forwarded development, of course," Lowenstein said.

"You got it, Dr. L. Here comes forty-eight hours compressed into a few minutes."

The unmanipulated spherule elongated into an ellipsoid ball, and an orderly phalanx of cells streamed from Spemann's organizer. After migrating through the geometric center and bridging the distance to the other side, the double column of cells split, one curvilinear ribbon burrowing upward toward the upper pole and the other delving down toward the lower pole.

"We've reached the two-layered stage. The top cell layer will develop into the central nervous system, and the bottom layer is the primordia, which will eventually specialize into all of the internal organs," Chris said.

"Instead of Spemann's organizer, it should be renamed Spemann's orchestrator," Lowenstein exclaimed, rocking back and forth in his seat like a child.

The upper surface undulated up and down forming a cleavage furrow, which was rapidly replaced with a long, notched groove.

The groove eventually deepened and was filled in from both sides with columns of migrating cells, which formed the tadpole's brain and spinal cord.

"We've almost reached the last stage," Chris said.

Seconds later, as the tissues lengthened and widened, Jon could now begin to distinguish the organism's top and bottom from its front and rear. In ordered sequence, the lower half enlarged and the internal organs branched and sprouted off from the deeper cell layers. In a period of one minute, a wiggling, perfectly formed, symmetrical tadpole with small eyes and a tail fluttered in front of them on the screen.

"Miraculous," Diane said.

"I'll second that," Jon added.

"And now on to the injected egg. The effects I'm going to show you only occurred when I transferred the smaller piece of stem cell DNA by itself. The larger piece had no effect," Chris said.

He freeze-framed the normal tadpole on the right and set the injected cellular ball into motion on the left. Within seconds, a wide ribbon of cells emerged from Spemann's organizer and raced toward the equatorial belt on the opposite side of the cellular ball. On their way, several columns of cells broke rank and split off from the main group, first wandering aimlessly in the sphere's cavity and then piling up onto one another.

"Hardly an orderly migration," Lowenstein remarked.

"It gets more intense," Chris said. "Compared to normal, there are more embryo cells migrating, and they're for sure speeding."

"More cells, fast cells, fast DNA, ninety percent of the functional genome activated. The story still fits," Jon said.

The organism continued to form at a rapid rate with the cells migrating, proliferating, and piling up in a disorderly manner. Finally, a bulky, malformed, distorted mass of tissue quivered in front of them on the left of the screen, contrasting sharply with the sculpted tadpole on the right.

Orchestrator   85

"Uncontrolled cell division with invasion of normal structures! It smells, sounds and looks like cancer to me," Lowenstein said. "And I have no doubt it will mimic the tumors we saw in Jose's autopsy tissue."

"How can such a small piece of DNA have such a disastrous effect on a whole organism?" Jon asked.

"I knew that you would ask me that, Dr. Drake, and I did a few more experiments and discovered it had attached itself to all the critical genes and literally drove the whole process of embryo formation," Chris said.

"More like cancerous malformation," Jon added. "You're blowing me away, Chris. What you're describing reminds me of Dr. Lowenstein's comment about Spemann's organizer."

"You mean changing the name from organizer to orchestrator?" Lowenstein asked.

"Right, this tiny piece of stem cell DNA is orchestrating the entire process, but it's doing it way too fast, and it's not self-regulating like it should," Jon said.

"A super-orchestrator, then," Lowenstein said.

"Yes, a gene that's capable of choreographing the development and specialization of the entire organism. Embryologists have hypothesized their existence and have tentatively called them *master orchestrator genes*. That would explain why we couldn't find a match in the human genome bank."

"Hypothetical? Tentative? Be more specific," Lowenstein demanded.

"Some have even hailed them as the secret of life, but they're extremely elusive, and no one has ever isolated or identified one," Jon said, almost breathless. "At least not until now."

"My god, man, if these orchestrator-rigged stem cells weren't breaking down and forming cancers, think of how they could be used to rebuild diseased organs!" Lowenstein exclaimed.

He thought some more, and an icy chill passed through him. Whoever had unleashed the orchestrator had done so by harnessing the power of the stem cell. But in the process, this master gene had overridden and silenced its own regulatory controls with a result that was truly horrifying. The images of the malformed boys flashed in his mind like a neon sign.

CHAPTER—10

Jon was awakened by a ringing sound. When he opened his eyes, he saw his beeper blinking on the coffee table. It was eleven-thirty P.M. He must have fallen asleep on his couch. He called Elliot's number.

By midnight, Jon was walking into the White Dog Coffeehouse in Old Pasadena. Elliot was waiting for him on the brick-walled patio, mug in hand and a manila envelope on his lap.

"What are you drinking? It smells good," Jon said.

"The house herbal tea—they say it soothes the soul."

"Man, am I ready for that. I'm still feeling pretty ragged."

After the waitress brought Jon his tea, Elliot removed the photos from the envelope and handed them over with a deep breath. "Here they are, negatives and all."

Jon thumbed through the prints one by one.

"You'll keep a set in a safe place for me?" Jon asked.

"Can do," Elliot answered.

The first dozen photos included shots of Elliot and Yolanda posing in front of Don Buckingham's Cessna, some wide-angle shots of the Sea of Cortez and the arid Baja desert, as well as several group pictures of the clinic personnel in front of the Santa Inez medical clinic. He saw Mona smiling from the back row.

The remaining photos depicted multiple interior shots of the abandoned Baja lab and, finally, the decaying remains of a young child lying inside the thawed freezer.

"I can see more here than I could there."

"Good flash, good detail," Elliot said.

"I'll say. What do you think the lab was used for?" Jon asked.

"Well, from what I've seen so far, the inventory goes like this: an ultracentrifuge, bottles of phenol/chloroform, multiple power sources, gel boxes, a CO_2 cell incubator, and a state-of-the-art microinjection setup. It must have functioned at one time as a sophisticated DNA isolation facility with the added capacity for gene-transfer experiments," Elliot said.

"Failed gene-transfer experiments," Jon said.

"So, you're sure this is Jose's younger brother?"

"It's circumstantial, but I can make a good case for the thick skin, at least what's left of it. What's your take?"

He handed the picture to Elliot, who held it close to his face.

"It's a bit of a stretch, but I have to agree with you. It could fit with icthyosis," he said.

Jon poured himself some more tea, as he briefed Elliot on the latest findings from his lab.

"That's huge! How do you piece it all together?" Elliot asked.

"I think that these two kids failed some sort of DNA injection/stem cell implantation procedure," Jon explained. "And if you couple it with the thick skin and upper-body muscle development, I think it points to some kind of water-adaptation experiment."

Elliot looked at him in amazement.

"Come on, Elliot, everyone knows that pathologists are part detective."

"Still, pretty good."

Elliot pondered his monogrammed White Dog mug for a moment before placing it on the wooden tabletop.

"So, Jon, by favoring a DNA injection/stem cell implantation procedure, you're excluding the possibility that these kids were genetically altered before birth."

"These kids couldn't be transgenics because I can only detect the abnormal DNA in certain tissues."

"But if they weren't transgenics, what were they?"

"Two previously healthy kids who were grafted with a robust DNA program that went bad over time."

"I thought that kind of genetic add-on technology wasn't yet possible in humans," Elliot whispered.

"Not anymore," Jon said, feeling sad for the two victimized children.

As if she sensed an energy change, the coffeehouse's canine namesake meandered up to Jon wagging her tail. "What do you think, girl?" Jon asked. The Samoyed pushed closer.

"If it was a water adaptation experiment that would explain the proximity of the lab to the water hole, huh?" Elliot asked.

"I think so. Something went wrong and poor Jose shipped water through his skin and down into his lungs via the connecting structures," Jon said.

"If the structures malfunctioned like Dr. Lowenstein said, and the kid literally drowned through his skin, what were the structures originally intended for?" Elliot asked.

"My best guess is that these kids were genetically engineered for prolonged underwater submersion."

"How?"

"Lowenstein did a rough calculation on how much air the connecting structures and all their anastomosing ducts would have held if they had been fully functional."

"You mean if they hadn't been filled with water and cancer cells," Elliot said.

"Right, and he came up with a figure that was at least ten

times to twenty times the normal lung capacity of a seventy-kilogram adult."

"Harry Houdini cubed, huh."

"At least, and it definitely gives a new meaning to self-contained underwater breathing apparatus," Jon said.

"Right, the old SCUBA acronym. And the thick skin?"

"Think of it as kind of a permanent wet suit."

"And the increased size of both the chest and back muscles?"

"They were doing the breast stroke—a lot."

"You've really thought this through, haven't you?"

"There's more, and it's a blockbuster," Jon said, telling Elliot about the unregulated master orchestrator gene and its activation of the boy's genome. "And if we can reconstitute the regulatory sequences, we should be able to stop the cancers from forming."

Elliot's mouth was agape. "A cure for cancer! What's your strategy for isolating—this, this ... *regulator?*"

"Hold on, someone's paging me," Jon said, feeling his beeper vibrating on his belt. He checked the number and stood up. "I need to find a phone—I left mine in the car. It's my lab."

"Here. Use this." Elliot pulled his from his shirt pocket.

Jon dialed the number and waited.

"Drake lab, Diane speaking."

"Diane, what are you doing back in the lab?"

"We've had a break-in."

§

Diane, Chris, and two security guards were waiting for Jon when he strode into the lab at one A.M. Diane spoke first.

"Well, it's not as bad as we first thought. Chris came back from Caltech and found the lights on and the freezer alarm sounding. He called me, and I came in from the Valley," she said.

"Did you see anyone, Chris?"

"No, not a soul, Dr. Drake."

"What's missing?"

Orchestrator 91

"Nothing that we can tell. Somebody rummaged through the big freezer, and the stuff was shuffled around a bit, but we can't identify anything as actually missing," Diane said.

"What about the Gonzalez DNA? It's still here, right?"

"Yes, it's safe. It was originally double-coded and, for good measure, stored in a satellite freezer down the hall. My lab notebooks are locked up in here," she said, patting a stainless steel cabinet in the main lab.

"And the computer? Has anyone messed with it?" Jon asked, performing his own inventory of the lab.

"Doesn't look like it, Dr. Drake. And even if they got into our files, the autopsy DNA findings are encrypted and scrambled," Chris said. "Nothing to worry about, I took care of that."

"How did they get into the building?" Jon asked, focusing his attention on the two security guards.

"We're checking into it, Dr. Drake. No leads so far. In the meantime, my boss authorized us to give your lab around-the-clock coverage," the taller one said.

"Thanks, that helps," Jon said.

"Jon, there's a message for you from Dr. Lowenstein on the lab voice mail. Something about the Baja water sample. Do you want to hear it?" Diane asked.

"Yeah, let's go into the office."

He closed the door behind them and listened to the message on the speakerphone.

"Jon, Abe Lowenstein here. Your hunch was right. The sample you gave me from the Baja water hole is a chemical match with the fluid sample from the boy's lungs. That's where he shipped water, all right." The line crackled and then cleared up. "Something else, Abner Woods, the L.A. county coroner, wants to meet with you to discuss the Gonzalez boy. I'll get you an appointment. He's an old friend."

"Man, when does Lowenstein rest?" Jon said.

"Speaking of rest, it looks like you could use some," Diane said. "Still got that headache?"

"I'm hangin' in there, but the back of my head is still killing me. Elliot's referred me to a neurologist who's taking a look at me in the morning."

"Sounds like something you should do. Don't worry about us. With the twenty-four/seven security, we should be fine here."

"Diane, you can't be too careful. Somebody out there is more than interested in the autopsy material. They already tried to claim the body, and now they've tried to break into the lab. We could be targeted again."

Diane nodded and began to push him out the door. "I agree, and we'll be careful. Now, go home and get some sleep. I'm going to do the same, I'm exhausted. Let's talk tomorrow after you've seen the neurologist. We should have some more data on the orchestrator gene and Bright Star's blood sample by then."

§

The waiting room of the Valley Neurology suites was a veritable gallery of Impressionist reproductions. Jon scanned them all and paused at a Monet painting of the French countryside. He attempted to fix his vision on the shocks of wheat, but as hard as he tried, he couldn't focus. The golden-yellow strands seemed to vibrate and undulate. He closed his eyes and gave in to the dull ache in the back of his head, which seemed to keep time with his heartbeat.

A plump, smiling nurse in her mid-forties opened a door and led Jon from the waiting room down a long corridor.

"You'll be seeing Dr. Goodman instead of Dr. Johnstone," she said, ushering him into a small office. "Dr. Goodman, Dr. Jonathan Drake to see you."

The lanky Aaron Goodman stood up and shook hands with Jon.

"Welcome," he said, pointing to the cushioned chair.

"I know you were expecting to see Dr. Johnstone, but he's not feeling well, so you're going to have to put up with me instead."

"Not a problem, thanks for seeing me on such short notice. Elliot Adams sent me here," Jon said, settling into the chair.

"Elliot was a grad student in the Johnstone lab when I did my postdoc training. We spent a lot of late nights together. So, you were hit in the back of the head two days ago in San Diego. What are you feeling now?"

"Mainly a dull headache and ringing in my ears."

"Taking any meds?"

"Only Advil."

"Okay. I'm going to do a complete neurological exam, followed by X-rays and a CT scan of your head."

It was two hours of mildly rigorous tests later before Jon rested on an examining table in a wood-paneled room. The neurologist returned holding his medical chart with a smile on his face. "Good news, Jon. The X-rays and CT scan are normal. No fracture, no significant bleeding. But you did sustain a mild concussion, which means you need to lay low and take it easy for a few days."

"And the neurological exam?" Jon asked.

"Okay except for one thing," he replied.

"What's that?"

"I'm not a legitimate ophthalmologist, so I'm not even sure if what I'm seeing is abnormal. Let's have another look."

He removed the ophthalmoscope from the wall, turned off the room lights, and looked into Jon's right eye.

"Okay, look straight ahead," he said. "It's probably an anatomic variation, but it's hard to ignore. Have you ever had any trouble with your vision?"

"Never."

"Hello, there it is. It's a small blue rectangular spot at the periphery of the retina at about one o'clock. And you have another one just like it on the other side," he said, looking into Jon's left eye. "And because they're bilateral, I'm convinced now that they're normal anatomic variants; nothing to worry about."

Jon felt relieved.

"Your main job right now is to rest, take it easy, and get better. You should take at least two days, maybe three off work. Keep taking the Advil as needed, and I'd like to see you again in a week. Any problems, give me a call, night or day."

CHAPTER—11

After leaving the Valley Neurology offices, Jon took Dr. Goodman's advice and drove home to rest. Elliot, who was in Pasadena seeing a patient at Huntington Hospital, called to find out how his appointment had gone, and Jon invited him over for a coffee. When Elliot arrived, they sat on Jon's enclosed patio, which faced the snow-capped San Gabriel Mountains. On one of the side walls was a series of topographical maps with an array of trails highlighted in bright colors.

"Man, you really are into backpacking and hiking, aren't you? Keeps you sane, huh?"

Jon nodded.

"So, Aaron said your headaches were nothing to worry about, right?"

Jon nodded again. "I don't know if I can sit around for a few days resting. It's going to drive me crazy before it's over."

"Use it as an excuse to chill out for a while. It looks like you're working way too hard anyway."

"What's going on with Brett Johnstone? Why couldn't he see me today?" Jon asked.

A pained look came over Elliot's face.

"What happened to him?"

"He suddenly came down with an accelerated form of dementia. It's totally bizarre. I found out this morning when I scheduled your appointment. He was fine when I visited him last week. I need to talk to you about it. It's getting to me. Ever since we came back from Baja, I've been feeling stressed out, and this makes it much worse."

"Sudden-onset dementia. Due to what?" Jon asked.

"To be determined. He's being monitored at home, but he'll be admitted to University Hospital tomorrow for a complete workup."

"Wow, what a shocker," Jon said.

"It's awful, I can't stand it. I feel responsible," Elliot said, looking despondent.

Jon reached for Elliot's shoulder and tried to comfort him. "Come on, man, how could you possibly be responsible for something like that?"

"It's my fuckin' do-gooder anarchist side getting people in trouble again."

"Does this have something to do with your history of civil disobedience?"

"How did you know about that?" He sat up straight.

"Mona told me it came up on their DEA security check."

"Meddling bastards!" He put his head in his hands.

"Elliot, get a grip, what's going on?" Jon asked.

Elliot took a deep breath. "Like I told you, I haven't been a hundred percent lately." He exhaled slowly, then went on. "It's some kind of anxiety reaction. I'll be okay."

"You sure you're up to talking about it?" Jon asked.

Elliot nodded.

"So what do you feel so guilty about? You couldn't have caused Johnstone's dementia? It's preposterous."

"Well, I didn't directly cause it, but I convinced him to make a decision that most likely backfired on us."

"What decision?" Jon asked.

"It's got to do with a hold on the patent rights to the gene therapy vectors that Johnstone and I developed for our clinical neurology protocols." He looked directly at Jon. His eyes were red and misty.

"I'll be all right as long as I stay calm," Elliot said.

"Agreed, stay cool. I'm listening."

"My main thesis project as a neurobiology M.D./Ph.D. student at U.C.S.F. was to genetically engineer viruses so that they would physically target the tissues of the eye and ear."

"Customized gene-therapy vectors?"

"Right. We originally designed the viral vectors so that they would carry the correct genes into the diseased eye and ear tissues."

"Man, your group pioneered that technology? That was a real breakthrough!"

"We thought so, too. Anyway, I fine-tuned the vectors, worked out an animal model, graduated, and went into pediatrics. During my residency, Johnstone and I pieced together the protocols for staging a relevant clinical trial. We relocated to Southern California and were just steps away from initiating a blockbuster clinical trail."

"One that had the potential to cure most forms of hereditary blindness and deafness, right?" Jon asked.

"Something like that."

"What happened? What knocked you off track?"

"We had applied for the patent rights on the vectors early on in the process. But just as we were about to submit the final paperwork to the U.S. Patent Office, our lawyers were approached by several lawyers from a prominent biotech company."

"Which one?"

"Pathgene."

"Pathgene!" Jon exclaimed.

"It a big one all right. Multinational, endless assets, huge clout, and…"

"And a CEO named David Kreeger," Jon said.

"Jesus, Jon, you know him?"

"Only by name until recently. He wants access to my transgenic mice and gene-transfer technology."

"How so?" Elliot asked.

"He's been personally harassing me, and just yesterday, he personally confronted me after my presentation."

"No surprise there. All he cares about now is money and power," Elliot said. "Big science and big bucks. It's hard to fathom that he was once a distinguished professor of pediatric surgery at Stanford."

"I remember some of his papers," Jon said.

"Somehow he became disgruntled with academia, stopped seeing patients, and left the ivory tower. Go figure," Elliot said.

"So what did his lawyers want?" Jon asked.

"It was a bombshell. They told us that they had a similar set of vectors and wanted to share the patent rights with us."

"They wanted to negotiate a copatent. Why didn't they just try to patent them on their own?"

"Because they stole them from us."

"But even if they stole them, why wouldn't they claim them as their own invention and not even bother to contact you?"

"They're desperate for our patients, our clinical expertise, and our FDA-approved clinical trial. Without us, they can't commercially develop the vectors for world-wide distribution. In other words, they can't make their bloody big bucks," Elliot said.

"How do you know they stole the vectors, and *who* stole them from you?" Jon asked.

"First of all, the structures they had were virtually identical. Second, we had a postdoctoral fellow suddenly leave under unusual circumstances. After he left, we discovered that we were missing an early passage of vectors along with a computer file that structurally identified them down to the last nucleotide."

"A traitor," Jon commented.

"I didn't want anything to do with Kreeger and Pathgene.

Johnstone was on the fence. They made us a big money offer, but I convinced Johnstone that they were greedy thieves, that they had no right to cash in on our science, and that the vectors belonged to no one but the sick patients who received and benefited from them. He eventually agreed. We turned them down, and then came the threat to block our patent with theirs, and so it went. Those mother-fucking corporate assholes!" He hit his fist on the table again.

"Calm down. Remember, you need to stay cool."

"Okay, cool," he answered.

"Then what?" Jon asked.

"Then came the wining and dining, and then the lost time." Elliot took a sip of coffee.

"Keep going."

"So, a month ago, the invitation came down from the big dog that we were to be his dinner guests at his private estate."

"David Kreeger?" Jon asked.

"That's right. He owns his own winery on the skyline ridge overlooking Portola Valley."

Jon gawked in amazement, feeling a slight tinge of jealousy.

"He's also got a degree in viticulture and enology from U.C.–Davis."

"Jesus, a wine science degree? What doesn't this guy do?" Jon said.

"Well, for one, he doesn't give a shit about human beings." Elliot put his cup down.

"So he wined and dined you and then tried to get you and Johnstone to change your minds about the copatent."

"A fancy limo picked us up at the San Jose Airport and drove us up to the Ridgetop Winery estate. What a location, what a dinner, what great wine, what a royal asshole."

"So you turned him down again, huh."

"You bet we did. But on the way back to the airport, something strange happened. Somewhere along the way, my vision blurred and I lost consciousness. The next thing I remembered, we were pulling up to the Southwest Airlines Terminal."

"What about Johnstone?" Jon asked.

"He experienced the same thing. We asked the driver what had happened. He said we'd both fallen asleep and joked about how much wine we had drunk."

"How long do you think you were out?"

"My best guesstimate was that we were out of it for about an hour, and that only about half of that could have been actual driving time. We couldn't have been stuck in traffic, because it was late. We were catching the last flight back to L.A."

"Do you remember anything at all?"

"I do remember a funny smell in the limo. Johnstone's not so sure."

"Do you think it could have been some kind of anesthetic gas?"

"Could be. The driver had the plastic barrier up, so that would explain why he didn't get exposed. Johnstone and I woke up with mild headaches, and I haven't been the same since. My anxiety reactions started after that episode."

"And now Johnstone comes down with accelerated dementia," Jon said.

"Jon, I'm terrified. I might be next."

CHAPTER—12

After meeting with Elliot, Jon wrestled with whether or not to return to the lab. Although he was tired, there was just too much going on to stay away.

Thirty minutes later, he was walking past the security guards, trying to enter his lab without being noticed. Diane, who was in the walk-in cold room setting up a column, spotted him through the glass panel and came out into the main room.

"Jon, how did your appointment go?"

"Nothing too serious; just need to rest for a few days."

"So what are you doing back *here* then?"

"I've got Abe Lowenstein's disease. I can't stay away," he said, sheepishly.

"Well, since you're here … I've been working on the Baja blood specimen. The preliminary screen on the white blood cells shows an extra protein, so I'm trying to extract and isolate it."

"Any hunches?" Jon asked.

She produced a photo from the vest pocket of her lab coat and handed it to him.

"Lovely, aren't they?" she said.

101

Jon looked at the photo, which showed a dozen or more cockroaches gathered in a small area.

"Didn't think we had so many in the lab did you?"

"The Health Department's going to love this one. It's disgusting," Jon said, feeling a shiver up and down his spine.

"They're huddled on a drop of Bright Star's blood that fell on the floor next to the centrifuge."

"Cockroaches don't feed on blood. There must be some type of chemo-attractant in it," Jon said.

"I think it's a pheromone."

"That would make sense. Those wasps definitely targeted him for a reason."

"But how does a pheromone find its way into blood cells?" she asked.

"I don't know. Could be he was part of another human experiment."

"This is getting more and more sinister," she said, shaking her head. "Jon, someone called you from the L.A. coroner's office to confirm a two P.M. appointment with Dr. Woods. I wrote the number down next to the phone."

"Thanks. I'll call back."

As they walked through the main room, Jon could see the security guard standing in front of the lab's main entrance.

"Where's Chris?" Jon asked, suddenly realizing that he wasn't in the lab.

"I convinced him that it wasn't safe to do the frog experiments at Caltech, so he's bringing them back to our lab. I even got him a security escort. He should be back in about an hour."

"Good thinking. Does he have any more info on the autopsy DNA?"

"Not that he's told me, but I'll ask him when he gets back. Where are you gonna be?"

"Back at the hospital for a while, and then to the coroner's office. After that, I'm goin' home to rest. Doctor's orders, ya know." He smiled at her. "If anything comes up, page me."

§

After checking his mail, making several phone calls, and arranging with the chief pathology resident for some sick days, Jon pulled out of the hospital parking structure and headed for the L.A. coroner's office.

As he drove through Elysian Park, he could see the light standards of Dodger Stadium peeking over the hills surrounding Chavez Ravine. Spring training wasn't that far off, and driving by the stadium always reminded him of the good times he and his father had spent there. It was their time to talk baseball and enjoy each other's company.

After driving through Chinatown, Jon neared the coroner's office, which was a complex of three whitewashed cinder-block buildings. Jon pulled up to the kiosk and checked in with the attendant, who made a phone call and raised the parking gate for him.

"Park in the back of the main building next to that pair of mortuary vehicles," he said, gesturing in the direction of the largest building. "Dr. Wood's office is just off the loading dock area."

After negotiating a maze of ambulances, official coroner's vehicles, and hearses, Jon found a place to park. He climbed up the steps to the loading dock and saw morticians in black suits directing the placement of zippered body bags into the rear compartments of their polished hearses. He walked down a long echoing hallway past autopsy rooms and morgues, finally entering an office bearing a plaque that read *Chief Medical Examiner, Los Angeles County.* A petite, middle-aged receptionist wearing dark eye shadow and bright red lipstick greeted him.

"You must be Dr. Wood's two o'clock."

Jon nodded.

"He's expecting you. Come this way," she said, opening the door to the inner office.

A large man smoking a cigar and dressed in green surgical

scrubs sat at his desk. The walls of his office were covered with authentic, full-size American flags, and on his desk was a large wooden replica of a wild boar with the words *University of Arkansas Razorbacks* branded on its right flank. Next to the boar was a black-and-white print of Li'l Abner and Daisy Mae conspicuously autographed by Al Capp: "To the One and Only Real Abner."

"Hello Jon," he said, extending his hand for a shake. "Abner Woods. Sit down and stay awhile. Abe Lowenstein told me all about you."

He puffed on the cigar and pointed to a black leather easy chair across from his desk.

"I need some more info on the boy you and Lowenstein transferred to me," he said.

"Fire away."

"What was left of him looked like he had been dead in the water for a while. We were more than surprised when we couldn't grow out the usual bacteria that cause tissue putrefaction."

"But he died in the hospital," Jon said.

"I know that now. Abe called me the next day and told me that you had done the autopsy the night before on a kid who had died that afternoon. No way in hell he could have been a floater. Abe said you had examined some of the tissues in your research lab?"

Jon went on to describe the autopsy findings and then the fast DNA that was present in the boy's abnormal tissues.

"So, if this fast DNA was responsible for the rapid tissue breakdown, it explains the absence of bacteria in the boy's corpse."

He puffed on his cigar a while. "Very screwy," he said, hitching his feet up onto his desk. "Jon, there's something else that might interest you. I'm online with all of the California coroners, and a colleague of mine in Mono County autopsied a Native American boy whose body underwent rapid breakdown and liquefaction."

"Really?" Jon leaned forward in his chair. "Were there any abnormal tissues?"

"I don't have the complete report, but I'll find out for you."

"Maybe I should review the case with him."

"Now there's an idea. He lives in the Eastern Sierra Nevada in a town called June Lake. I hear the skiing is pretty good this season."

"I know the area. I've backpacked there."

The door opened, and his secretary popped her head in.

"Dr. Woods, someone from L.A.P.D. is calling about the two bodies they found in the Los Angeles Street sewer. He wants to know if you have a preliminary."

"Sorry to run, Jon, but duty calls," Woods said and stood up. "Jen, Dr. Drake needs a phone number and an e-mail address where he can reach Lucas Faust."

He shook Jon's hand, then handed him a report.

"Here's what we've got on your kid so far. Have Jen make a copy for you on the way out. I'll be in touch if I need any more information, and you do the same."

As he walked back to his car, Jon scanned the autopsy report on the boy and saw that the narcotic screen was negative.

§

As soon as Jon got home from the coroner's office, he shot off an e-mail to Lucas Faust and then phoned Elliot, briefing him on his encounter with Abner Woods.

"If Faust agrees, why don't we go together," he offered. "You know we both could use a break. What do you say?"

"Okay, deal. I need the rest, and I know someone who has a condo in June Lake. I'll give him a call."

"Any more news on Brett Johnstone?" Jon asked.

"None yet. He was supposed to be admitted this afternoon. I'll let you know once I've had a chance to check in on him."

Jon hung up and deliberated a moment. He had to call Mona

and tell her about the negative drug screen on Jose Gonzalez and also about the Native American autopsy in Mono County. Her answering machine picked up. "Mona. Call or page me ASAP. It's Jon Drake in L.A." He repeated his phone and pager numbers and hung up.

It was getting dark and the house was cold, so Jon took the opportunity to build a fire in the living room. By the time he had sprawled out in front of the hearth with Chelsea, the phone rang. It was Mona.

"Jon, it's me. I was hoping you would call. But I can't talk too long. I'm at a pay phone."

"A pay phone? What's going on?"

"I think I'm on to something pretty big, and I'm afraid my phone's been tapped." Her voice came through as clearly as if she were sitting in the room with him.

"What happened?"

"After you left, I got to thinking some more about the Baja drug connection, the decomposed body, and those abandoned lab buildings that we found. So I started digging around at work, and lo and behold, I found out that Stringfellow and a few of his higher-up DEA buddies have been collaborating with the U.S. Air Force on a series of biology projects. You were right on—the drug connection was a ruse. I knew that son of a bitch was up to no good."

"Roger that. The coroner's drug screen on Jose was negative. I just saw the report. And why the U.S. Air Force/DEA collaboration? What kind of bio projects were they?"

"Not sure yet, I'm still digging. You're going to have to translate the science for me. You're my ticket out of here."

"Mona, let's get together and talk then. I have some more info, and I'll help you any way I can."

"Okay. I'll page you tomorrow then and we'll work something out. Can't talk now. I've got to keep moving. I think I'm being followed. Talk to you soon."

He set the receiver down and took a deep breath. Finally, he

Orchestrator   107

had reconnected with her, but now he wondered whether or not she was digging too deep. Getting a promotion was one thing, but double-crossing Stringfellow and his cronies was a risky proposition at best. He was scared for her, but looking forward to being with her again.

Feeling a chill, he moved closer to the fire. He patted Chelsea and drifted off into sleep. With time, he felt his father's fingers twirling and curling his hair. Then he heard the dry logs crackling in the fireplace of his boyhood home while Benjamin Drake read *The Night Before Christmas* aloud. Jon was awaiting Santa's arrival when his pager sounded. He jerked up and returned the page.

"Jon, it's Elliot, something terrible has happened. Brett Johnstone is dead."

"Dead?" Jon asked.

"His brother found him at home. He never made it to the hospital."

"Any witnesses?"

"He lived alone. Divorced," Elliot said.

There was a long pause, and he thought he heard Elliot sobbing.

"I know it's awful, Elliot, but try and get a hold on yourself. You must."

There was another pause.

"Okay, I'm trying to relax," he said.

"What are they doing with the body?" Jon asked.

"Since he died at home, it's a coroner's case. The body's already there, and the autopsy will be done tomorrow."

"God, and I was just there. Any evidence of foul play?" Jon asked.

"No. He had a gash on his forehead, but the deputy coroner thinks that he had an epileptic seizure and hit his head on the edge of the coffee table when he fell. His mouth was frothy, which fits with epilepsy."

"So they're treating it as natural causes at this point," Jon said.

"They are, but I know Kreeger is involved, which means I could be next. And, Jon, you might not be safe yourself." Elliot was speaking so quickly he lost his voice and coughed into the phone. "But I don't know how we're gonna prove it."

"Let's make sure Abner Woods knows the whole story. I think Abe Lowenstein can help us with that. Lowenstein's tight with him. I'll call him and give him a heads-up," Jon said.

"I want to be there for the autopsy, but I don't think I can stomach it in my present condition. I'd feel better if Lowenstein were involved," Elliot said.

"I'll see what I can do. Hang in there, Elliot."

Jon wouldn't allow himself to think about all the ominous possibilities. He immediately dialed Abe Lowenstein's work number and got a busy signal. He headed toward the kitchen. Passing by the study, he saw his e-mail inbox blinking on his computer. It was from faust@HAPPEN.org.

Dear Dr. Drake,
Greetings from June Lake. Delighted to show you the case you're interested in. Give me a call anytime and we can set up an appointment. All I need is a few hours advance notice. I'm not going anywhere for the holidays, so if you're in the area, that works too.

Regards, Lucas B. Faust

P.S.—I also have teleconferencing capability if you can't make it.

Jon replied that he'd be in touch soon and did a quick online search on Lucas B. Faust. A bibliographic listing of forensic pathology articles came up, one of which was coauthored by Dr. Abner Woods. There was another link that listed him as the founder and director of Health Allied Professionals for the Protection of the Environment and Nature (HAPPEN). So,

Orchestrator   109

Lucas Faust was an environmentalist with a knack for acronyms in addition to being a coroner. Jon was definitely looking forward to meeting him.

It was after nine P.M. when Jon finally got through to Abe Lowenstein to inform him of the circumstances surrounding Brett Johnstone's demise. Abe immediately said he would call Abner and make arrangements to assist him with the autopsy at the coroner's office.

"Jon, give me some ideas. What do you think we're looking for?"

"Well, from what I've heard so far, his signs and symptoms all point to central nervous system pathology, so the neuropath examination should be the most revealing," Jon said.

"Agreed, then."

"Is there any way to get some fresh tissue for my lab?"

"I think I can arrange for that. Before we fix the whole brain in formaldehyde, I'll get a couple of needle biopsies from several areas of the cortex. How do you want them to be sent?"

"On dry ice. I'll tell Diane that you'll be calling her. Or maybe I should be there to help you," he said.

"Jon, Diane told me you were taking a few days off. Doctor's orders, she said."

"It's driving me crazy."

"I understand. It's hard to keep a good man down. Get some rest. I'll call you when I know something."

Jon decided he had to try to sleep. He dozed on and off for several hours, then tossed and turned for another. He couldn't take it anymore; he had to tell Mona what was going on. He had to call her. He was worried about her. It was risky, but maybe she could call him back on a payphone.

He dialed the number and waited for her to answer. After multiple rings, a prerecorded phone company message stated that the number was no longer in service. He slammed down the phone and fumbled with his wallet for Mona's work number. At least he could leave her a voice message. After a couple of rings, a canned male voice announced "Agent Larsen is on extended leave. Please leave a message, and another agent will return your call as soon as possible."

He hung up and started to pace. What should he do next? She believed someone was following her, and now her phones were either disconnected or forwarded. He had no choice but to drive to Solana Beach and find her. Thirty minutes later he was on the road.

CHAPTER—13

The high beams of Jon's BMW pierced the blackness as he pulled into the parking lot at the Solana Beach Vista apartment complex. He killed the engine and turned off the lights so he could think for a moment. Even though Mona's phone was out of order, there was still a possibility that she was home.

He got out of the car, walked to the common entryway, and quickly scanned the black-and-white directory. M. Larsen, Apartment 14. His adrenaline pumping, he crept down the dimly lit concrete path toward Mona's garden apartment where the wind chimes out front hung motionless. Jon conjured up a vivid picture of her standing there, and moved in the direction of her apartment.

The door was slightly open. When he put his ear to the crack, he thought he could hear faint voices toward the rear of the apartment. As the voices got louder and closer, he stepped back from the door, jumped over the metal railing, and ducked under the suspended walkway next to a stand of sego palms.

"Where do you think she went? The boss is gonna be pissed that we didn't find her," a voice said.

"I agree, he's really hot about something. She must'a split though," another voice said.

As they walked down the pathway, Jon saw that both men were in uniform and the man on the right was wearing a baseball cap. From his voice and mannerisms, Jon was pretty sure it was the helicopter pilot he had met in Baja. He breathed a deep sigh of relief when, minutes later, he heard a car start up and drive off.

Jon retraced his path and found Mona's front door still slightly ajar. He tapped it open, listened for a full ten breaths, and cautiously entered the apartment. The sky was beginning to get light, and Jon could see the vague outline of her living room furniture. He took out a penlight and went into the bedroom. It was clear that her bed hadn't been slept in and was still lined with stuffed animals. He walked over to the dresser and shined the light onto a pair of framed photos. The smaller one showed a much younger Mona posing with an older man dressed in a police uniform, while the larger depicted an adult Mona with two women, one older and one younger, dressed in sweat suits. The three stood in front of a 5K race sign entitled "Run for Breast Cancer Awareness." He guessed that the man was her father and the women, her mother and sister.

Feeling uneasy about staying much longer, he decided to look for anything that might give him a hint of how to find her—an address book, a scrap of paper with a phone number. With this in mind, he began by going through Mona's dresser and then the drawers in her desk. After finding nothing of interest, he spotted a vial of pills on the floor. He picked up the plastic container and studied the label. It was a recent prescription for the beta-blocker Atenolol, with Mona's name on the label. Wondering if she had high blood pressure, he put the vial in his pocket. She must have been in quite a hurry to leave.

Next he went into Mona's walk-in closet and parted her clothes in the middle. He looked behind them and found nothing. He shone the light on the upper shelf of the closet. A thick red book lying on its side caught his eye. Its cover was neatly engraved with block letters spelling *New American Standard Bible.* A medium-sized, manila envelope was wedged between the middle pages. He removed it and took out the half dozen 5 x 7 black-and-white pictures that were inside.

They were nude photos of Mona in a variety of provocative poses. Maybe Stringfellow was blackmailing her after all. He held his breath and examined the photos, each of which clearly highlighted and accentuated her natural beauty. As he put them back in the envelope and then back into the book, he noticed that the envelope had been stamped in the upper left hand corner with the words *VELA Estudio Fotografico, Tijuana, Baja California Norte.* On the address label was Mona's name and address and a recent postmark. Seconds later, he was out the front door, bible in hand.

§

Jon sat in his parked car on an unnamed Tijuana side street watching the entrance to the VELA Estudio Fotographico. The Via Insurgentes, one of the main traffic arteries connecting the north and south sections of the Mexican border town, was twenty yards to the east. He watched as several barefoot Mexican children ran back and forth across the dirt-covered street kicking an old soccer ball. Jon followed the trajectory of the ball to the other side of the street and noticed an old, ramshackle one-story building with a bilingual sign saying *Clinica del Cancer, Receta Medica No Necesaria—Cancer Clinic, Medical Prescription Not Necessary.*

He watched the ball bounce back and forth, back and forth, until a white stretch limousine rounded the corner with its brakes screeching. As if this were a routine occurrence, the children gracefully leapt out of the way and stood watching as the limo stopped in front of the studio entrance. The ball rolled to a standstill near one of the rear tires. The back door opened

and out stepped an attractive, dark-haired Latina in her mid-
twenties wearing red high heels and a low-cut, black-satin dress.
A tall, well-dressed, Latino male who wore his jet-black hair in
a ponytail accompanied her. The woman picked up the tattered
soccer ball and, smiling, tossed it to the children. After the couple
disappeared into the studio, a young Mexican man in blue jeans
and a Hard Rock T-shirt emerged from the studio entrance and
became engaged in conversation with the couple's chauffeur, who
was wiping down the windows of the limousine.

It was now or never. Jon took a deep breath, got out of the
car, and walked in their direction.

"*Permisso,*" he said looking directly at the man in the
T-shirt.

"*Como?*" he answered.

"Do you speak English?" Jon asked.

"*Si.*"

"I'm looking for a woman."

"How much do you wanna pay, *senor?*" he said with a wide
toothy smile.

"No, that's not what I mean. I'm trying to find *this* woman.
Do you recognize her?" he asked.

He held up a photograph of Mona, who was standing in
front of the Santa Inez Medical Clinic with the rest of the clinic
personnel.

"*Si, senor,*" he answered.

"Do you know where I can find her?"

"*No se.*"

There was a long pause.

"I have to find her. I'm her doctor," Jon said.

"*No se,*" the man repeated.

He lit up a cigarette.

"Is there anyone inside who knows where I can find her? It's
an emergency."

"*Que es su problema, senor?*" another voice said.

The man with the ponytail had reemerged from the studio

entrance and was approaching the limousine with his female companion. After a short exchange in Spanish with the other man, he turned to Jon.

"Who are you looking for?" he said in perfect English.

Jon showed him the photo, which he took and examined more closely. He showed it to the woman who nodded in agreement.

"We are friends of Miss Mona. Is she in some kind of trouble?" the man asked.

"I'm not sure. I'm trying to find her. I'm her doctor. She has a medical condition, and I'm worried about her," Jon said, sincerely.

"Why do you think she came here?" the man asked.

"I have reason to believe that she might have been doing some modeling at this studio," Jon said, hoping that his story sounded believable.

"So, you're a doctor?" the man asked.

Jon reached into his pocket for his wallet. He took out both his California medical license and driver's license, showing it to the stranger, who introduced himself as Roberto Garcia. He shook hands with him.

"Dr. Drake, Maria and I manage the studio, and you are correct. Miss Mona is one of our models, and we want to help her. We'll take you to someone who will know how to find her."

§

Jon surveyed the Tijuana streets as the limousine weaved through its cluttered roads. The woman's slender legs touched his as the driver took the corner sharply, and then swerved in the opposite direction narrowly missing an antiquated school bus parked on the side of the road.

"So, where are we going?" Jon asked.

"To a private club on the west side of town near the ocean," Roberto said.

"Relax, Dr. Jon, and enjoy the ride. You can trust us," Maria said, inserting a pop music CD into the stereo.

While Jon leaned back and tried to relax, he wondered if he had made the right decision. These two seemed well intentioned enough, and genuinely concerned about Mona. What choice did he have?

The limousine soon left the crowded city streets and made its way up to the top of a hill where a complex of high-rise buildings overlooked the bluish-green waters of the Pacific.

After entering an underground parking garage lined with an array of closed-circuit TV cameras, they got out of the limo and boarded an elevator. Jon was still nervous, and his feelings of claustrophobia didn't help matters.

"When we get to the top, stay close to us," Roberto said, pushing the top button.

The elevator picked up three Japanese businessmen, who bowed and smiled several times until the doors finally opened on the twelfth floor. They walked out into a lavishly decorated bar and casino. Disco music throbbed. Nude dancers in suspended wire cages, looking more possessed than sexy, gyrated to the pounding beat. The wood bar was adorned with art deco tiles, and a panel of glass aquariums teeming with tropical fish served as a multicolor backdrop for the two animated bartenders who were dressed in black tuxedos.

"You want your own private dancer, Dr. Jon," Maria joked, moving her hips back and forth.

"You're embarrassing our guest," Roberto said.

"But he's so cute, and he has such nice dimples," she said, lightly pinching him on the cheek.

"I'm going to see what I can find out. I'll meet you by the blackjack tables in a half-hour. Maria will take good care of you," he said.

"I'm sure she will," Jon replied.

§

Orchestrator 117

Thirty minutes later, Roberto escorted Jon to a private office in the rear of the casino.

"Make yourself comfortable. Rodrigo will be along to talk to you in a few minutes. I'll be waiting out front," Roberto said.

Jon gazed out the window at the wide expanse of ocean and tried to calm his nerves. He had partially succeeded by the time a tall Latino man in his late forties or early fifties with a medium build and a bushy black moustache opened the door and entered the room.

"I'm Rodrigo Escheverria, the manager of Club Paradise."

He shook hands with Jon, a little more rigorously than Jon was used to.

"Roberto tells me you're looking for Mona."

"That's right. She left her job, abandoned her apartment, and forgot to take her medicine. I'm her doctor and need to find her," Jon said taking out the vial of Atenolol and handing it to Rodrigo.

"What happens to her if she doesn't take these?" he asked.

Rodrigo studied the label, then handed the vial back to Jon.

"Patients with untreated hypertension have an increased risk of stroke and heart disease."

"That does sound serious. In all the time I've known her, she never told me she had high blood pressure."

"Most patients keep that information pretty private."

"Agreed, Dr. Drake, but I was married to her."

"I'm sorry, I didn't know," Jon said, suddenly feeling awkward and not wanting to disclose his shock.

"She's quite a woman. Let's say it just didn't work out. No hard feelings. Let's call it past history."

Jon could barely manage a nod in response.

"Which brings me to another question, how does one become so fortunate to have her doctor personally deliver her medications? Are you her lover, perhaps?" Rodrigo asked.

"Just good friends with some common interests," he answered.

"So you've developed a working relationship," Rodrigo said with a smile.

"That's a good way of looking at it."

"Well, Roberto assures me you came a long way to find her, and I, too, am worried about Mona's health. She and I are still friends, and she calls me when she's in trouble."

"Is she in TJ?"

"No. She called me last night and told me she had to get out of San Diego. Your story fits with what she told me. 'Trouble with work,' but she didn't go into any of the details. One of my business partners owns a hotel-casino complex in North Vegas. I told her to lay low at his place for a while. She should be there by now. Here's his card. He can help you if there's a problem. And here's mine for good measure."

He pulled out a bottle of Commemerativo Gold Tequila, poured two shots, and handed one to Jon.

"To Mona's health," he said.

"To Mona's health," Jon echoed.

As they drained their glasses, Jon was surprised how easy it went down.

Before beginning the long drive ahead of him, Jon text-messaged his sister to ask her to take care of Chelsea. Then, realizing she would be worried, he called her saying that he had hastily arranged a surprise vacation and would be back for Christmas. Everybody in her house, she said, was preparing for the holidays and their mother's visit to Southern California from St. Louis.

§

Jon had been driving for several hours. He switched on his high beams as he left the desert plateau and started down the long steep grade into California's Anza-Borrego basin. The lights of Borrego Springs twinkled in the distance. According to his map, it was twenty miles ahead. He was tired and had to sleep. He would find a motel there, and drive the six hours to Vegas in the morning.

CHAPTER—14

It took Jon most of the afternoon to find Mona, finally locating her with the help of Rodrigo's partner. When he entered the private guesthouse at the periphery of the Palms Tropicana pool in North Las Vegas, he had found her fully clothed and stretched out on a couch in a semi-drunken state. He quickly packed her belongings and got her into his car.

As they raced away from Las Vegas going north on U.S. Highway 95, he glanced over at his passenger. It had been an hour since the black coffee and aspirin had started to take effect, and she was beginning to come around. He slowed down, turned right and parked on a local ranch road.

"Jon, how did you find me?" Mona asked, her speech slightly slurred.

"Solana Beach with a stop in Tijuana. We can talk about it later. How are you feeling now?" he asked.

"I'm a little dizzy, and I've got a pretty good headache."

"Here, take one of these. You left them in your apartment," he said, handing her the vial of blood pressure medicine and a bottle of mineral water.

"My apartment? How did you get in?" she asked.

119

"Somebody left your door open. I think they were DEA."

"How do you know?"

"I got a glimpse of them when they were leaving and one of them looked like the pilot that rescued us in Baja."

"Figures it was them. They were tailing me pretty close."

She swallowed the pill with a swig of water, closed her eyes, and took a deep breath.

"You better sleep some more," he said.

"Okay," she whispered, her eyes still closed.

He pulled back onto the main highway. He checked his rear mirrors for any suspicious vehicles but saw only a lone semi a mile back, so he relaxed and settled into driving. Mona had fallen back to sleep, her blonde hair hanging across her forehead like a schoolgirl's.

Jon continued north on U.S. 95 and then turned west onto Nevada State Highway 157, which led to Charleston Peak through a forest of pinion and ponderosa pine. After passing the seven-thousand-feet sign marker, he stopped at a roadside pullout with a sunbathed picnic table. Even though there were two more hours of daylight remaining, the air temperature had dropped at the high altitude. As he retrieved his down jacket and sleeping bag from the trunk of the car, he could feel the fresh air and smell the sweet scent of pine. He unzipped the down bag and placed it over Mona, who had woken up and was still groggy.

"Why are we stopping?" she asked.

"I need some fresh air and a stretch, plus we need to talk."

"Where are we?"

"Fifty miles out of Vegas. That's Charleston Peak over there with the snow on it. It's twelve thousand feet high." He pointed to the large snowcapped mountain.

"You sound like a fucking tour guide," she said, pulling the sleeping bag around her shoulders in the front seat of the car and looking away.

He opened the thermos and poured her another cup of coffee.

"Here, drink this, it'll warm you up. You're starting to act like the real Mona." He paused. "And that's a good sign."

She took a sip and looked up at him from the corner of her eye.

"How did you find me?"

"I located your ex-husband in TJ."

"You're more resourceful than I thought."

"You forgot to take your medicine. He was just as concerned as I was."

She glared at him.

"Then fuck both of you. What makes you think I want to be saved? My professional life is over. I have nowhere to go, and I don't want to talk about it." She bit her lower lip, and tears rolled down her cheeks. "I just want to be left alone."

"Stringfellow's not going to leave you alone. Those guys were looking for you, and it's only a matter of time before they catch up with you ... and me. We've gotta stay ahead of them. We're onto something really big, and he's involved."

She looked up at him and made eye contact.

"I want to nail that mother-fucker to the wall! What have you found out?"

"Remember what I told you in Solana Beach about the autopsy DNA?"

"Yeah, the stem cells, the super-fast DNA, the implants," she said, dryly.

"My lab's isolated a hyperactive master orchestrator gene that choreographed the implants and caused the cancers. I'm trying to isolate the regulator sequences that slow the orchestrator down and stop the cancers from forming."

"*A cure for cancer*, you didn't tell me that," she said. Her eyes brightened.

"I didn't know until I got back to the lab on Monday. Somebody's been experimenting on these kids with a 'super-gene' and whoever *they* are, *they* don't want anyone to know about it. My hunch is that Stringfellow is covering it up," he said.

"I think I may have a handle on the *they*," she said, warming her hands on the coffee container.

"Let's hear it then." He moved closer to her.

She nodded and gulped down the rest of the hot drink.

"Okay. I've got a friend at work who supervises the information system in the regional DEA office. Before I filed my report on Monday, I asked him to search the existing DEA data base for any mention of biological experimentation in the Baja drug zones."

"What did he find?"

"After a little work, he retrieved a cross-referenced, classified U.S. Air Force file that had something to do with molecular biology experiments in unique ecosystems. I can't tell you any of the specifics because we could read only a small part of the file. Most of it was scrambled. But we did verify that the USAF had formally notified the DEA that they were operating in the smuggling/trafficking area of central Baja."

"Whoa, the Air Force, that's big. Did it mention the Santa Inez area?"

"No, not by name."

"Do you have a hard copy?"

"Too risky."

"How can we link the operation to Stringfellow?" Jon asked.

"There was a personal e-mail from him to the Air Force lead officer ensuring that the DEA would respect their space."

"What did you do next?" Jon asked.

"I went ahead and filed my report saying that I brought you along as medical support for the old Indian, that we used one of those buildings as a temporary shelter to keep the wasps away, and that we were rescued pronto. End of story."

"What was Stringfellow's reaction?"

"Suspicious and paranoid, and fueled no doubt by some sort of story the good old boys furnished him. He's always viewed me as a dangerous person."

"You told me you had threatened him at one time with a sexual harassment suit."

"Right, and then he counter-threatened me saying he would expose a part of my past that would force me to resign. I dared him to do it and warned him that if he did, I would pay him back in spades. It worked, 'cause he backed off and left me alone. It also makes me think he has something to hide."

"Like what?" Jon asked.

"Like the word on the street is that he's on the take with some of the Mexican drug lords—you know, top-level profit-splitting."

"Do you think he's in on the Air Force experiments?"

"Can't prove it yet, but if it's got anything to do with money and power, he would be the first in line. He sure seemed interested in what we were doing."

"I'll say he did. He was pretty riled up," Jon said, cringing when thinking about his inquisition at Brown Field.

"Remember, he knew you were an M.D. scientist, and was probably suspicious of your motives for being there."

"Makes me wonder if he knew about the L.A. autopsy."

"It wouldn't surprise me," she answered, stretching her arms and then yawning. "Wouldn't surprise me at all." She yawned some more. "So where are we going?"

"June Lake, California, in the Sierra Nevada near the eastern edge of Yosemite."

"Why there?"

"The Mono County Coroner, a guy named Lucas Faust, did an autopsy not long ago on a prematurely decomposed Native American boy. I'm hoping it might be related to the L.A. autopsy."

"Boy, you pathologists have a real thing for corpses."

"We ghouls just can't get enough," Jon said, smiling. "Anyway, he's willing to show me the case and said anytime was okay to visit him. So that's where we're headed. I figure it's about six to seven hours from here … if the weather holds."

A bank of dark clouds was moving in from the west.

She took another sip of hot coffee.

"Feeling warmer now?" Jon asked.

He pulled the sleeping bag a little tighter around her shoulders and put his arm around her.

"I think so," she said, smiling back.

"I like it when you smile. It's a keeper, for sure." He held her closer.

§

Mona fell back asleep again as Jon drove down Lee Canyon's icy grade toward U.S. Highway 95. The weather had changed. Dark cumulus clouds had rapidly brought snow flurries to the higher elevations and a mixture of sleet and rain below. As he approached the intersection with the main highway, the precipitation had lightened to a misty rain. He headed north on U.S. 95 toward Indian Springs, Lathrop Wells, Beatty, and Scotty's Junction.

An hour later, at twilight, he sped past the deserted Phillips 66 station and the gravel pits of Lathrop Wells. In the distance, he could see the silent flashes of lightning illuminating the desert landscape, followed seconds later by the muffled sound of thunder. As he drove into the storm, the mist enveloped his car and brought with it the musky scents of the desert. Staccato flashes of light danced around the car, appearing to startle the surrounding Joshua trees, whose spiny arms reached up to the firmament as if in prayer.

The smell of ozone permeated the air and sharpened his senses, heightening his awareness of time and place. The fingers of his psyche reached out, grasping for an explanation—what was the biological mystery they found themselves immersed in? Was it genetic engineering with noble intentions gone awry? Or was it genetic manipulation for power and profit? Who was behind it, where did they get their resources, and how did they develop such

Orchestrator 125

an advanced technology? Eventually, his high beams illuminated the Beatty city limits sign. The rain had stopped, and the town was cloaked in darkness.

"Where are we?" Mona asked.

"Beatty, Nevada, but I think there's been a power outage."

"I think I see some light over there. Pull over, Jon, I need to make a pit stop."

Jon slowed down and turned into a gravel parking lot where a Victorian mansion was silhouetted by lightning flashes. A high gabled tower protruded from the center, and twin turrets projected from both sides. Jon drove closer and saw candles flickering in the windows. A sign out front read *The Sherlock Holmes Inn, An Authentic Bed and Breakfast.*

"Norman Bates has a new home," she said, then opened her door and got out.

They walked up the front steps and entered the inn, happy to be out of the cold wind's clutches. The heavy oak door closed behind them. The lobby's warmth embraced them and cut the frigid air that had followed them inside. Two velvet armchairs were positioned on either side of a black marble fireplace, which was alive with a wood fire. A lavishly decorated Christmas tree occupied one of the corners. A candle-laden chandelier lit the Victorian sitting room, and an alcove of antique books was visible at the far end of the main lobby.

"Greetings, travelers, what brings you here on this stormy eve?" a voice said.

In a candle-lit alcove to their right, a tall, thin man stood in front of a wooden counter, smoking a pipe with a long thin stem. Behind him a cape-backed overcoat and deerstalker cap hung on a peg. On the wall above, the sign read *221B Baker Street.*

"Good evening. My friend needed to make a stop. No one else in town had lights."

"Ah, yes, the inconvenient power outage. It's been known to happen in these parts."

He walked out from the alcove and bowed. "Please, my lady,

the powder room is this way. Could I interest the both of you in a spot of hot tea, and perhaps some dessert?"

"Sounds pretty good to me. How about you, Mona?" Jon asked.

"Well, okay, but I don't think we can stay too long."

"Delighted, ma'am," the man said as Mona disappeared down the hall.

"My name's Thackery, Wendell Thackery, I'm the innkeeper here."

"Jon Drake, pleased to meet you."

They shook hands. Jon was struck by the intensity of the man's gaze when he made eye contact.

When Mona returned from the bathroom, their host led them down a long candle-lit passageway along which a spectacular series of dioramas depicted the adventures of Sherlock Holmes.

"We have all fifty-six short stories and the four novels recreated in the boxes on these walls," Thackery said with delight.

"Recognize this one?" He puffed on his pipe and covered the placard with his hand.

Jon moved closer and saw two men—one younger and one older—leaning over Holmes. John Watson and another man were looking on from a distance.

"Give up." He took his hand off the plaque. It read *The Reigate Squires*.

"These two despicable characters are the Alec Cunninghams, senior and junior, of course, and they're trying to retrieve the torn letter clue from Holmes's fist."

Jon and Mona lingered at the exhibit studying the details.

"We must move along, though," Thackery said.

As they walked the rest of the long hallway, Jon lagged behind a bit, examining the remaining dioramas—he even thought he spotted Sir Henry Baskerville and the infamous luminescent hound. The innkeeper opened the mahogany-carved door in theatrical fashion. Before them was a spacious dining room with several lines of adjoining tables lit with candles and covered with white lace tablecloths. Thackery gestured toward a stocky waiter.

"George, please seat this handsome couple and bring them some hot tea and the dessert tray."

"Of course," he answered.

"And if I may be of any further assistance, I can be found in the main lobby." Thackery spun around and left.

At a nearby table sat a middle-aged man and an elderly woman with frizzy hair. The tea arrived almost immediately, and Mona ordered a crème *brûlée*. While sipping her tea, Mona leaned over and whispered to Jon.

"What's going on around here? It's like we stepped into a different world. It's giving me the big-time creeps."

"Me too," Jon answered.

"You folks spending the night?"

Jon jerked his head to his right and faced the man from the next table.

"No, just stopped for a rest. We're headed for California. Quite a power outage, wouldn't you say?"

"They say it was ball lightning that went through the power station near the Rhyolite mine road. There are downed power lines all over the main highway. You may have to stay the night," he said.

The old woman fidgeted in her seat. "That sounds like somethin' the sheriff would say to cover his backside. I know he's in cahoots with those flyboys who operate the test site. Lots of funny business goin' on in these here parts," she said.

"Now, Mother. These young folks didn't come to Beatty to hear your crazy stories," the man said.

"Isn't ball lightning kind of rare?" Mona asked.

"Not around these parts, young lady. It floats, hovers, changes directions, and moves fast. Isn't that right, Horace?" the woman said.

He frowned. "Now, Mother, I'm not gonna argue with you in front of these nice people. It's not polite." He struck his fist against the table and sank back into his chair. "You know that the mayor has told us not to worry about the lights. Just the Air Force testing new aircraft at the Nellis Base." Then he chuckled. "Don't make it sound like we're being invaded by aliens."

"Well, all the decent folk in Nye County have done moved away, and that sniveling sheriff and his henchman, Mayor Samuels ... "

The man stood up.

"That's enough, Mother, we're going. You're scaring these people when there's nothing to be scared of. Put your coat on."

While she struggled with her coat, the man looked at Jon and Mona. "Don't mind her. She's a little crazy in the head," he whispered, drawing big circles with his right index finger near his right ear.

Then he put on a cowboy hat, followed by a gun belt and a brown service jacket. The jacket was decorated with a patch that read—*Nye County Sheriff.*

CHAPTER—15

While Wendell Thackery scurried about and fussed over the preparation of their room, Jon and Mona sat together on a sofa in the front lobby beside the fireplace. The winter storm had intensified, and a call on his cell phone to the highway patrol verified that the highway leaving Beatty in the direction of June Lake had been closed because of the downed power lines.

"I guess we're stuck," Mona said. She leaned back into the cushion and closed her eyes. "And what's with the Holmes gig, anyway?" She sunk lower in the sofa, tucked her legs against her chest, and locked her arms.

Jon leaned closer. "You're still tired, huh? I can tell."

She nodded, eyes still closed.

"So, what was going on back there in North Vegas? You were a different person."

"You ever hear of too much Wild Turkey? My whole world collapsed."

"Your whole world?" he asked, trying to put his arm around her.

"That's right, my whole fucking world!" she snarled, pushing him away.

129

He pushed back and looked squarely at her. "Look, I might not be the most eloquent person in the world, but I want to help you. I really care about you, and that's not going to change."

Her eyes became glassy, and she began to tear up. "You think it's easy when you're the family breadwinner and then, bingo, your job is history?"

"I'm sorry, that is a tough one, and I can relate," he said, moving closer and putting his arm around her again. This time she didn't resist.

"You can?" she said, her eyes still misty.

"You bet I can," he said, going on to tell her about the circumstances surrounding the death of his father and the continuous financial support that he had given to his mother and sister for years afterward.

She broke down and cried for several minutes, then gazed up at Jon with a sad but determined look.

"Dad was in law enforcement and was murdered by a scumbag junkie. That's why I went into the DEA. I wanted to put every low-life drug dealer behind bars. I'm a real easy read, now with nothing to show for it." She leaned her head on his shoulder.

"This is just a temporary setback Mona. Everything's going to be okay. Trust me," he said, squeezing her hand.

She went on to reveal that her mother had been diagnosed and treated for breast cancer. He also learned that her sister was still in college, and Mona had been sending them money on a regular basis, which explained her modeling job. The situation with her family, along with that of Stringfellow and the DEA, made her diagnosis of high blood pressure more understandable.

Thirty minutes later, Wendell Thackery entered the lobby carrying a set of keys.

"Third floor at the top of the stairs, Room 313," he whispered, handing them to Jon. "We'll settle up tomorrow. Rest well."

Jon let Mona sleep by the fire a little bit longer while he retrieved their bags from the car. Shortly thereafter, they entered the plush Victorian room and gazed at the oversized bed.

Orchestrator   131

"We're pretty lucky. Thackery said this was the last room."

"Lucky us!" she yawned. "He's probably downstairs at this very moment trying to contact Sherlock Holmes on a Ouija board."

"Well, the sign did say it was an *authentic* bed and breakfast," Jon said with a grin.

Mona grimaced, put her finger in her mouth, and pretended to vomit.

"You are bad, aren't you?" he said, laughing.

"I hope so," she said with a little-girl smile. She dropped her bag and bounced on the end of the mattress. "At least the bed's comfortable. I could use some more shut-eye."

"Same here," Jon said.

"I was thinking some more about what the sheriff said. Isn't Area 51 somewhere on the Nellis Air Force Base?" she asked.

"That's what I've heard." He thought for a moment. "There you go. The sheriff's senile mother is a bona fide space case and thinks she's been seeing alien craft. That would explain it, wouldn't it?"

They both laughed.

After a period of awkward silence, Jon felt self-conscious and began to unpack his suitcase. "Mona, I can sleep on the floor, no big deal." He pulled out some clothes and rummaged through the bag looking for his toiletries case. Mona leaned over and looked into the bag.

"My Bible! How did you get that?" she said, reaching in and extracting the red book with the manila envelope tucked in between the middle pages.

"In your apartment. I wanted to return it to you," he said trying to remain cool.

"You looked through these, didn't you?" she said, pulling out the envelope and studying its contents.

"Well, they were hard to ignore."

"Stringfellow thought so too."

"So he was blackmailing you. I figured as much."

132   *Paul K. Pattengale*

"What difference does it make now? I'm out of a job."

"Forget about Stringfellow, the photos are beautiful, and so are you," Jon said, sitting down next to her. He kissed her on the lips. He moved closer. "You're amazing." He kissed her again. She smiled and pulled him toward her.

§

After sleeping in and finding out that the roads were still closed, Jon and Mona used the time to relax, recuperate, and enjoy each other's company. They found a variety of board games in the lobby and soon found themselves by the fire in the midst of a Scrabble tournament. True to form, Mona was a fierce competitor and matched Jon game for game. After an afternoon nap, they had dinner and waited out the storm, finally getting ready to leave Beatty by eleven. Before they left the inn, Jon reconfirmed with Elliot their rendezvous point in June Lake and learned from him that Brett Johnstone's autopsy findings were still pending.

As they traveled north on the main highway, a parade of highway patrol cars passed them, heading in the opposite direction. A short distance later, they could see a number of emergency repair vehicles still working on the high-tension wires next to the asphalt road.

"What's our route to June Lake?" Mona asked.

"I learned from Thackery that the shortest route to California is through the Westgard Pass. Here it is on the road map."

He switched on the overhead map light and pointed to the exact spot.

"From the pass, we drop down into the Owens Valley, and June Lake is a couple of hours from here."

"Just get us there in one piece," she said.

He switched off the light, and they drove in silence for a while.

After filling up at the last gas station and checking that the

Orchestrator 133

Westgard Pass was still open, they drove several miles north on U.S.95 and then turned west onto a two-lane road. According to the map, the road weaved through the Inyo and then the White Mountains, starting in Nevada, and ending up in California's Owens Valley.

They drove for an hour and a half without seeing another car and found themselves on a long stretch of road that paralleled a large dry lakebed. On the far side of the white flats, a yellowish orb gleamed in the distance through the light mist.

"How far away do you think that light is?" Mona asked. It was the first thing she had said in nearly an hour.

"I'd say a couple of miles at least. I've been watching it too. It's probably a ranch," Jon said.

Her eyes were wide, and she looked cold.

"What's wrong? You look scared," Jon said.

"This place reminds me of a nightmare I had when I was a kid."

"What was it about?"

"It starts with me riding a bicycle next to a deserted field in the middle of the night. After riding for a while, I see a bright pulsating light on the field's surface. I get off my bike, walk toward it, and discover that it's a glowing light ball with a porthole on the side closest to me. I'm drawn to look into the porthole to see what's inside and … "

She stopped.

"And what?" Jon asked.

"And this *thing* is seated in there with its back to me. I can't stop looking. I feel paralyzed and can't move. Suddenly, it turns around and looks me directly in the face. It's horrible-looking and deformed, with skin heaped up in mounds all over its face. It's staring at me, and I'm trying to scream, but I can't. And then I wake up screaming and cold."

She shivered.

"Sounds pretty scary," he said, turning up the heater setting.

As the car approached the far end of the dry lake, a blanket of mist extended across the road ahead.

"The guy at the gas station said there might be pockets of fog on the road," he said. "At least it's not snowing."

"Better slow down," Mona said.

After entering the fog bank, he decelerated and switched on the BMW's fog lights.

"Man, it's like pea soup out here," he said.

Jon slowed even more and kept his eye on the centerline, barely visible in front of them. Suddenly, he heard a roaring sound overhead.

"What's that?" Jon yelled.

He steered the car while looking up through the windshield.

"Get us outta here! I want to see what's going on," Mona said.

He saw the mist clearing in front of them and sped up. After emerging from the fog, they looked up. A jet was flying behind a dimly lit circular object about three times its size in the night sky.

Mona strained to see what was above them.

"It looks like some kind of experimental aircraft," she said.

The circular craft made an abrupt turn, and the jet banked right trying to keep up with it.

Mona reached into her backpack and retrieved a large pair of binoculars.

"Stop the car, Jon. I want to have a better look," she said.

She quickly got out and pointed them in the direction of the aircraft, which were still visible in the western sky near a setting quarter-moon. Jon could see the craft in front oscillating from side to side and the plane behind following in a straight line. A minute later, they had disappeared behind the mountain range ahead.

"What did you see?" Jon asked.

"Looks like an F15 that was having trouble keeping up with the other plane. It might have been trying to chase it."

She continued to scan the terrain in front of them. "Maybe the sheriff's old lady wasn't so far off after all. And there's more fog up there."

"Great, and that sign ahead on the right about fifty yards, can you read what it says?" Jon asked.

"It says 'Caution—Temporary Military Activity. USAF Checkpoint, Three Miles Ahead, Be Prepared For Long Delays.'"

She flipped a switch on the underside of her binoculars and rescanned the terrain ahead.

"Okay, I'm getting a couple of good heat readings on the infrared scanner. Probably some flyboys ready to inconvenience us for a couple of hours. I don't like the looks of it."

In the meantime, Jon had pulled out a detailed topographic map of the area and laid it out on the hood of his automobile.

"The map shows there's an alternate route. It's a Forest Service road that weaves through the Ancient Bristlecone Pine Forest and then reconnects with the Westgard Pass road on the California side of the White Mountains."

He pointed with his right index finger while holding a flashlight in the other hand.

"Where's the road?" Mona asked.

"If my calculation's right, it's about a half mile back."

She redirected the binocs and viewed the area they had just come from.

"Let's boogie, then. There's some kind of emergency vehicle with a blinking red light coming up the road. If I'm right, it should be here in about ten minutes," she said.

Ten minutes later, Jon and Mona sat in the idling BMW with the lights out on the dirt road watching a speeding ambulance make its way up the asphalt road they had just been on. When it entered the fog patch near the road's summit, Jon switched on his lights and proceeded on the unimproved road in a northwesterly direction.

"I hope you know where you're going," Mona said.

"I didn't teach a summer orienteering course for nothing," he answered.

"Am I blessed, or what? Just get me to California without being abducted," she said.

About fifty miles later, they had climbed into the Ancient Bristlecone Pine Forest and encountered heavy fog near the summit.

"I can't see a thing, and I don't want to get lost. I vote that we stop and get a few hours' sleep," Jon said. "I have enough sleeping bags and blankets. You can have the back seat; it's more comfortable."

"What time is it?" she asked.

"Three A.M. It should be light in about four hours, and hopefully the fog will have lifted by then," Jon said.

"All right, you've convinced me, but I expect breakfast in bed," she said, leaning over and kissing him hard on the lips.

He pulled the car to the side of the road, killed the engine, and crawled into the back seat with her.

CHAPTER—16

Jon peered out the car window at the nearby stand of trees. Water droplets glistened like crystals on the pine needles in the dim morning light. There was a fine mist, and it looked like the sun might break through at any time. Feeling a chill, he decided to start the car to turn the heater on, but when he turned the key he discovered the car was dead. He tried several more times but could only elicit a clicking sound from the ignition.

Mona began stirring in the back seat. "What's going on?" she asked.

"Car won't start. I don't get it. It was fine last night," he said, pushing his body back into the seat in frustration.

He pulled the hood latch and got out of the car. As he lifted the hood, he heard a rustling noise in the woods and looked in the direction of the sound. A tall, sinewy figure emerged from a grove of pine trees. As he came closer, Jon could see it was an old man with a white beard dressed in a beige trench coat carrying a threadbare backpack. He wore stereo headphones, which were attached to a tape deck on his waist belt. He was uttering rhythmic guttural sounds and reading a paperback. Though the light was dim, Jon could see it was *The Dharma Bums* by Jack

Kerouac. On the side of the old man's backpack was a sign that read, "Beebop Spoken Here."

When he saw Jon, the man stopped and took off his headset with his left hand. "*Utcha*," he said holding up his right hand, palm forward.

"Do you know where the main road is? I'm having car trouble," Jon said, hesitating to say anymore until he found out if the man spoke English.

"Artemus Twitchell, at your service, and, by the looks of things, I would venture to say that your battery terminals might have collected too much moisture last night. It's a common problem in this part of the world," he said. "Allow me to assist you."

The old man put down his pack and took off his trench coat, revealing green lederhosen underneath. He put on his stereo headset, walked up to the hood, and leaned over the motor. He twisted the battery cables back and forth on the terminals while gyrating his hips and humming aloud to the music. Meanwhile, Mona had gotten out of the car and spotted the unusual man.

"Where did he come from?" she whispered.

"He sort of … came out of the woods," Jon said.

"*Utcha, userit*," the old man said, now addressing Mona. "Artemus Twitchell, mountain mechanic, at your service, ma'am. I think I've solved the problem."

He pointed at the interior light, which was now shining brightly. Jon got into the car and turned the key, and the engine started. Several minutes later, it was purring at a low idle.

"How can we repay you, Mr. Twitchell?" Jon asked.

"Take me back to civilization. I know the way. And call me Artemus." He gestured dramatically with both hands.

Mona pulled Jon aside while Artemus busied himself with his tape deck.

"Look, Jon, I know he's probably a sweet old man, but I'm not sure we can trust him. And what's that gobbledygook that he's babbling? It's not a language I've ever heard, and that's saying something."

"I know it sounds weird. We should take him up on his offer, though. I think we're lost. I didn't tell you last night."

"How did that happen?"

"My calculations from the map didn't jibe with our actual compass course. I can't explain it—plus the Beemer GPS stopped working. You were sleeping, and I didn't want to bother you."

"Some Boy Scout you are. Next time remind me to bring my own GPS."

"Okay, next time, then," Jon said.

"Do we have enough gas?"

"Enough if we don't spend too much time finding our way back to the main road. And I don't think I want to take that chance. He said he knows the way."

"All right, you win, but he rides in front. I want to keep an eye on him."

§

Much to his surprise, Jon enjoyed the company of Artemus, who was a competent navigator, an engaging conversationalist, and straight-ahead jazz devotee. In between the "Go, Satchmos" and the "Groovy, Birdmans," he managed to take off his headphones long enough to give them the history of the Ancient Bristlecone Pine Forest.

He said that at two miles above sea level, the pines, technically called *Pinus longaeva*, had been growing for almost five thousand years and were the oldest and longest living organisms on the planet, even outliving the giant sequoias by almost two centuries. He had told them that the oldest tree in the Methuselah Grove was exactly 4,768 years old, and had sprung into existence during the third Egyptian dynasty of the Old Kingdom. It was then, Artemus noted, that the chancellor Imhotep had designed and built the step pyramid at Saqqara. Not only did Artemus

Twitchell have a passion for Egyptian history, but they also learned he was an accomplished linguist with a special interest in Egyptian hieroglyphics. When asked, he told them that in ancient Egyptian *utcha* meant "greetings" or "hail" and that *userit* translated to "goddess." His intellectual prowess reminded Jon of his ancient history professor in college.

After several hours, the sun broke through as they drove on the paved road in the direction of Highway 168 near the Westgard Pass summit. Although Jon now felt confident that they were on the correct route, the terrain had gotten more rugged and the road steeper. As he negotiated a series of ascending switchbacks, he saw that there was snow on the sides of the road. Since there were no guardrails, he proceeded cautiously. Fortunately, the road had been plowed, and despite a light mist, they had no problem making their way to the top. Mona had been quiet for most of the ride, but Jon knew from her facial expressions and body language that she was on full alert, a cat ready to pounce.

"How far are we from the main road?" Mona asked.

"If we're right, only about one mile," Jon said.

"I dig you, Monkman," Artemus said, snapping his fingers in time.

Jon looked back at Mona and smiled.

"It's more Thelonius, travelers, and he's definitely in the groove," Twitchell said, lifting the earphone away from his right ear.

The BMW negotiated another sharp turn, and when the car came around half circle, a parked white van with two men standing in front of it blocked the road ahead. The one on the right pointed a pistol.

"Both of you freeze," the other one yelled.

Jon put on the brakes and did what he was told.

"Okay, you two, get out with your hands up and do it slow," the man on the right said, brandishing his firearm.

"Jon, try and distract them when you get out of the car," Mona said in a low voice.

"Okay," he replied, trying to maintain his composure.

He surmised that she must have been on the floor of the back seat since he couldn't see her in his peripheral vision.

"You on the driver's side, get out of the car now," the bigger one said.

Jon responded and did what they asked him to do.

"Now it's your turn, old man," the smaller one said, motioning to Artemus, who exited the car with hands in air, the bottom of his unbuttoned trench coat pulled upward, exposing his bare legs above the green lederhosen.

"What are you wearing, your underwear?" the bigger man chuckled.

"I come in peace and carry no weapons with me. I will prove it to you."

"We've got ourselves a flasher," the little man said.

Artemus grabbed the lapels of his coat and extended his arms upward like a giant bird, the dingy trench coat cloaking his outstretched arms and partially obscuring the man's view of the car. In the split second that followed, Mona leapt out of the car, planted her feet behind Artemus in a karate stance, then sprung forward and blindsided the bigger man with a skipping roundhouse kick to his left temple. As he crumpled and fell to the ground, Artemus hovered over him with arms still outstretched and temporarily blocked the other man's view of Mona, who was now taking cover behind the white van. The man fired several shots at her but instead hit the rear of the vehicle.

Jon threw a roll block into the man's backside directly behind his knees. His adversary fell backward, almost in slow motion, firing two rounds into the air as he went down. Before he could get up, Mona pounced on him, first kneeing him in the groin and then knocking him out with a palm thrust to the face. While Mona and Jon searched the two unconscious men, Artemus grabbed his pack from the backseat of the BMW and set off into the woods on the other side of the road.

"Artemus, come back, where are you going?" Jon yelled.

"Let him go, Jon. He's spooked and we don't have time to waste. These two probably have friends."

"But he helped us," Jon said.

"Get over it." Mona took the loaded gun from the man's hand.

Jon kept an eye on the bodies, while Mona rummaged through the van, finding several ammunition clips and two pairs of handcuffs. Together they dragged the two men to the side of the road and cuffed them at the ankles. Mona took off their shoes, throwing them to the bottom of the ravine on the other side of the road.

"That should keep them from going anywhere too fast," she said.

Next she got into the van, put the gearshift into neutral, released the emergency brake, and proceeded to steer the vehicle downhill toward the steep embankment. As the car picked up momentum, she jumped out and let it careen over the cliff. It stumbled and rolled down the mountain, disappearing from sight and exploding in a canyon far below.

"Jon, you're not gonna like this, but your car's next."

"My car! You're not doing that to my car!"

"Yes, we are. I'm sure it's been bugged with some kind of tracking device. How else could they have found us here in the middle of nowhere? And it means they've probably got an air unit close by."

"Why can't we find the device and remove it?"

"It could be anywhere in the car and we don't have the time to go looking for it. We've got to create a diversion and fast. Let's get the stuff we can carry out of the car, and then we'll hightail it to the main highway on foot. We'll hitch a ride from there. We have no other choice."

After grabbing what he could from the trunk, he retrieved his parka from the back seat and found a hardcover notebook in the front seat where Artemus had been sitting. He opened it to the title page, which, in exaggerated, flowery longhand, read *Artemus*

Orchestrator 143

Twitchell's Prescription for Survival. Underneath was a line of hieroglyphic characters. He placed the notebook in his bag and reluctantly joined Mona on the driver's side of the car where she was getting in position to push it toward the edge. Minutes later, with the BMW at the bottom of the canyon, they were climbing up the steep road in the direction of Highway 168.

CHAPTER—17

Jon and Mona stood together on the shoulder of Highway 168 several hundred yards below the California side of the Westgard Pass. There was no traffic in either direction. A light snow had started to fall.

"At least we've got a good view of the downgrade from here," Jon said, grieving the loss of his car and still reeling from their violent encounter.

"How much more daylight do we have?" she asked.

"Not much, maybe less than an hour with this cloud cover."

"Jesus, where is everybody?" Mona asked.

"I don't think this road's very well traveled in winter, and when you factor in the holidays … "

"That's right, I totally forgot. Christmas is only a few days away," she said. "We'll just keep walking until someone comes along. How far is the next town?"

"Big Pine is twenty miles or so, but it's all downhill. We better keep moving though or we're gonna freeze to the pavement." Jon shivered in the cold air.

"Here, this'll help," Mona said.

Orchestrator 145

She moved closer, dusted the snow off his shoulders, and took out a half-pint of Wild Turkey from her purse.

"Drink."

"You really come prepared, don't you?" He nuzzled closer to her.

"Don't leave home without it," she said, handing him the opened bottle.

He took a long swig and felt the liquid heat soak through his core.

"Man, that's got a kick to it," he said.

"Happy Holidays," she said, taking another swig.

They decided to walk, to stay warm as much as anything else. Jon checked his watch. Four o'clock. Thirty minutes had gone by, but no cars. It was darker, and the snow was falling harder when Mona suddenly turned toward the uphill grade.

"Do you hear it? It sounds like a truck," she practically squealed.

Jon looked up into the dim light and saw a pair of powerful headlights break through the low-lying clouds cloaking the pass. As the vehicle snaked down the grade, he could hear the driver downshift.

"We gotta get him to stop. Hold my stuff, I'm gonna try and wave him down."

She tossed him her backpack and smeared on a fresh coat of lipstick, then strutted onto the pavement and straddled the centerline. As the truck approached, she jumped up and down on the asphalt, waving her hands back and forth. In response, the black semi with its brakes screeching veered to the left and came to a halt about twenty yards ahead of them.

"Yee-ha!" the driver yelled as he rolled down the window.

With Jon following, Mona ran up to the truck's cab and hopped onto the chrome running board.

"Our car's broken down; we need a ride," she said.

"You've got it, ma'am. The two of you hop on in, there's plenty of room in here," the driver said, with a twang in his voice.

146   *Paul K. Pattengale*

When he leaned over and opened the truck's door, Jon could see that the driver was in his early fifties, had graying brown hair, and was wearing a black cowboy hat. He was smoking a cigar.

"Let's get a move on before this weather gets any worse. There's already a white-out at the top of the pass," he said.

The warm interior of the cab was filled with the sounds of Dwight Yoakam as they headed down the California side of the White Mountain range toward Big Pine and the Owens Valley.

"We was worried about you, Agent Double-Eleven," the driver said, as he turned down the volume on the radio.

Mona immediately pulled the confiscated gun out of her right pocket and pointed it at the trucker. Jon, who was sitting between them, pushed his body back into the seat as far as it could go.

"It's former Agent Double-Eleven to you, cowboy, and who's we?" she asked.

The man bobbed his head and laughed.

"Jamie-Boy was right on the mark. You are a feisty one, aren't you?"

"You know JB?"

"Used to work with him in the Agency before the big change."

"You mean, before Stringfellow?" she said, quietly.

"That's what I mean, ma'am."

Though she looked more relaxed, Mona continued to aim the gun at the man.

"Prove it then," she said, waving the gun.

"Well, ma'am, after Jamie's leg injury at the San Ysidro border crossing, he's gotten real familiar with computers and supervises information systems for the Agency. He hates Colonel Stringfellow. His wife's name is Clara. He met her in Dubuque, Iowa, and they have two boys named..."

"Okay, okay I'm convinced. And who exactly are you?"

"Otis Sweeney, ma'am, former DEA pilot. Some people knew me as Sweetcakes."

Orchestrator 147

"You're Otis Sweetcakes! Jamie did tell me about you. You're a legend."

"That would be me, Miss Mona."

After he smiled and tipped his hat, she returned the gun back to her right pocket. He nodded at Jon.

"And pleased to make your acquaintance, Doc Drake. Call me Otis. I'm a trucker nowadays and I work outta Reno, and sometimes Ely, Nevada."

He shook hands sideways with Jon, who was still unwinding from the confrontation.

"How did you know to find us up here, Otis?" Jon asked.

"Well, to start with, Doc, JB gave me a heads-up on your location, and you must be some kind of VIP, 'cause someone, and I think it was Stringfellow, went to the trouble of bugging your Beemer with a transponder. For an old pilot like me, the rest is easy. It's just like finding a socked-in airport using IFR!"

"IFR?" Jon asked.

"Instrument flight rules," Mona chimed.

"Something must have happened to your car, though, 'cause I lost the signal about an hour ago. But I knew you had to be around here somewhere."

"Well, here we are." Mona said.

"So where's the car?" Otis asked.

"It met its maker," Mona said.

"It's at the bottom of a ravine about a mile from the pass," Jon said, feeling pained.

"Wowee, sounds like you two had quite a tussle back there."

"Oh, yeah," Jon said, flashing back onto the blur of karate blows, gunshots, and tumbling vehicles.

While Jon listened, Mona described, agent to agent, what had happened.

"Well, that explains why I lost your Beemer signal. And it's this little device that led me to you," Otis said, patting a piece of electronic equipment on the dashboard. On it was a magnetized, pin-up photo of Marilyn Monroe.

"Hope you don't mind my picture of Norma Jean. She keeps me company on long trips," he said.

Jon glanced at the black-and-white of a young Marilyn posing in the surf.

"JB said that you kinda looked like her, ma'am. And ya know, I think I gotta agree with him."

Mona looked at the trucker and glared. "I'm not wearing a bathing suit, Mr. Sweeney."

Otis looked flustered and began to fidget in his seat. "Don't get me wrong, ma'am. I mean your face. Norma Jean had a beautiful face."

Otis pretended to wipe his brow with his right hand.

"Mmmm-hmmm, what else did JB tell you?" she asked.

"He told me they figured that the Doc here would lead 'em to where you were hiding."

"Which is why they left you alone when you drove to Solana Beach, Jon. They were trying to get to me," Mona said.

"So they had to have planted the transponder sometime before that," he said, irritated. "Bastards, it's against the law."

"That never stopped Stringfellow," she said.

"Boy, Miss Mona, you sure musta got under Stringfellow's skin real good," Otis said.

"You've got that right, Sweetcakes, and I'm not done with his ass yet," she said, checking the bullets in her gun.

"Oohee," Otis howled. "I wouldn't want you mad at me for very long."

"So why didn't they pick us up right when we left Vegas?" Jon asked.

"Good question, Doc. There are a couple of reasons. My guess is that it's partly a jurisdictional thing. By that I mean Stringfellow's operation is mostly Mexican border-based, and he's gotta convince someone else to do or go along with his dirty work in another location. That can be kinda tricky and it takes time."

"And the other part?" Jon asked.

Orchestrator   149

"The other part, Jon, is that you're a well-known physician, and if you were detained, there would be too many questions asked by the local authorities," Mona said.

"Couldn't have put it any better myself, Doc."

"Why do they have to detain us at all. Why don't they just kill us both?" Jon said, looking despondent.

"You're a fast learner. It's because you probably got something they want, something they need you alive for, something to do with your science knowledge. JB didn't go into detail, but it sounded like you stumbled onto something pretty hot."

"Makes sense. And what about you, Mona?" Jon asked.

"Stringfellow doesn't want to do me in just yet. Somewhere in his perverted, bloated state, he still wants to get into my pants."

Otis glanced at Mona, drove some more, and glanced at her again. "You are a direct one, Agent Double-Eleven, I mean former Agent Double-Eleven. I will say that about you," he said.

"I never would have noticed," Jon said with a grin.

"Lay off, you guys."

It was snowing harder now and Otis slowed the truck by downshifting into a lower gear.

"Big Pine's about an hour from here in this kind of weather. Shouldn't be a problem though. Black Beauty'll get us there safe and sound." He patted the dashboard with pride.

"You two should get some shut-eye. You've been through a lot. Maybe a little music'll help," he said, turning up the volume on the radio dial.

"Amen," Mona said.

Jon leaned back against the cab's plush red interior and tried to empty his mind, but as hard as he tried, it swirled with the recent events. Was JB the same "inside" person who had researched the Air Force's biological link to the DEA for Mona? Did that linkage have anything to do with the appearance of the mysterious craft the night before or possibly with the U.S. Air Force roadblock they had evaded? Was there a connection with the aircraft he and Mona had seen when they were night-stalking the old Oaxacan

Indian in the Baja desert the weekend before? And who were those two men in plain clothes they had just pummeled? What were they after? Were they DEA? Were they Air Force? And, finally, what was with Otis and his sudden appearance onto the scene? There was something about the scenario that seemed too tidy.

Mona leaned into him, half asleep already, taking his right hand in her left, and wedging their hands between their bodies. Finally, his exhaustion overtook him. As he started to doze off, he heard the lyrics of the Johnny Lee song Otis had tuned in on KKOW, the country voice of the Eastern Sierra.

"Picking up strangers, let me tell you 'bout the dangers."

§

Jon awoke to the gentle bounce of the truck. Mona was still asleep. He glanced at Otis who was concentrating on the road ahead. The cab's powerful headlights illuminated a curtain of falling snow.

"Doin' okay, Doc?" Otis said with a smile.

"Doing well," Jon answered.

"You two were both sleeping, so I drove on through Big Pine. We're traveling north on Highway 395, and we'll be stopping in Bishop in about another hour or so. Try and get some rest."

Jon closed his eyes and thought about Otis, who was a good twenty years older than he. Despite Jon's uncertainties regarding Otis's true identity, the man's calm and reassuring demeanor made him think of his father. Physically, his sharp features, aquiline nose, graying hair, and constant smile also reminded him of his dad. After reflecting on their similarities, he decided that it was the "everything's gonna be okay" smile that he missed most about his father. Even after his father had been diagnosed with advanced cancer and was living in considerable pain, he still managed to eke out a smile. Jon didn't understand how he could have remained cheerful through such an ordeal, but he was

Orchestrator 151

Dad, and that was the way it was. That's why his suicide was so unexpected, so mind-blowing. It just didn't fit.

As he tried to fall back to sleep, the results of his dad's autopsy took center stage in his mind. It was familiar territory; he had replayed it hundreds of times. It had taken him a full eight years, until after he had graduated from med school, to muster enough courage to request the results from the coroner's office. It confirmed that the aggressive, drug-resistant leukemia had spread to his brain, which likely explained the rapid onset of his blackout spells and his despondency. The depression and drug overdose naturally followed, the report had said.

But if that wasn't enough, a genetic screen on his father's blood cells at the time of his autopsy found that he was carrying a susceptibility gene, which had likely accelerated his chances of getting cancer. Jon had become well versed with this cancer susceptibility gene, since several of his colleagues at U.C.L.A. had cloned and characterized its DNA mutation.

He eventually revealed the situation to his sister telling her that they each had a fifty-fifty chance in the Mendelian draw of carrying the same cancer susceptibility gene. And if they did, they were at high risk of developing leukemia and other forms of cancer at a much younger age than most other people. He and Cathleen both had the test performed. He carried the mutation. She did not. After that, his life just wasn't the same—Jon could never get serious about having a family—and he began to pursue in earnest, the Holy Grail of modern medicine, a cure for cancer. He was a driven man, he repeated to himself, as the truck bounced up and down on the pavement, lulling him back into a light sleep.

"Wake up Jon, we're about to stop," Mona said, shaking him.

Jon woke up cold.

"Geez, Doc, are you alright?" Otis asked.

"I'm okay. Just a bad dream. Where are we?" he asked.

"On the outskirts of Bishop, California. We're lookin' good.

The snow's stopped and it looks like we got a clear shot to June Lake," he answered.

Five minutes later, Otis Sweeney had pulled the rig into a Bishop truck stop and was outside filling the tank with diesel fuel. Finally, Jon had his chance to talk with Mona.

"What's happening?" he asked.

"While you were sleeping, I told him you had business in June Lake, and he offered to drop you there."

"You're not coming with me?"

"Not tonight. Otis has a car that he can lend us. I'll ride with him to Reno and then drive back down to June Lake some time tomorrow. Maybe I can catch up with you and Elliot at the Mono County coroner's office."

"I'm not sure we should split up."

"We definitely need a car, and I want to do a license plate check on the van and run their IDs through the system. Otis said he would help me. Probably won't turn up much, but you never know until you try."

"So you think he can be trusted?" Jon said.

"I do. Otis is on our side, and JB's a reliable source." She looked him square in the eye. "He's my inside connection."

"I thought so. Sounds like Otis is still pretty tight with him."

"Sounds that way," Mona said.

"What's in it for Otis? Why is he so motivated to help us?"

"That's what I'm going to find out." She leaned over and gave him a long, hard kiss. Before he knew it, Otis had returned from paying the cashier and was opening the door on the driver's side.

"Don't mean to interrupt you two, but we need to be moving on. We're working on some good weather," he said with a grin.

Ninety minutes later, Jon and Elliot were waving goodbye to Otis and Mona from the front porch of the June Lake condo where Elliot was staying. Mona waved back, and Otis tooted the horn as he steered Black Beauty onto the main road, then honked once more for good luck.

§

Jon sat on the living room couch at midnight, drinking a cup of hot chocolate. Elliot was tired and had gone to bed after listening to the details of Jon's trip. Before retiring, he had told Jon that Abe Lowenstein was sending the Johnstone autopsy report care of Lucas Faust. Jon tried to call his lab, but no one answered. It was Saturday night, and Christmas was the following Wednesday.

Next, he decided to leaf through *Artemus Twitchell's Prescription for Survival*, which consisted of a potpourri of quotations, newspaper clippings, and cartoon-like drawings. At the top of the first page was a quotation ascribed to Robert Louis Stevenson, which read *"We are travelers in the wilderness of the world, and the best thing we can find in our travels is an honest friend."* Underneath was a clipped-out, faded newspaper article entitled *"The Relationship of Dada Surrealism to Heavy Metal Rock."*

Jon chuckled and paged through the notebook. There was a quote at the top of each page. *"I hear of Sherlock everywhere since you became his chronicler."—Mycroft Holmes to John H. Watson, M.D., The Greek Interpreter.*

On the next page, it read: *"Go for the prize."—Henry James.*

Then there was a detailed scrawl of Egyptian hieroglyphic characters, which continued for an additional ten pages. Artemus was some kind of Egyptologist after all. Jon would have to find a way to translate the passage.

On the last page, it read: *"Live forever."—Ray Bradbury.*

Further down was a prominent black-inked diagram consisting of a triangle and an adjacent five-pointed star positioned above a half circle, and underneath it, an inscribed phrase that read

"Sopdet rising." What did this stand for, he wondered? Jon went into his bedroom and nodded off to sleep.

Then the nightmare began. He was lying in a hospital bed in a sterile, white room. He looked to the side to see his parents wearing surgical masks and looking at him through a glass window. He called to them, but they didn't respond. A white-garbed figure with a green surgical mask entered the room carrying a stainless steel tray covered with a green towel. The figure uncovered the tray, exposing a long hypodermic syringe. Jon tried to scream as the figure approached him with the dripping needle, but no words would come out of his mouth. He tried to move but couldn't. The semisweet smell of medicinal alcohol permeated the air as the figure came closer.

"This won't hurt," the garbed figure said, lifting up the loose-fitting nightgown with the other gloved hand and squeezing his lower abdominal skin into a bunch, causing his scrotum to retract.

"No more. I can't take it anymore!" Jon screamed in abject terror.

He awoke suddenly, covered in sweat.

CHAPTER—18

With Elliot at the wheel, the metallic green Land Rover weaved through the leafless aspen groves along the June Lake Loop road, passing a chain of partially frozen lakes on the right, followed by the June Mountain ski area on the left. They pulled into the parking lot of the log cabin–style building situated in what the locals called the down canyon area of the loop. Jon tried to call his lab, but again there was no answer.

"What am I thinking? It's Sunday," he said, closing his cell.

"It doesn't stop Lucas Faust," Elliot remarked.

As they walked up the cedar steps to the Mono County Coroner's office, Jon saw a silver placard hanging on the overhead beam. Health Allied Professionals for the Protection of the Environment and Nature (HAPPEN).

"So this is where it's happening," Elliot joked.

"You mean *happenin'*, don't you, man?" Jon retorted.

The wooden front door was decorated with a festive green-and-red-ribboned pine wreath, and as they made their way down the long rustic hallway, a chorus of Handel's *Messiah* could be heard emanating from an open doorway. Inside was a man in his mid-fifties with a salt-and-pepper beard wearing a red and gray

156   *Paul K. Pattengale*

flannel shirt, faded blue jeans, and hiking boots. He looked up and addressed them. "Jon and Elliot, I presume."

"And you must be the legendary Dr. Faust," Jon answered.

"I am. Come into my office."

He turned down the volume on the wall stereo, which was perched on a shelf above a well-worn leather couch.

"Too many hallelujahs for me. Make yourselves comfortable," he said, gesturing toward the sofa.

Elliot shook Faust's hand and said, "I was telling Jon that I've met some of your mover-and-shaker colleagues at the Earth Summit Action Coalition. Your work on environmental degradation is seminal."

"*Our* work," he replied. "It was a collaboration in the true sense of the word. I have great colleagues. And I've heard about your leadership in anti-nuclear circles, Elliot. We featured your group in a recent HAPPEN newsletter. I'll find you a copy before you leave."

Before settling into his seat, Faust handed Jon a package addressed to him c/o Dr. Lucas Faust from Dr. A. Lowenstein.

"It came by special courier earlier this morning. Pretty good service for a Sunday. Must be important," Faust said.

"Wow! He didn't waste any time, did he?" Jon said examining the parcel.

"It's Brett Johnstone's autopsy report," Elliot said, nervously. "I gave Lowenstein our June Lake itinerary."

"That's old Abe, going a mile a minute, never stopping to look back," Faust said.

"You know Abe Lowenstein?" Jon asked, looking surprised.

"When I was working at the L.A. coroner's office with Abner Woods, Abe would come over and look at all of the interesting pediatric autopsies."

"Well, I can report that he's still doing that," Jon said.

"Excuse me for a few minutes. I'm in the process of putting together the autopsy material that you asked for in your e-mail. It shouldn't take too long." He left the room.

"No problem," Jon said.

Jon opened the envelope and eagerly pulled out its contents. Elliot tried to be patient but was obviously preoccupied with the outcome.

On top was a hand-written letter from Lowenstein, paper-clipped to several eight-by-ten black-and-white photos.

Jon read the letter out loud.

Dear Jon and Elliot,

The neuropath findings on Brett Johnstone were highly unusual. Something wasn't right when we sectioned the brain with the cutting knives. Abner and I both thought it had a gritty, metallic feel to it. The thalamus was the most involved, followed by the cortex and the brain stem. The retinas in both eyes also had a similar gritty consistency to them. In addition to routine light microscopy, I submitted the involved tissues for electron microscopy and have enclosed several relevant prints, which are magnified 10,000 times.

Jon handed the photos to Elliot and kept reading.

As you can see from the pictures, there are hundreds of small crystalline structures inside the nerve and retinal cells. I searched the literature, and discovered that the tiny crystals are magnetite, a naturally occurring, iron-containing magnetic mineral that miners and mineralogists call lodestone.

"Magnetite. What's he doing with ferromagnetic crystals in his body?" Elliot exclaimed.

Jon continued to read, his own heart pounding with the news.

The immediate cause of death was an intracranial bleed

secondary to a skull fracture. With all that magnetite in his brain, Abner and I think he had a massive seizure, and that the fracture occurred when he hit his head during the fall. The rest of the autopsy was unremarkable. Give me a call when you have a chance and we can talk some more. I gave your research lab some fresh brain tissue, and Diane will send you something under a separate cover. Maybe she'll find something of interest.

Regards, Abe Lowenstein.

"I don't believe this. I'm in shock," Elliot said.

Jon put his hand on his shoulder. "If it's too stressful for you, we can take a break. I want you to feel comfortable."

"It's okay, Jon, I'll be alright. It's probably better that I talk about it."

"Let's talk then. The thalamus determines whether we're asleep or awake and functions like a command center for the brain, doesn't it," Jon said.

"Right, and that would fit with some of Johnstone's symptoms. He was falling asleep at work," Elliot said.

Jon examined the pictures some more. "Abe amazes me. Where did he dig up the information on magnetite?"

"He probably found it in the *Journal of Comparative Biology*. Magnetite's been found in other species," Elliot replied.

"Really? Fill me in."

"It's kind of esoteric, but I've kept up with the field. I did a master's degree in comparative bio before I went to med school. My thesis advisor had shown that certain species of aquatic bacteria like *Aquaspirillum* contained magnetite crystals."

"What function do they serve?" Jon asked.

He handed the pictures back to Elliot.

"Magnetite transforms them into compass needles so that they orient and swim along the incline lines of the earth's magnetic field."

"Does that give them some kind of adaptive advantage?" Jon asked.

"Unclear in bacteria, but in higher species like birds, the magnetite allows them to use the earth's geomagnetic field to find and maintain direction."

"Like what homing pigeons do," Jon said.

"Right, they navigate with magnetic maps," Elliot said.

"What about humans?" Jon asked. He was now sitting on the edge of the sofa.

"There have been a few disputed studies that reported trace quantities, but none with any real certainty, and nothing like this."

As Elliot held up the photos of Johnstone's brain cells, Lucas Faust reentered the office, carrying a pot of hot coffee in one hand and tray of glass slides in the other.

Jon explained what they were seeing in the photos, and Faust nodded, a concerned look on his face. He looked at each one of them intensely.

"Your case is going to be a hard act to follow. Are you sure you're up for this one?" He glanced at the tray of slides next to the multiheaded microscope.

"We're game. Let's get started," Jon said, answering for himself and Elliot.

"Okay, the kid that I autopsied was a ten-year-old Native American orphan boy. Two Paiute elders found him floating in the shallow water at Navy Beach on the Mono Lake shoreline, near the South Tufa preserve."

"Navy Beach?" Elliot asked.

"The Navy conducted amphibious war exercises there in the early 1940s," Faust said. "Here are the photos of the body when we pulled it out of the water." He took out a set of color Polaroids from his shirt pocket.

Jon and Elliot stood on either side of Faust as he flipped through the pictures, which showed the distorted corpse of a young child.

"It was odd. The body had a luminescent reddish orange color to it. It almost looked like it could have glowed in the dark," Faust said, shuffling through the photos. "The pictures don't do it justice, though."

"The boy Dr. Lowenstein and I autopsied decomposed into a similar color," Jon said excitedly.

"I remember you saying that in your e-mail."

"Could you tell if the skin was thickened?" Jon asked.

"Not really. Mono Lake water is so corrosive that the outer skin layers were missing by the time the body was retrieved."

Jon studied the photos for any abnormal skin openings near the collarbones on the child's upper torso but could discern nothing on the bloated and disfigured body.

Faust pulled out another set of photos from his shirt pocket.

"By the time the body was brought back to my office, it had started to liquefy and looked like this."

Lucas pointed to a relevant photo and handed it to Jon.

"It's almost like the alkaline lake water had inhibited it from liquefying. I can't pinpoint the exact time of death, but the kid had to have been in the water for a few days," Faust said.

"Abner Woods told me about the liquefaction. My case did the same thing," Jon said.

"I rushed the autopsy and got most of the internal organs out before they turned to soup," Faust said.

"Was the boy an orphan?" Elliot asked.

"That's what the elders told me. He had been missing from the Indian school for about a month."

"And the local authorities didn't know about this?"

"The Paiutes are a proud people and close-knit community. They don't report anything to the local authorities."

"The Baja boys were orphans, too," Elliot said.

"Poor kids, let's have a look at the slides." Faust put down his coffee and placed a slide under the scope.

"Jon, I really didn't pay much attention to your e-mail the first time around, but I reread it again this morning and it really grabbed me. Do I have it right? Was it icthyosis, skin-lung connecting structures, multiple lung tumors, and enlargement of both the scapular and pectoral muscles in an eight-year-old boy?"

"You've got it. Pretty wild, huh?"

"I'll say! I want to say there's cancer in this kid's lungs, but the tissue sections are so full of artifact that I can't be completely sure," Faust said.

He moved the glass slide back and forth across the microscope stage.

"What did the lungs look like when you opened up the body?" Elliot asked.

"Heavy and bubbly with the suggestion of whitish tan nodules on both cut surfaces, but it was hard to tell," Faust said.

"So you think he drowned?" Jon asked.

"I think the physical evidence strongly supports it, but the lake water that he took into his lungs was so caustic that it digested his lung tissues."

"I agree. With all that distortion artifact, it's hard to be certain, but if it resembles the L.A. case, my best guess is that these lung nodules are malignant tumors," Jon said. He took the slide off the stage, and returned it to the tray.

"So if these are truly malignancies, we definitely have some real similarities between the two cases. They both drowned, they both have multiple lung cancers, their body consistencies were similar, and they both were orphans," Elliot said.

"And his body and tissues were so disfigured that we'll never know if he had icthyosis, skin-lung connecting structures, or enlarged upper body muscles," Faust emphasized.

Jon briefed Faust on the foreign DNA findings that he and his staff had encountered in the L.A. autopsy material. He also told him about Jose's younger brother.

"So, you've got a stem cell–derived, revved-up 'super-gene' that can cause tissue malformations, cancer, and eventually liquefied bodies? Where did it come from, and how did it get into those Mexican children?" Faust asked, shifting restlessly in his seat.

He poured himself another cup of hot coffee. "What about my case, then? It's probably too late to check out the DNA? I'm guessing it's too poorly preserved."

"Agreed," Jon said.

"We've even speculated that the Baja boys may have been test subjects in a genetic engineering experiment aimed at water adaptation and prolonged underwater submersion," Elliot said.

"So, you think someone implanted a supercharged genetic program?"

"That's the best we could figure," Jon said.

"And it went bad and malfunctioned, and the kid and his sib drowned in the Baja water hole?"

"That's what we think, based on the evidence," Jon said, feeling suddenly very sad for the affected children.

"That's outrageous! Who would do something like that and why?" Faust asked.

"We don't know," Jon said.

Faust took a long sip of coffee.

"If you think this Pauite boy may have been engineered like the others, why would *they*, whoever *they* are, choose Mono Lake? Isn't it too harsh and corrosive?" Faust asked.

"Not necessarily, I would argue the opposite—that it represents the ultimate water-adaptation challenge. Remember the icthyosis, it's pretty good protection. It's like a wet suit," Jon said.

"Well, if you put it that way, it makes sense. Sounds like my case is related to yours," Faust said.

"I'm definitely suspicious. Any other missing Pauite orphans?" Jon asked.

"Funny that you should ask. The elders informed me there was another boy, a six-year-old, who disappeared from an after-school care facility about three weeks ago."

"Any clues?" Elliot asked.

"The tribe's freaked out. They're linking the disappearance with something they think is happening on Paoha Island."

"Paoha Island?" Jon asked.

"It's the bigger of the two islands in Mono Lake. Paoha means 'children of the mist' in Paiute," Faust said.

"So they chose to share that information with you and not with the sheriff."

"They trust me. I've championed their interests in the area ever since I came here as an environmental activist."

"So what are they saying about Paoha Island?" Jon asked.

"Well, it's a little crazy. They say they've been seeing strange colored lights around the island at night."

"What's out there?"

"A lot of volcanic ash and pumice, a hot spring or two, a few dilapidated animal pens from an abandoned 1920s goat farm. Not much else. Nobody's allowed to go out there anymore."

"Why not?" Elliot asked.

"Mono Lake's a protected national scenic area. The only boats allowed on the lake are certified brine-shrimp trawlers and U.S. Forestry–registered canoes traversing the shoreline. You can't even rent kayaks anymore."

"And that's really enforced?" Jon asked.

"I sit on the Mono Lake Conservancy, and we're pretty fanatical about it."

"How far is Paoha Island from Navy Beach?" Jon asked.

"About twelve miles as the gull flies," Faust said.

"So it's incredibly isolated. Sounds like a prime location for a water-adaptation experiment," Elliot said.

"Okay, let's argue that the dead boy was engineered out there and that he was being tested in the water around the island," Jon said.

"And he tried to escape. So he headed for the shore, but didn't make it. And he washed up on Navy Beach," Elliot added.

"That would fit with the prevailing-wind pattern," Faust said.

"So maybe the other boy's out there," Elliot said.

"What do you think, Lucas?" Jon asked.

"I think we'd better go find out. And soon."

CHAPTER—19

After their meeting with Faust, Jon and Elliot drove to Mono Lake to meet Mona. She was traveling south from Reno in a car she had borrowed from Otis. They had agreed to meet at the National Scenic Area overlook on the lake's western shore at two P.M.

They skirted the eastern edge of Yosemite National Park on U.S. Highway 395, cruised through the town of Lee Vining, drove another mile, and turned right into the Mono Basin Visitor Center. As they turned into the parking lot, Jon's cell phone rang again.

"Jon, it's Lucas Faust. You're a popular guy. Just after you left, another piece of mail came. It's from someone named Diane Peterson. Thought you might want to know about it. Where are you now?"

"Just checking out the sights at Mono Lake," Jon said, trying to stay low-key.

Faust offered to have someone bring the letter to them at the Visitor Center. No big deal, he said—his friend was headed that way anyway.

"How will I recognize him?" Jon asked.

165

"He's a Paiute paramedic. Name's Ethan Bearskin. You can't miss him," Faust said.

After parking the Land Rover, they walked to the scenic overlook.

"The lake's enormous. I didn't realize it was so huge," Jon said.

He looked from left to right and scanned the black basaltic rock from the distant north shore past the two islands—one small and black, the other larger and light tan in color—to the tall, wispy, stalagmite-like tufa towers on the south shore. The landscape was stark, and the water was gray-blue.

"They say that the basin is the same size as San Francisco Bay," Elliot said.

"It's spectacular," Jon remarked. "So, which island is Paoha?"

"It's the big one on the right," a female voice said, over his shoulder.

Jon looked back and saw a glowing Mona smiling at him. She wore a black parka, khaki pants, and hiking boots.

"See, Jon, look what you've done to me. We're dress twins," she said, giving him a warm hug and then shaking hands with Elliot.

"He's been known to have that effect on people," Elliot remarked.

After the formalities, they settled into a picnic lunch at a table situated near a self-guided nature walk, which meandered its way down a slope toward the lake.

Mona had picked up sandwich makings at the Lee Vining General Store. She set out an assortment of cheeses, cold cuts, bread, condiments, soft drinks, and bottled water. During lunch, Jon and Elliot told her of their conversation with Lucas Faust and summarized the autopsy findings on the local boy. They also discussed the other missing Paiute boy and the possibility that Paoha Island was the setting for a genetic experiment involving water adaptation.

"So how do we get out there?" she asked.

Orchestrator 167

"Faust said he would work on it," Jon said.

"What does that mean?"

"From what we can tell, his status as an environmental guru in these parts has led the Paiutes to hold him in high regard," Elliot said.

"So what's that got to do with getting us out to Paoha Island?" she asked.

"There's some federal environmental agreement that limits access to the islands. Only indigenous peoples like the Paiutes are allowed to go out there. I'm guessing he'll try to find us a ride," Jon said.

"I guess we'll have to see what he comes up with. What's the time frame?" Mona asked.

"We're gonna talk again later tonight," Elliot said.

"Did you and Otis turn up anything on the van?" Jon asked.

"As a matter of fact, we did. Their IDs and license plate took us nowhere, but we traced the vehicle identification number to a bogus lease agreement with some company called Pathgene International. They're supposed to be located in Palo Alto. Sounds like a biotech company, but who knows?"

Jon and Elliot stared at each other. Mona looked up from her sandwich.

"So, you've heard of them?" she asked.

"Yeah, unfortunately we have," Elliot answered.

"You look like you've seen a ghost or something. What's going on? I don't know jack-shit about biotech. Educate me," she said.

"Elliot's had a bad experience with Pathgene, and so have I," Jon said, folding his napkin over and over to fill the silence.

"Looks that way. Tell me about it," Mona said.

After some hesitation, Elliot gave Mona the short version of David Kreeger's attempt to cash in on their clinical trials. Then Jon told her about his verbal clash with Kreeger after his cancer biology talk and Kreeger's prior attempts to obtain his transgenic technology.

"Man, that guy's got major-league cajones. First he steals your viruses and then wants in on your gene-therapy trials. Plus he's after Jon's human leukemia mouse," Mona said.

"I had the exact same reaction," Elliot said, jerking his hands and spilling his soft drink on the table in front of him. "I told him to take a hike!"

Jon reacted by setting the aluminum can upright and throwing a pile of napkins onto the liquid.

"You okay?" he asked.

"Not really. Whenever I hear Kreeger's name, I start losing it, big time." He was flustered and visibly shaking.

"So why would Kreeger and Pathgene try to pick Jon and me off on the Westgard Pass road? Otis thought those two guys were connected to Stringfellow. Now he's not so sure," she said.

"I don't know why," Elliot said, rubbing his temples. "This headache just keeps coming back." He took a long sip of bottled water. "I'll be okay. Don't worry about me."

"Sorry, Elliot, but I *am* worried about you. You haven't been the same since you and Johnstone had the run-in with Kreeger," Jon said.

"Run in? What exactly happened?" Mona asked.

Elliot frowned.

"Elliot, try and relax." Jon put his hand on Elliot's back. His shirt was soaked with sweat. "I'll tell her. I think she needs to know. She can be trusted. We're all friends here."

Jon explained the circumstances surrounding Elliot's and Johnstone's return trip to the San Jose Airport from Kreeger's estate. He then told her about Johnstone's rapid demise and the relevant autopsy findings.

"So you're saying that Johnstone is in excellent health before you experience this missing-time episode in the limo," Mona said.

Elliot nodded.

"And in a relatively short period of time, he develops acute

Orchestrator   169

dementia and then is found dead with magnetic material scattered throughout his brain and in his eyes."

Elliot nodded again.

"That's scary! How does that happen to somebody?" she asked.

Elliot sat up straight and crossed his arms in front of him.

"I don't have a clue," he said. "Not a clue, but I've got a feeling that I'm next."

Before anyone could react to Elliot's comment, Jon looked up and saw a man standing by the table—a tall, dark Native American man in a navy blue paramedic uniform.

"Dr. Jonathan Drake?"

"That's me. You must be Ethan Bearskin."

He nodded, handed Jon the letter, and walked away just as Jon was about to invite him to sit down and have a drink.

"The strong silent type, huh?" Mona said. "What's in the envelope?"

"It's a letter from Diane, care of Faust, who had his friend bring it to us."

"You're right, Faust is connected around these parts," Mona said, as Jon opened the letter. "And who's Diane?"

"She's my lab tech. Lowenstein got her a piece of Johnstone's brain for a molecular analysis, and I'm hoping she came up with something brilliant."

He read out loud.

Dear Jon,

You're not going to believe this. I did a DNA screen on the material obtained from Johnstone's brain and found something that didn't belong there. We isolated it and sequenced three kilobases [see attachment].

Later, Diane

"Three what?" Mona asked.

"Sorry, three kilobases is three thousand subunits of the DNA code," he said.

Mona nodded as if she understood.

Jon said that Diane and Chris had determined the DNA to have human viral sequences at both ends, a brain-targeting sequence internal to the virus, and finally, a gene that coded for an iron-binding protein called ferritin.

"This can't be a naturally occurring virus. I've never seen anything like it before. What's it doing with a ferritin gene in its proviral DNA?" Jon wondered.

"Let me see the sequence," Elliot said.

Jon handed him the attachment.

"It's definitely engineered," Elliot said, studying the printout. He stroked his hair with his right hand. "Jesus, it gets worse."

"What do you mean?" Jon asked.

"The viral sequences are the same ones that Pathgene stole from us."

"How can you tell that? That printout looks like alphabet soup," Mona said.

"Both ends of the virus that Johnstone and I engineered have identical sequences. They're called terminal repeats, or TRs, and they have a characteristic GCAT repeat sequence called a signature repeat. Here's the signature at either end of the construct," Elliot said, pointing to the multiple GCATs at the top and bottom of the page.

"Holy shit, I see it. It actually makes sense," Mona said.

"It's starting to make sense to me too. It means that Johnstone and I were infected with the stolen vectors and that his and my neurological symptoms are related to the infection," Elliot said, still perspiring.

"But I thought you said that your vectors were aimed at curing diseases, not causing them," Mona said.

"That's what they were originally intended for, but Kreeger and his buddies obviously re-engineered them for something different. They added a brain-targeting sequence and rigged them with a ferritin gene," Elliot said, looking pale.

"What does a ferritin gene do?" Mona asked.

"It codes for a protein that binds iron. And it looks like this brand of ferritin captures and stores so much iron that it renders it magnetic," Jon said. "That explains the magnetite in Johnstone's brain cells, but it doesn't explain why. Why did they choose magnetite? What's behind that? What's the bloody rationale?" Jon asked.

Mona's eyes were wide. "Okay, let me see if I have it right. If you're injected with this engineered virus, it seeks out the cells in your brain, jumps into your DNA, and then makes a protein that generates a kick-ass amount of magnetite."

Jon nodded back at her, impressed. "That's one way of looking at it, and it's exactly what we're dealing with here."

"It also means that Kreeger's one scary, evil mother-fucker," she said, standing up and pacing near the picnic table. "He makes Stringfellow look like a Cub Scout."

She paced some more. "So what do we do now?" she asked.

"I need to go back to the condo. I can't think about it anymore. I'm feeling pretty rocky," Elliot said.

"Okay, then, we're out of here," Jon said.

§

After leaving the Mono Lake visitor center and driving on Highway 395 for thirty minutes, Jon, who was driving Elliot's Land Rover, took a right at the June Lake junction and headed for the Mono County Coroner's Office. Meanwhile, Mona had taken Elliot to the condo in Otis Sweeney's borrowed Oldsmobile. It was five-thirty and starting to get dark when he rang her up on his cell.

"How's Elliot?"

"He's sound asleep and looks comfortable. I think those Advil finally kicked in."

"I'm going to get him some local help. I'm really worried about him."

"So you're pretty sure he's infected with the same virus that killed Johnstone?" she asked.

"It's a good bet."

"So why do they have different symptoms—Johnstone had dementia, and Elliot's got a bad headache?"

"Probably individual variation, meaning that different people react differently to the same virus. It's not uncommon."

"I didn't want to push it back there at the lake, because Elliot looked so fragile, but is Kreeger trying to kill them?"

"If it was meant to be a killing virus, Mona, magnetite wouldn't be my first choice. There's got to be some other reason behind their selection."

"Well, whatever it is, it killed Johnstone dead. And Elliot's not far behind!"

"Don't go there. I think he's got a much better chance of surviving."

"How can that be?"

"I just got through to the lab, and they're preparing an antidote. If my experimental design is right, we should have it in a day or two."

"So soon? How does that work?" she asked.

"We're lucky enough to have the complete DNA sequence, so we can rapidly customize antiviral sequences that neutralize the effects of the virus. It's called an 'antivirus' and it's given as an intravenous infusion."

"Are we going to have to take him back to L.A. for that?" she asked.

"I think so," Jon answered. "That's why this meeting with Faust is so important. Somebody needs to get out to Paoha Island and look for that missing child ASAP. I'll also find out what can be done around here for Elliot while we're waiting."

"Okay, see you later," Mona said, ending the conversation.

Hoping that he had made the right decision not to stay with

Orchestrator   173

Elliot, Jon steered the car toward the brilliant red sunset, which lit the western sky and highlighted the jagged, snow-covered peaks of the Sierra Nevada range. No wonder John Muir called it the range of light.

CHAPTER—20

Jon waited impatiently for Lucas Faust in a wood-paneled room with logs glowing in a fireplace, the light reflected by an enormous illuminated aquarium. An old wooden Victrola in the corner softly played Duke Ellington's "Mood Indigo." The tank, whose pH measured 8.2 on a digital meter, contained large numbers of small, translucent, worm-like organisms that undulated to the music. Faust had described the room as his "environmental study" and had explained to Jon that brine shrimp were the only creatures that could both survive and thrive in the alkaline waters of Mono Lake.

He scanned the lower bookshelves, stopping at a small porcelain statue of a bearded man holding a long stick and standing above a quote by Archimedes that read, "With a lever long enough, I can move the earth." Next to this small statuette was a little placard that read "Think Globally, Act Locally."

The shelves were full of the stuff—the makings of an activist, an environmentalist, and an intellectual.

- *Power of Place*

- *The Origin of the Los Angeles Aqueduct: A Biography of John Mulholland*
- *Sacred Native American Sites*
- *The Impact of the Michaelson/Morley Experiment on Einstein's Theory of Relativity*
- *Water and Power*
- *Deochronology: The Study of Tree Ring Dating*
- *A Dictionary of Egyptian Hieroglyphics (Volumes 1 and 2)*

He reached up and plucked down the first E.A. Wallis Budge volume and began to leaf through the pages of hieroglyphic symbols.

"Interested in hieroglyphics, are you?" Lucas soon emerged from the far side of the room.

"Well, funny that you should ask. I may need someone to help me translate a document that I ran across," Jon said.

"How's that?" Faust asked.

Jon told him about his encounter with Artemus Twitchell on the Westgard Pass road near the Bristlecone Pine Forest.

"He does sound strange, but weird things happen in these parts." He paused and thought for a moment. "His name has a familiar ring to it. Can't place it though. Spell it for me," he said grabbing a yellow Post-it note from his desktop. "Got the diary with you?"

"No, it's back at the condo."

"I have a 'translator' software program from UC Santa Cruz. Make me a copy and I'll see what I can do."

"So you're into Egyptology?" Jon asked.

"An ex was, and I kind of got bitten by the bug," Faust said.

Faust unrolled a large map, placed it on the wooden table in the center of the study, and pointed to the larger of the two islands. "Paoha's about an eight-mile trip from the brine shrimp pier here on the northwest shore of the lake." He pointed again.

"Brine shrimp pier?"

"It's where the brine shrimp plant moors its boats. The Paiute

176   *Paul K. Pattengale*

Council is the principal business partner. They trawl for the shrimp, dry them at the plant, and sell them as aquarium food. It's unusual, but there's a pretty good market for it."

"So, we'd leave from the pier on a brine-shrimp trawler?" Jon asked.

"That's right, and I want to get out there as soon as possible. The tribe is acting pretty spooked, and I'm wondering how long it will be before they decide they don't want to go out to the island."

"Why, what's going on? What are they scared of?"

"Well, like I told you this morning, they're upset about the missing boy, and now they're getting themselves all worked up about the lights they've seen around the island."

"What are they saying?"

"They're saying that the Hav-Musuvs have returned."

"The Hav-Musuvs?"

"Paiute legend has it that the Hav-Musuvs were gods who came down from the heavens in silver canoes," Faust said.

"And they're afraid of them?" Jon asked.

"Yeah, and they've got good reason to be. The legend says that they paralyze their victims with poison darts."

"So these gods aren't the benevolent, ancient astronaut types," Jon said with a smile.

Faust grinned back at him. "I guess not. Anyway, why don't you hold on to this map for a while."

As Faust rolled up the map, Jon's cell phone rang.

"Hello," he said.

"Jon, Mona, here. Elliot woke up and his headache's worse. I'm worried about him."

"We're on our way," Jon said, putting the phone back into his pocket.

"What's going on?" Faust asked.

"Elliot's got a medical problem. Do you mind having a look at him?"

"A medical problem? What kind?" Faust asked.

"It's a long story. I'll brief you on the way."

Fifteen minutes later, Jon and Lucas, black bag in hand, hurried into the Gull Lake condo to find Elliot lying face up on the couch with the lights dimmed and a wet washcloth across his forehead and eyes. Mona was at his side.

"I gave him another dose of Advil. Hope that was okay," she said.

"No problem," Jon said, moving closer to Elliot. "Hey, buddy, sorry to hear that you're feeling worse. I brought Lucas with me. Mind if he takes a look at you?"

Elliot nodded, and Faust opened his black bag, taking out an ophthalmoscope.

"I know you're probably light-sensitive, Elliot, but bear with me. I need to have a quick look at your optic nerves." He lifted up the washcloth and looked first into the right eye and then into the left. Elliot tolerated the eye exam but was noticeably uncomfortable when Faust shined the bright beam onto his retinas. "Okay, all done. We won't bother you anymore," Faust said, repositioning the washcloth over his eyes and then motioning for Jon and Mona to meet him in the bedroom.

"What did you see?" Jon asked, closing the bedroom door behind them.

"He's got significant papilledema. His intracranial pressure must be sky high," Faust replied.

"Translation, please," Mona said.

"It's when the optic nerves get pushed into the backs of your eyes due to increased pressure inside the brain. No wonder he has a bad headache," Jon said.

"I saw something else. His retinas were discolored and had funny bluish spots all over them. That plus the increased intracranial pressure must be the effects of the magnetite virus infection. Johnstone had eye involvement, according to the autopsy report, right?" Faust asked.

Jon, who was stunned by the news, felt a wave of nausea come over him.

"Jon, you still there? Hello! You're as pale as a ghost," Faust said.

"Sorry, I'm in shock. I've been in denial about the seriousness of his illness. It's hitting me pretty hard."

Mona moved closer to him and rubbed his back. "I understand, Jon. It must be terrible to see your friend so sick."

"We need a plan. What do you think we should do, Lucas? You know these parts better than I do," Jon said, trying to regain his composure.

"He needs to see a hospital-based neurologist before he has a major seizure. Reno's a lot closer than L.A., and I know the docs up there. I'll call ahead and make the arrangements. It's about three and a half hours from here."

"I can attest to that. The road was good," Mona said. "Plus, Otis can help us if we need him."

"You think he'll tolerate the car ride?" Jon asked, the normal color returning to his face.

"I'm going to give him some stronger pain meds. That should work. Grab his stuff and let's get going."

"Okay, we'll stabilize him in Reno. I just spoke with my lab. They'll have the antidote to him by tomorrow morning."

§

Twenty minutes later, after packing their bags and deciding to leave Otis's car at the condo, they left June Lake in Elliot's SUV. Mona rode shotgun, while Jon tended to Elliot in the back seat. The stronger pain medicine had taken effect, and now, wrapped in a blanket, he seemed comfortable, his head resting on a pillow.

"I need to make a five-minute appearance at the Paiute tribal council," Faust said. "Not to worry, it's on the way. I need to make the final arrangements for us to get out to the island. The big chief will be at the meeting. It's our only chance."

Forty-five minutes later, they pulled into Bridgeport,

California, whose main street was adorned with a brightly painted Victorian-style courthouse lit up like a Christmas tree.

"The meeting is in the elementary school," Faust said, pulling into the school parking lot, whose broken asphalt was populated with an assortment of RVs and a cadre of old, dilapidated cars. A Mono County ambulance and a volunteer fire-fighters' truck sat parked near the open door of a schoolroom. Inside, various people were standing or sitting.

"Wait here. If anybody asks, you're with me."

Faust got out of the SUV and made his way to the meeting. Jon, who was still feeling a slight twinge of nausea, rolled down his window and breathed in the damp, cold night air. The vintage Mercury across from them had its windows open, and several Native Americans with jet-black hair fastened in ponytails sat in the car grooving to the Doors' rendition of "Roadhouse Blues." The smell of marijuana permeated the air. Sensing that he might be invading their privacy, Jon rolled up his window.

"Weird energy around here," Mona said. "What's with these people?"

"Shafted by Uncle Sam and the American Dream—the crime of the millennium," Elliot said, yawning and stretching in place.

"Man, you're sounding better! It's good to see you up and about. You had us worried. How are you feeling?" Jon asked, putting his hand on Elliot's arm.

"Still sleepy but a lot better. Faust's medicine is definitely strong."

"That's great," Jon said.

Elliot reached down into his day pack and pulled out a packet of papers. "I've been meaning to show you this. It's a dossier on Kreeger."

Jon stared at him with a quizzical look.

"And don't worry about me. I'm not going to fall apart. I'm keeping my cool."

He handed the packet to Jon, but before he could delve into it, Faust, true to his word, had returned from the meeting.

They headed north on 395 in the direction of Reno. Jon had switched seats with Mona, who now sat next to Elliot in the back.

"Man, they've really got themselves worked up over that missing boy," Faust said. "They're building a sweat lodge next to Mono Lake."

"Why? Do they think that will bring him back?" Mona asked.

"They think the evil spirits have attracted the ancient gods and that these sky deities called the Hav-Musuvs are punishing the tribe by taking the boys from them," Faust said.

"It sounds like a UFO-abduction myth, Native American–style," Elliot added.

"I agree—it does have that ring to it. Makes you wonder about what they've been seeing in the vicinity of Paoha Island, I mean, with the colored lights and all," Faust said.

"Man, what a story." Jon replied.

"And it's still unfolding. Ethan is going out there tomorrow with his brother in a brine-shrimp trawler. We're invited if we can get back in time," Faust said.

"I feel bad about holding you guys back," Elliot said.

"Don't! Your health comes first. We'll find a way out there," Jon said.

After Elliot had fallen back asleep, Jon pulled out his penlight and began to page through the paperwork on Kreeger.

"What's that?" Faust asked, looking in Jon's direction.

"It's a partial dossier on David Kreeger. Elliot's been putting it together. I haven't had a chance to look at it yet," Jon said.

"So, this is the guy who stole his gene-therapy viruses, reengineered them with a magnetite-capturing protein, and infected him and his mentor; son of a bitch!"

"Terrible business," Mona said. "It's so malicious. What's driving that man?"

"Elliot told me he lost it and cornered Kreeger in his winery

Orchestrator   181

estate office like a wild animal. He called him a thief and threatened to expose him to the FDA and the NIH."

"Elliot did that? He seems way too mellow," Mona said.

"Up to a point. But when one of his causes is challenged, he morphs into a tiger. He was one of the founding members of Physicians for Social Consciousness," Jon said.

"I can vouch for that. He's definitely a go-getter in antinuclear circles," Faust added.

"Kreeger has pretty impressive credentials, though." Jon thumbed through Kreeger's dossier. "Ph.D. in Physics, Princeton, then an M.D. at the University of Oregon; member, National Academy of Science; distinguished pediatric surgeon and physician scientist in cancer biology at Stanford with a track record of seminal publications; then, suddenly, turns entrepreneur, forms own biotech company, and is subsequently shunned by the academic establishment, including the Nobel committee. Sounds like a guy with a chip on his shoulder and something to prove to the world. Fantastic scientist, though, in his early years."

"What did he do?" Faust asked.

"I remember his cell hybrid work and its effect on slowing the growth of cancer cells," Jon began. "It led to the discovery of the genes and their protein products that can inhibit malignant tumor cell growth."

"Tumor inhibitor genes, right? Now I remember," Faust said.

"Whoa, how did Elliot get hold of these?" Jon asked, holding up several sheets of medical records, each with a Children's Hospital of Philadelphia (CHOP) logo at the top.

"He has Kreeger's personal medical records?" Faust said, taking his eyes off the road just a bit too long. "He must have a good connection at CHOP."

"Jesus! Kreeger's a childhood cancer survivor. He had a malignant bone tumor on his right leg and was cured with amputation and chemotherapy. He's a lucky guy," Jon said. "And there's more. A recent bone-marrow biopsy report from a San Francisco hospital, dated six months ago, shows that he has microscopic evidence of a smoldering leukemia. This is too much! So he's got two malignancies, one that's cured and another that's about to declare itself. Take it back—he's not so lucky after all."

"Two cancers, isn't that kind of unusual?" Mona asked.

"It's been known to happen. Childhood cancer survivors have about a five percent chance of developing a second malignancy, and it's usually leukemia," Jon said.

"Can't leukemias be cured with chemotherapy?" Mona asked.

"A lot of them can, particularly in children, but not all of them. And certainly not the type Kreeger has—they're bad actors and resistant to chemotherapy," Jon said, twisting in his seat, thinking of his father's struggle. "I'll bet it motivates him to find a cure, and it might explain why he's been badgering me for my mice. I've been trying to cure these aggressive drug-resistant leukemias using my experimental transgenic mouse model."

"Makes sense to me." Faust said, staring out the window at the low-lying mist and snow flurries in the Walker Canyon corridor below Topaz Lake. He looked at Jon. "Feel like driving for a while? I need a break."

"Sure. Go ahead and pull over."

Not long afterward, Jon settled into a long stretch of clear, dry road, and both Mona and Elliot fell asleep in the back seat.

"If these road conditions hold up, we should be in Reno by midnight," Faust said, in a low voice.

"The sooner, the better," Jon said, glancing down at the odometer.

"Jon, I inquired about Artemus Twitchell."

"What did you turn up?"

"I knew the name sounded familiar and checked it out with some of my academic friends. He's listed as a professor at Deep Springs College, but he left after the spring term this year on a leave of absence."

Orchestrator 183

"Deep Springs College? I've never heard of it."

"You're not alone. It's an all-male, two-year liberal arts school that's located on a combined cattle ranch and alfalfa farm. It was founded in 1917 by a guy named L.L. Nunn, who believed that academics and manual labor should be part of the same curriculum. Faculty live on-site, and most boys go on to finish at world-class colleges and universities. *The New Yorker* had an article on it several years ago."

"Sounds interesting, where is it?"

"This is going to blow your mind. Not too far from the Bristlecone Pine Forest. It's next to the Deep Springs dry lake in the valley below."

"Wait a minute. It *is* blowing my mind. Mona and I saw some lights on the far side of a dry lake bed on our way into California that night before we drove up into the forest."

"That's the place."

"What did he teach?"

"I checked their Web site, and they listed him as a humanities professor with expertise in linguistics and ancient cultures."

"That would be Artemus." Jon said. "It's odd, though, that he would be wandering around in the Bristlecone Forest."

"I checked with the park ranger up there, and he told me they have had more visitors than usual and that a good number of them appeared to be New Age, modern-day-hippie types. He was checking with his colleagues to see if anyone had seen or heard of him."

"Artemus had some eccentric characteristics for sure, but I wouldn't classify him as a New Ager."

"Did you make me a copy of his diary?" Lucas asked.

"No, didn't have a chance with all the excitement. The original is in my day pack. Grab it," Jon said, pointing toward the floor of the back seat. "It's right on top."

Lucas reached back, retrieved the diary, and then paged through the well-worn notebook. "Very curious, for sure. I'll definitely run it through the 'translator' and see what we come up with. They certainly look like Egyptian characters," he remarked.

He looked at the successive pages of scrawled hieroglyphics. When he got to the last page, there was a large inked diagram containing a triangle, star, and half circle entitled "Sopdet Rising."

"Sopdet translates to Southis, which is ancient Greek for the modern-day Sirius, the brightest star in the sky."

"So, it's Sirius rising, huh?"

"Right. The rising of Sirius was a big deal for the Egyptians. When it rose on the eastern horizon just before sunrise, the priests knew that the Nile would flood a few weeks later. They called it the helical rising, and this is its diagrammatic representation in hieroglyphics. The star here is Sirius, and the half circle is the sunrise."

"And the triangle?"

"It's the character the scribes used for Egypt," Lucas said.

"What's Artemus doing with it in his notebook?" Jon asked.

"No clue. Maybe it had some special meaning for him. Maybe he was teaching it to his college students," Faust said, yawning. "I think I'm going to get some shut-eye. I've had enough excitement for one night."

Jon thought some more about ancient Egypt and wondered if he would ever see Artemus again. Why had he left Deep Springs College? He refocused on driving and felt a sense of wellness, his nausea now a distant memory. Moreover, he was happy that his passengers were resting comfortably, especially his friend Elliot.

CHAPTER—21

At midnight, Jon was navigating the SUV through the gleaming, multicolored jangle of Reno's gaming casinos, when he heard a series of throaty guttural sounds emanating from the rear seat. He glanced back and saw Elliot rolling his eyes, his body out of control and jerking the seat belt in a rhythmic, rapid to-and-fro motion. Lucas and Mona quickly awoke and witnessed the remainder of the episode, which culminated in a violent bout of vomiting followed by unconsciousness. Elliot lay limp in his seat when Jon pulled the vehicle to the side of the road.

"Oh, my God! What's happening to him?" Mona exclaimed.

"He's had a seizure," Jon said, opening his door and rushing to Elliot's side. He propped up his head, opened his froth-covered mouth, and pulled Elliot's tongue to one side. "His breathing is shallow. Lucas, call 911!"

"How far is the hospital from here?" Mona asked.

"A couple of miles. I know the way," Faust answered.

"I'm driving. I'll get us there faster than any 911 call." She jumped into the front seat.

"Okay, let's go then. Lucas, call ahead to your neurology buddies and have them meet us at the ER entrance."

"Roger that," he said, pulling out his cell phone.

After a wild ride through North Reno, they pulled up to the Washoe General ER entrance fifteen minutes later, where a team of doctors in surgical scrubs and white coats awaited them. After removing Elliot from the car and putting him on a stretcher, Jon parked the car while Lucas and Mona accompanied his friend into the hospital. Jon jogged the short distance to the entrance of the ER where Mona was waiting for him. It was midnight.

"Where did they take him?" he asked.

"To radiology for some imaging tests. Lucas is with him. He wanted us to wait here."

"I need to be with him," Jon said, a sense of panic in his voice. He looked into the open doors of the emergency room.

"Jon, there's nothing more you can do. Lucas said he would handle it. You haven't been feeling well yourself. It's better that you stay here with me," she said, first pushing him back and then trying to embrace him.

"I need to be with him," he repeated, dodging her and walking quickly into the ER entrance.

After showing his medical license to the triage nurse, he caught up with Elliot in an examining room where he lay unconscious on a stretcher with a team of health professionals surrounding him. Lucas Faust stood to one side. A nurse was starting an IV in his right arm. An EKG and chest monitor was in place and recording both his heart and breathing rate.

"This is Dr. Jon Drake, a friend of the patient," Faust said.

"He had a grand mal seizure in my vehicle about thirty minutes ago and never regained consciousness," Jon said, trying to remain calm.

"No wonder," the lead neurosurgeon said. "His intracranial pressure is off the charts. After the IV's started, we're taking him to the OR to relieve the pressure. His heart rate and breathing are slowing, which tells me his brain stem function is being compromised!"

"Affirmative," another M.D. chimed. "His heart rate is fifty-six and his respirations are eight."

"Mind if I come along?" Jon asked.

"I can't take you or Dr. Faust into the OR, but you can help us get him there," the neurosurgeon answered.

Seeing that the IV had started to drip, the neurosurgeon pushed the monitor in Jon's direction.

"Let's go!" he shouted to the cadre of health professionals.

After leaving the room, Jon vigorously pushed the heart-lung monitor, keeping up with Elliot on his transport stretcher. As they made their way down the long hallway in the direction of the OR, he glanced at the digital readout and saw that Elliot's heart rate had now dropped to thirty per minute and his breathing rate to four per minute. Suddenly, his heart rate went flat and the monitor flashed red and started beeping.

"Jesus!" the lead neurosurgeon said. "O'Reilly, call a code, and have the resuscitation team meet us in the OR. We'll give it our best shot!"

Jon and Lucas stopped short of the OR and watched as Elliot was wheeled through the swinging doors by the neurosurgeons. Seconds later, the Code Blue resuscitation team raced in behind them.

Jon felt faint and grabbed for Faust's arm.

"I can't believe it Lucas. We were just having lunch with him at Mono Lake today. It was all so sudden. He went downhill so fast."

"Jon, quit torturing yourself. It just happened that way. Let's go sit down."

Minutes later, Jon, Lucas, and Mona sat huddled around a small table in the hospital lobby.

After what seemed like an eternity, a masked, green-garbed man came into the lobby. He took the mask off and approached them. Jon looked up and knew by his expression that the news was bad. He braced himself as he approached and felt his stomach pushing up into his chest.

"We couldn't save him," the doctor said.

"Mona, this is Dr. Josh Whitaker, head of the neurosurgery team here at Washoe. They did everything they could," Faust said, sweat on his forehead.

"His intracranial pressure was so high that it pushed the lower part of his brain into his spinal canal. His breathing stopped, and his heart failed. He didn't have a chance," Whitaker said.

As Jon sank lower into his chair, Mona reached over and held his hand.

"I know it's a shocker," Whitaker continued. "Because your friend died so suddenly, I'll have to turn his body over to the Washoe County Medical Examiner. We need a proper autopsy to find out what happened. I have no other choice."

After his pager sounded, he excused himself and left the lobby.

After a period of silence, Faust spoke. "I know the county coroner up here and can brief him on Elliot's pre-existing condition. I can even help him do the autopsy."

Jon hit his fist square on the wood table and then slumped back down in his chair.

"Good. The more evidence we have on Kreeger, the better case we have against him and Pathgene," he said. His voice was resolute, determined. "I want to nail that son of a bitch on a murder one charge. The fucking magnetite! It must have caused his brain to swell."

"We'll get Kreeger," Mona said. "When will the autopsy be done, Lucas?"

"Tomorrow morning. They've got to complete the paperwork and transfer the body."

"What about his family?" Jon asked.

"You need to give the hospital the contact information? They'll be notified first thing in the morning."

Jon nodded reluctantly, then put his hands over his eyes and lowered his head. He felt nauseous.

"Jon, give me the info you have on Elliot, and I'll take it

to the supervising nurse. You need to take it easy and lay low," Mona said, leaning over him.

He nodded again, slowly reaching for his PalmPilot.

Five minutes later, she returned.

"Otis called. He's putting us up at his place. Let's get out of here," Mona said, extending a hand to Jon and pulling him up to a standing position.

§

Soon after, they were inside a large warehouse where Otis housed his big rig and where they could clean the insides of the SUV. There they found Otis busily shining the chrome trim on the cab of his black and silver semi to the sound of country-and-western music. The doors of the semi were neatly lettered: *Sweeney Shipping, Reno, Nevada.*

"Howdy folks. I'm so sorry to hear about your friend. It's a terrible bad thing, but the way I see it is that it's already done and we can't bring him back. My advice is that we stay focused. We've got a mystery to solve and a mission to accomplish. I've got some fresh coffee brewing back in my office, and there's somethin' I want to tell you and somethin' I want to show you," he said, tipping his cowboy hat.

He sang along to the music as he led them inside to a large Formica table where they sat and drank coffee and tried to relax. Jon was relieved that Otis was willing to do all the talking for a while. A double shot of Jack Daniels didn't hurt either.

Otis sat near them and worked at a computer terminal situated next to a CB, which crackled every few minutes with static and an occasional voice. The two-way, he explained, kept him in touch with a network of truckers on various types of jobs in California and Nevada. He took a long sip of coffee from a large shapely mug with Marilyn Monroe's face and breasts protruding from its surface.

"As you've probably heard from Miss Mona here, I used to be

190   *Paul K. Pattengale*

employed by the DEA as a field pilot. Helicopter or fixed-wing, north of the border, south of the border, it didn't matter. After the DEA, I was assigned to a classified U.S. Air Force project, but after a year or so I got thrown off for security reasons, or so they said. They blackballed me, and that was it for government flying jobs." He put his cup down on the table. "I've been trucking ever since."

"What Otis is really saying is that he's still super-pissed that he got kicked off the Air Force job, and he's been trying to find a way to get back at the bastards ever since," Mona said.

"What kind of job?" Jon asked, feeling more relaxed.

"Well, Doc, that's where it gets kind of interesting, 'cause the project I was working on might somehow relate to what you and Doc Faust have discovered in those unfortunate young lads you've autopsied," Otis said.

With the Mr. Coffee bubbling and burping a second pot in the background, Jon sat up straight, gripping his coffee cup. "We're listening," he said.

"You've heard of Area 51 on the Nellis Air Force Base?"

"That's where the U.S. government's supposed to be hiding UFOs. At least, that's what some would have you believe," Faust said.

"This may surprise you, folks, but the Air Force *wants* the public to believe in UFOs."

"So you're saying the United States Air Force is complicit with the tabloid press," Faust said.

"What I'm saying, Doc, is that, first and foremost, they are busy developing experimental aircraft. The UFO controversy and their systematic debunking of it provides them with a convenient smokescreen that obscures and deflects any real interest the public might have in knowing what they're really up to."

No one uttered a word as Otis continued with his story.

"I worked on the development of a circular stealth craft. We nicknamed her the Ebony Fox, and she functioned like you'd expect a UFO to function. She could change directions in a split second, she could go fast, she could go slow, she could hover, she could spin, she could land on a dime, she could elude radar, and she could fly at Mach 3. You should have seen that baby hum. She was an awesome flying machine, and I miss her."

Otis loosened his collar and took another long swig of coffee like he was drinking water on a hot day.

"And they let you walk away from a top-secret project, just like that, no questions asked?" Jon said.

"Me and another guy, a nuclear physicist, had words with the project manager, a higher-up Air Force brass named Patterson—a real control freak and a Nazi-poser type. Next thing we knew, we had lost our security clearances and were both out of a job. He gave us the standard 'national security' party line and warned that if we leaked anything to anybody, there would be dire consequences. We also found out they had a standard debunking protocol, which discredited and ridiculed anyone who tried to come forward with an experimental aircraft/ quasi-UFO story. Nobody believes you after they've done that to you."

"What did they mean by dire consequences?" Jon asked.

"I really didn't want to find out, Doc, so I've been layin' low in my trucking business. They even tapped my phone for a while. My nuclear physicist friend was so wigged out that he changed his name and took up a new profession. No matter though, we haven't forgotten and never will."

He stood up, poured himself another cup of coffee, and placed a box of donuts in the middle of the big table.

"C'mon, folks, there's plenty here. I can't eat 'em all. Heck, you can even dunk 'em if you're so inclined."

Jon looked at the box but had no appetite. "What does your project have to do with the dead boys?" he asked.

"Tell them what you just told me, Otis," Mona said.

"Well, Doc, it goes like this. Mona's computer buddy, JB, pulled a classified file off the Air Force server that looks like this."

He pulled several sheets of paper from the printer and handed them to Jon.

"What it is, Doc, is a summary briefing that says the Air Force has been conducting a series of biologic experiments in certain geographic zones," Otis said.

He handed the other document to Mona, who studied it like a map.

"What do these numerical zones decode to, Otis? I'm assuming they're located in the desert southwest."

"Don't know exactly yet, ma'am. I'm still working on that. But from what JB's told me and from what I can deduce so far, they map close to Baja and the Eastern Sierra, and that would be where those young boys died."

"Why would the Air Force be performing biologic experiments?" Jon asked.

"Don't know for sure, Doc, but rumor has it that this group splintered off from the main body and they're doing their own thing. It's been known to happen. Zealots on a higher mission."

"A rogue group!" Lucas said.

"So, you're saying, Otis, that these Baja and Mono Lake boys might be part of these biologic experiments?" Jon asked.

"I can't say for sure, Doc, but I'm suspicious that those 'aqua boys' were somehow involved."

"I'm more than suspicious," Mona said. "We know that Stringfellow and the upper-brass DEA were fronting for this group in the Baja desert. Of that I am sure."

There was silence.

"So, what's next?" Lucas finally asked.

"I need some shut-eye. It's been a long day and I'm on information overload," Mona said, twisting her neck back and forth and stretching her palms over her head.

"I vote for that," Jon said.

"All right then folks, here's what I've got for bedding. Follow me."

§

For Jon there was no chance of easy sleep. He tossed and turned on the back mattress in the rear of Black Beauty's cab, grieving the loss of Elliot and trying to digest the maelstrom of information that had just been revealed. If Elliot's death wasn't enough of a shock, the likelihood that the human experiments were being conducted by the U.S. military left him speechless. Whatever their intent, malevolent or otherwise, these experiments had broken new ground and needed to be understood better. Someone had tried to play God but with a disastrous result. Who were these people? His mind spun and he felt a knot forming in his gut. He needed to get a grip, but his mind wouldn't cooperate. He was still spinning out when the driver's side door opened, and Mona climbed into the cab carrying her backpack.

"Okay if I join you? That cot and air mattress combo he dug up for me really sucks," she said.

"Sure, no problem. There's enough room here," Jon said moving more toward the rear cab window.

Taking off her parka and removing her hiking boots, she lay down and pulled the covers up to her chin. "It's cold in here," she said rustling the blanket up and down with her body, her blonde hair bobbing back and forth under the double blanket. After a minute or two, she turned on her side and pushed close to him, taking his arm.

"I'm still cold," she said.

"You know, Mona, I've been thinking."

She snuggled even closer and nuzzled his cheek. "You think way too much. You need to relax, Jon. You're going to self-destruct if you're not careful. We've got a big day ahead of us. Besides you've gotta keep me warm."

She pulled him closer and he could feel her breath on his neck.

"Deal," he said, as she inched her face up to his and began to kiss him gently on the mouth.

"Think about me instead," she said, rolling on top of him.

"Double deal," he said.

CHAPTER—22

It was close to five in the morning when Otis woke them. He opened the door to Black Beauty's cab and informed them that a trucker had reported a hearse leaving the Washoe County Hospital with a body.

At five-twenty, Jon, Mona, and Otis were standing on the loading dock of Sweeney Trucking. It was still dark, and snow flurries filled the night air.

Lucas walked up and joined them, shaking his head. "I just double-checked with the coroner. They never picked up the body. They were planning to do it later this morning."

"Are we sure it's Elliot's body that the hearse took?" Mona asked.

"Yep, I just called the morgue office at Washoe. Whoever they were, they were dressed in black and posed as undertakers. They had the right paperwork, and Elliot's body was released," Faust said.

"Kreeger's a clever one, alright," Otis said.

"Kreeger! You think this is Kreeger's work?" Jon asked, astonished.

"That's who I've got my money on, Doc. I forgot to tell you,

195

but when I traced the Westgard Pass van to Pathgene, I also uncovered a lease agreement they had made with a commercial manufacturer in the Bay Area for a half dozen hearses. He's trying to get away with the evidence. I'm only puttin' two and two together," he said.

"The bastard!" Jon said.

Just then the CB radio crackled in the truck's cab.

"This is Road Runner. I've got a 10-20 on the hearse, Black Beauty. It just turned south onto 395 at the South Reno interchange, and it's a good bet they're headed for the California line. I'm right behind 'em though. Will keep you posted."

"Let's go folks! We don't want 'em to get too far ahead."

"What are we doing?" Jon asked.

"I'm pickin' up a buddy of mine at the edge of town, and you folks are following me. The plan for now is to see where they're going and what they're going to do with the body. And just so ya know it, I installed a CB radio in the Land Rover. Your code name is Saluki. Just keep the frequency open, and we'll be in touch along the way."

Otis hopped into the cab, started the engine, and turned on the country-and-western station. With the music playing loudly, he sang aloud to Joe Straight's "She's As Gone As a Girl Can Get."

Twenty minutes later, they were on the road traveling closely behind Black Beauty and headed south on U.S.395.

"Jon, are you awake enough to drive?" Mona asked.

"I'll be okay for a while," he answered.

"Let me know if you need some relief," Lucas said from the back seat.

"You know, after hearing what Otis had to say about Pathgene's lease agreement for the hearses, I'm wondering if it was Kreeger and his boys who were the ones trying to claim Jose Gonzalez's body the night I did the L.A. autopsy," Jon said.

"What makes you think that?" Lucas asked.

"Lowenstein reported that two guys dressed in black showed up with a hearse and tried to claim the corpse," Jon said.

"Sounds related to me. But if Kreeger's really involved, what could be the link between stem cell–implanted orphans like Jose Gonzalez and virally infected adults like Brett Johnstone and Elliot Adams?" Lucas asked.

"Goddamn!" Mona yelled. "What's the big surprise here! Kreeger's a megalomaniac. He's a fucking mad scientist. He's in on all the big-time stuff. He's like dog shit—he's everywhere."

"I guess that's one way of looking at it," Faust said sheepishly.

The radio sounded again, giving everyone an excuse to shut their mouths for a while.

"Black Beauty, do you copy? This is Road Runner again."

"I copy you, Road Runner. Your signal was breaking up. Can you hear me, over?"

"Loud and clear. These funeral homeboys are still hightailin' it down 395 and should be passing through Walker Canyon in a few minutes. They've gotta slow down some in the Canyon though. I've still got a good bead on them. What's your twenty, Black Beauty?"

"About thirty miles behind you. Keep your distance and don't blow your cover. And keep us posted Road Runner. Black Beauty out, 10/4."

"Roger, Black Beauty. I copy. This is Road Runner, 10/4," the gravelly voice said.

"Where do you think they're going with his body?" Jon asked.

"Hard to know, but one thing's for sure. At this time of year, with all the pass closures due to snow, they have to stay on 395 at least through Bishop," Faust said.

"Then?" Jon asked.

"Then they have a choice. Continue south through California or cut over on Highway 6 to Nevada. We'll have to see."

The ride during the ensuing hour was uneventful with the

exception of a spectacular sunrise, which had illuminated a series of jagged peaks called the Matterhorn range just to the southeast of Bridgeport, California. Somehow it countered the somber mood inside the SUV. Lucas was in the midst of describing the geologic features of the area when the two-way came to life again.

"Black Beauty, this is Roadrunner, do you copy?"

"You're a little fuzzy, Roadrunner, but we copy. Over," Otis answered.

"It looks like we've got some weather down here."

"Where's down here?"

"I'm at eight thousand feet on top of the Conway Summit about twenty miles south of Bridgeport looking down into the Mono basin, and it's completely covered in fog. I've still got the hearse in sight, and I'm following it down. Will be in touch. This is Roadrunner. I'm out."

"It's called a *poconip*," Faust interjected.

"What's a *poconip*?" Jon asked.

"It's an Indian name for an atmospheric inversion. There's no wind to blow the fog out of the basin. It doesn't surprise me. The conditions were right for one when we left June Lake last night," Faust said, reaching for his alphanumeric pager, which was vibrating on his belt. He read the display, "It's from Ethan. They're leaving for the island at eight A.M."

Then he put the pager back on his belt and checked his watch.

"So we're going to the island?" Mona asked.

"If we hurry, we'll have enough time to meet them at the northwest dock near the brine-shrimp plant. It might be our only chance to visit the island, and the *poconip* will give us a good cover. I vote that we go with them," he said.

"What about the hearse?" Jon asked.

"Let Otis and his buddies handle it. They're competent. Tell him we'll hook up with him later," Mona said.

"But what about Elliot?" Jon asked, feeling terrible about abandoning his friend.

"Jon, he's dead. He'd want us to find out what's happening on the island. It might explain the mystery of the boys, and who knows what else. Otis has it covered," Mona said.

Jon hesitated for a few moments and then reached for the radio transmitter. "Black Beauty, this is Saluki. We've had a change of plans."

§

The Land Rover passed the signpost that read *Mono Scenic Basin, 6500 Feet Above Sea Level* and broke into the dense fog of the *poconip*, which clung to their vehicle like a wet shroud. It muffled the sound of their engine like heavy snow. As Jon strained to see the road ahead, the dark shade of gray gave way to a wave of lighter grays, which illuminated the surrounding landscape with an eerie silvery glow. Were his eyes playing tricks on him, or was the *poconip* allowing more light to enter into its inner recesses? Whatever the scenario, he remained mesmerized as they traveled deeper into the cloud's interior.

"Slow down, the turn's not far from here," Faust said.

They reached the intersection of the main highway with a dirt road and turned at a battered signpost for the High Sierra Brine Shrimp Processing Plant. It was a long dirt road to the gravel parking lot where a blue-and-white-striped paramedic vehicle waited near a hazy boat dock.

"There's their ambulance. Ethan and Levi can't be too far from here. Let's get a move on," Faust said.

Jon, Mona, and Lucas, along with Ethan and his brother Levi Bearskin, boarded the *Mark Twain* and set off onto Mono Lake. Their compass was set at 113 ESE, a calculation Ethan said would put them at the northwestern shore of Paoha Island, conditions permitting, in approximately one hour. Ten minutes into the trip, Jon isolated himself on the top deck next to the wheelhouse where he could collect his thoughts for what was to come.

As the shrimp trawler snaked between the tufa towers and sliced though the mist that covered the prehistoric alkaline lake, Jon drifted through a jumbled stream of conflicting feelings and images. They ranged from stark terror to downright exhilaration.

What had haunted him from the beginning was the fact that they had stumbled onto a complex series of biologic experiments that targeted helpless children and involved genetic manipulation using a new species of DNA. Kreeger's potential involvement, though, was most disturbing. Mona was right—he seemed to be everywhere, and they were heading into unchartered scientific territory. And what was awaiting them on Paoha Island? Or who?

To Jon, this constellation of menacing circumstances was counterbalanced by the confidence and good feelings that his traveling companions engendered in him. He didn't have to look far to verify this as he watched Ethan Bearskin keep a silent vigil at the ship's helm with his head high above the boat's windshield like a wolf sampling the ambient air. His brother, Levi, had positioned himself in the ship's bow on the lower deck and was busily scanning the murky waters ahead. Directly below him, on the side deck of the starboard side, Faust was explaining to Mona that Mark Twain had spent time at Mono Lake in the mid 1860s and had even made the trip to Paoha Island with his mining partner, Cal Higbie. Jon listened to Mona hypothesize that Sam Clemens had relocated to the western territories from Missouri to avoid serving in the Civil War on the Confederate side.

As the time passed, he concluded that it was a unique time and place with a set of extraordinary circumstances and people.

Mona pointed the double-barreled, binocular-like device at the silvery void in front of them and clicked several buttons on the panel. "I'm getting a reading on the infrared scanner. How far are we from the island?"

"Less than a mile," Ethan said.

"There's an image about three thousand feet directly in front of us," she said.

"What is it?" Jon asked.

"It's kinda funky. It looks wispy and unstable. And when I zoom in, it breaks apart," she said.

"You're probably picking up water vapor from a fumarole vent. There's also a pretty good-sized hot spring on the north end of island," Faust said. "These islands are dormant volcano cones, and it wasn't that long ago that they were active. There's a lot of geothermal activity around here."

"Looks that way on the screen." Mona continued to scan the area in front of the boat.

Several minutes later, Ethan, Levi, and Lucas converged on the top deck, cut the engine, and then let the *Mark Twain* drift silently through the haze. Jon joined Mona on the side deck near a tangle of fishing nets, and watched the others as they studied their surroundings like a team of scientists on a field trip, especially Ethan and Levi, who were adept at using all their senses while processing the particulars of their immediate environment.

Slowly, the mist began to clear to the point where Jon could begin to discern a brown landmass with several smaller islands positioned in front of it.

"The big one must be Paoha Island. Looks pretty quiet from here." He stepped back behind her, put his arms around her, and rested his chin on her head.

"We'll see, Professor," Mona said, reaching up and touching his face.

Ethan restarted the engines after drifting several hundred yards, and slowly steered the boat toward the northern end of the island. Faust joined them on the side deck.

"Levi thinks we'll find something on the northeast shore. He's trawled out here before and thinks there may be a hidden cove on the far side. So we're going to put in on the north-northeast end and walk the shoreline."

A series of low-pitched, rhythmic sounds emerged from the helm, where Ethan and Levi were softly chanting to the gray water ahead of them.

"What's that?" Jon asked Faust.

"They're praying to the spirit of the lake for safe passage," Faust whispered.

"I hope he or she's listening," Mona whispered back. "This place gives me goose bumps. I feel like I'm on another planet."

They rounded the northern tip of the island. Levi brought the boat as close to shore as possible before dropping anchor about thirty yards out. He stayed with the *Mark Twain*, while Jon, Mona, Lucas, and Ethan rowed ashore in an inflatable Zodiac craft across the wind-still water. As they approached the pumice-covered beach, the *poconip* began to reappear and filled in their view of the shoreline like the snowy relief of a wispy Currier and Ives lithograph.

Once they had beached the Zodiac and unloaded their backpacks, Mona rescanned the shoreline with the infrared device. Nothing of any significance showed, so they made their way down the narrow rim of beach, flashlights in hand. They went several hundred yards and were forced to climb up a gradual rise of black volcanic rocks, which extended to the water and blocked their way onto the beach. They descended to the other side and came upon a large circular depression, which was about twenty to thirty yards in diameter and had a black sandy bottom. Jon and Mona shined their flashlights through the mist, illuminating the expanse before them.

"What is it?" Mona asked.

"It's a crater. You've gotta remember we're perched on top of a volcano," Lucas said, taking a topo map out of his pocket and unfolding it. "According to this, there's supposed to be another crater not too far from here. Let's keep moving."

Taking Faust's advice, they walked another hundred yards of beach and, when it looked like they were approaching a deep indentation in the shoreline, headed inland. They crossed a second wide outcropping of black rock and found themselves staring at another minicrater. Ethan Bearksin hiked into the cone and stooped down to examine the black sand. There were three imprint markings located about twenty yards apart near the periphery of the crater's inner ring.

"It looks geometric. What are they?" Jon asked, directing the beam of his flashlight across the diameter of the crater cone.

"They're each about the same size and distance apart, and they'd form a tripod if you were to look down on them from above," Ethan answered.

"So you think it's an aircraft footprint?"

"I don't know of any aircraft that leaves a print like that," Ethan said.

"We do," Mona interjected. "Do you think Kreeger and Patterson have enough balls to use that experimental aircraft for their perverted experiments?"

"It fits alright," Faust offered. "Otis told us the Ebony Fox put any conventional stealth aircraft like the F-117 Nighthawk to shame. Plus, it could land vertically on a dime."

"A crater landing site with a perfect black-on-black camouflage. Means we've got to be close to the lab site," Jon said.

Mona took another reading on the infrared scanner. "Still not picking up anything."

Jon noticed through the haze that Ethan had gone ahead and was motioning them to come his way. By the time they reached him, he had trekked over another rise of black rock and was standing at the top of a path, which led to a deeply recessed cove of water. The cove housed a sunken black concrete building, which straddled the shoreline and the water. Ethan went ahead to reconnoiter the site.

"Looks like nobody's home," Jon said.

"Don't be so sure," Faust said.

"I'm not taking any chances." Mona pulled the Glock from a shoulder holster beneath her parka.

Ethan returned several minutes later.

"What did you find?" Faust asked.

"Three smaller buildings on the other side, and this one's built into the lake," he said.

Ethan shined his light on the structure and illuminated what looked like a Plexiglas wall—thick and transparent, it formed the sidewall of the building and plunged directly into the lake.

"It's show time," Jon said, raising his fist in the air. He picked up a chunk of black obsidian rock and smashed it against the padlocked latch on the building's entrance. One smash for Elliot, another for Johnstone, three more for the orphaned boys, and the last for anyone else who had been harmed. He finished off the door by kicking it in with the heel of his boot.

Mona, a gun in one hand and the flashlight in the other, was the first to enter. After checking in all directions, she relaxed her stance and looked back at them.

"All clear," she said.

Once inside, they dimmed their lights, went down a flight of stairs, and began to scan the structure's interior with their strong lights. As they moved deeper into the belly of the building, Jon perceived a heavy, humid feel to the air, and he strained to see what was on the far side of the room. Was it water, or was it something else?

Ethan was the quickest of the bunch, darting off to side rooms, and running back to the main stairwell to report. The discovery of a generator was his biggest find yet, and they all filed in to witness it. A few minutes later, the large room was bathed in light. They had found more than a generator.

Jon took a deep breath and looked at the scene in front of him. At the far end of the colossal room was an Olympic-size swimming pool, which directly connected with Mono Lake through a large porthole-like opening in the transparent wall that comprised the east wall of the building.

"Anyone for a swim?" Mona quipped.

"I didn't bring my goggles," Jon replied, approaching the water.

An assortment of wet suits and scuba gear hung on the south wall, and in the area opposite the pool toward the west wall were several workstations with computers.

"What were they doing in here?" Faust asked. "And where is everyone now?" It was a question none of them had allowed themselves to ask aloud.

"Maybe this will tell us something. Let's cue up this video camera," Mona said, pointing to the electronic device, which was connected to a computer.

"I'll do it," Faust said. "It should work off the generator," He stepped up and turned on the computer. "Okay, it's booting up." He sat down at the desk and then clicked his way into the appropriate video-cam software program. The others milled around waiting for something to happen.

"There's something recorded on the camera. Let's see what it is. We even have sound." Faust flipped on the stereo-speaker equipment. "Here we go."

The video started, beginning with a shot of several adults in full wet suits and scuba gear surrounding a young, muscular, boy in only a partial wet suit. The wet suits were glistening and water was dripping from them onto the floor. The indoor lake-fed pool was in the background, and the date, 12-20, and time, 14:30, registered in the lower left corner.

Ethan leaned in for a better look. "Ephraim," he said, almost to himself.

"Some way to spend the holidays," Mona said.

"That was just three days ago. They cleared out fast and for a reason," Jon said.

"Ethan, you recognize the boy?" Lucas asked, freezing the frame.

"Yes, he's the one who disappeared from the Paiute day-care center. His name is Ephraim Northstar."

"He doesn't look sick to me," Mona said.

"He's gotta be okay. He's only wearing a spring wet suit. If

206   *Paul K. Pattengale*

he's got thick skin like the others, it must insulate him enough so that he doesn't freeze in the lake water," Jon said.

"Let's see if we can get a closer look at him," Lucas said as he froze and then amplified the image.

"Look, the wet suit's cut away at the clavicles, and there are the skin openings right where we would expect them to be," Jon said.

"And they must be functioning. It looks like they just got back from a dive. Let's see what else is on here," Faust said.

He clicked the mouse several more times, and the video continued to play. One of the adults motioned back to the camera with the thumbs-up sign.

"We did it," he said.

"Is the next experiment here or back at Nellis?" an unidentified voice asked in the background.

"Nellis. Dr. Kreeger wants to run some more genetic tests on the boy," another voice said.

"Son of a bitch," Jon growled.

Suddenly, Mona looked up at the ceiling and pulled the automatic out of her holster.

"Shit, I thought I disarmed the security system. They must have an override mechanism. Everybody down," she yelled.

As Jon retreated to the side of the room, he looked up and saw the bright red indicator light on the surveillance camera as it panned in their direction.

"It just kicked in," she said, unloading several rounds into the device and disabling it.

Everyone crouched silent for a long minute, catching their breath, checking one another's eyes.

"Do you think it saw us?" Faust asked.

"I don't think so," Mona said. She reloaded her gun.

"How could it transmit to a remote site when this place runs off a self-contained generator?" Ethan asked.

"Probably works off a satellite connection," Mona said.

"I think we better get out of here," Lucas said.

Orchestrator 207

"Yeah, Nellis Air Force Base is only a few hundred miles from here by air. If they're motivated, they can get here pretty quick, is my guess. And they definitely know someone was here," Mona said.

"Okay, then, let's shut this place down," Jon said.

It was a mad dash from the lab facility to the *Mark Twain*. Jon, Mona, and Lucas huddled on the starboard deck as Levi and Ethan set the correct compass course and put the main engine at full throttle.

§

Three quarters of an hour had passed. The *poconip* had begun to thin out as they neared the northwest shore of Mono Lake.

"We've got a west wind of about five miles per hour and slightly better visibility. We might not have our cover for very long," Ethan said.

Jon thought he heard a thrumming sound above them, which seemed to intensify as he listened more intently.

"And it looks like we could've used it too. Do you hear what I hear?" Mona asked, looking up at the mist above them. "It sounds like a chopper."

"The timing fits with a unit traveling from Nellis," Faust said.

"We better be ready," Jon said, bracing himself on the railing.

"It's for sure they know we're down here. If it's a Cobra, they've got infrared and state-of-the-art radar tracking. But they can't really see us, yet," she said.

Ten minutes later, just as they were approaching the dock, the *poconip* began to break up and the throbbing sound intensified. The helicopter peeked through the breaks in the haze and descended in their direction.

A voice over the loudspeaker blared. "This is the U.S. Air

Force. Moor the boat on the dock, and get out with your hands up. Your lives are in danger."

Jon could now see a medium-sized chopper with several people inside. One of them aimed in their direction. As it hovered near them, the mist settled back in and the aircraft disappeared back into the haze.

"This is our chance. Everybody out of the boat. We're gonna run for it and try to make it to the parking lot," Mona said. She leaned toward the dock. Levi tossed one of the mooring ropes to Ethan, who tethered the *Mark Twain* to a wooden piling.

"Let's go," Jon said. He jumped off the boat with Mona, Lucas, and then Levi following close behind.

When they reached the gravel parking lot, the chopper had reappeared again and was attempting to set down on a level spot near the plant's loading dock.

"Freeze!" the voice over the loudspeaker announced.

"Fuck you!" Mona shouted back.

Jon was digging into his pocket for the keys to the Land Rover when he felt a sharp pain shoot across his forehead passing through both temples and then over his entire scalp. A millisecond later, a wave of nausea rocked his abdomen. The symptoms were so intense that he had to stop what he was doing.

"What's going on, Jon?" Lucas asked.

"All of a sudden, my head is killing me. I feel dizzy and nauseous. I'm not sure I can make it." He tried to regain his balance by reaching out and grabbing Ethan's shoulder.

"Let's get him into your ambulance," Lucas said looking at Ethan and Levi.

While the Bearskin brothers and Faust helped Jon move toward the ambulance, he extracted the Land Rover's keys from his pocket and handed them to Mona.

"You may need these," Jon said.

"You guys keep moving, I'm gonna try and hold 'em off," she called. She ran in the direction of Elliot's SUV.

From the rear of the paramedic vehicle, Jon could see that

Mona had climbed into the Land Rover just as the chopper was setting down next to the loading dock. He could also see Levi running after her, but by the time he reached the car, she had taken off and was racing toward the helicopter. Although he was dizzy and disoriented, the last thing Jon experienced before blacking out was the sight of the Land Rover colliding with the helicopter and a loud thunderous sound.

CHAPTER—23

Jon opened his eyes to find his body being wheeled on a stainless steel litter down a long hallway by three masked figures dressed in surgical greens.

A deep masculine voice responded to his movement. "He's waking up. I thought you gave him enough sedative."

"I did," a female voice responded.

"Give him another dose then."

"Where are you taking me?" Jon slurred, trying to sit up, the IV dangling from his right arm.

"You have blue spots on your retinas and you're having a series of unexplained seizures, Dr. Drake. We're getting a baseline magnetic resonance image on you. Lie down. You're not well. We want to help you."

"You have the wrong person. You must mean Dr. Adams, Elliot Adams. You've made a horrible mistake," Jon said.

He thought about the ferromagnetic particles in Elliot's brain, and then in his, and what effect the MRI procedure would have on his cerebral tissue. He could visualize the tiny shards of magnetite moving to and fro in the magnetic field and lacerating his central nervous system into a bloody puree.

"No, Dr. Drake, we have the right person. Now please lie down. This procedure doesn't hurt."

"I didn't give you permission to do this!"

"Nurse, he's getting agitated. Give him more Valium," the larger male figure said.

He pinned Jon's right arm to the bed and turned the litter into a smaller room on the left side of the hallway where a large hollow cylinder loomed. Jon couldn't quite bring the sign into focus, but he knew what it said: *Danger, High Power Magnetic Field In Use (10 Tesla). Secure All Metal Objects In Immediate Area.*

"Push ten milligrams IV," the masked figure said, pointing to the plastic reservoir beneath the hanging bag.

"I'm going to activate the magnet," the other male said, adjusting a large chrome rheostat.

"What's taking you so long, Nurse? If you won't do it, I'll do it myself."

The larger of the two tried to grab the loaded syringe from her.

"Over my dead body!" she cried.

She pulled the man's arm forward and sank the syringe deep into his right shoulder muscle.

"What do you think you're doing!?" he yelled.

He ripped off her face mask and cap with one swing of his left arm.

"Sedating a pig in heat," Mona said, her blonde hair falling onto her shoulders.

"Don't waste any more time. Put him in the machine. I'm turning up the power," the other grunted.

"Mona, stop them!" Jon cried out.

As the man tried to push the litter closer to the hollow cylinder, he was intercepted by Mona, who now stood between him and the magnetic resonance imager.

"Get out of my way!" he said, rushing toward her with a pair of scissors raised like a knife.

As he lunged toward her, she grabbed his outstretched arm, tripped him with her right leg, and, with the help of his own weight, slung him into the mouth of the open cylinder like a sack of potatoes into the back of a truck.

From his supine position, Jon looked over his shoulder to see that the man was deep inside the metallic steel drum with the scissors and a silver pen spiraling over his head. Seconds later the steel objects were swirling around the machine's insides and making loud clanging sounds, followed soon by the muffled screams of the man within.

"Mona!" Jon shouted.

"Snap out of it, Jon, you're having a bad dream," said Faust. He was nearby.

Jon woke up in the framed bed, with Lucas Faust and Ethan Bearskin standing over him. He looked around the room and saw several windows and a door.

"Where am I?"

"In my house, in the guest bedroom," Faust answered.

"Where's Mona?" he said, sitting up.

"She was captured back at the boat landing."

"How did that happen?" Jon strained to maintain his upright position.

"Careful, Jon, remember your head," Faust said.

He fell back on the pillow and rubbed both temples.

"The last thing I recall was seeing Elliot's Land Rover hit the chopper, and then hearing an explosion. At least, that's what I think I remember." He rubbed his head some more. "I feel like I'm going crazy. How long have I been out?"

"About nine hours. It's Monday night," Ethan said, looking out the window as if gazing at the stars.

"What happened to her? I need to know."

"Levi figures she must have put the Rover in cruise control, jacked up the speed a few notches on the column controller, and then bailed out on the driver's side. The military guys jumped out and scattered just before the car broadsided the chopper," Faust said.

"She blew up a helicopter. It's insane."

"She's one amazing woman. She tried to escape but was limping when they surrounded her," Ethan said.

"So she hurt herself jumping out of the car?"

"That's what we thought. There wasn't much we could do. Since we knew there had to be another air unit on the way, we split," Faust said.

"It's my fault. I slowed everyone down." Jon rolled onto his side and buried his face in the pillow.

"Take it easy on yourself, Jon." Lucas tried to console him. "There's nothing you could have done differently. What happened, happened. She was overpowered." Lucas smiled, grimly. "We were able to escape because of her."

Jon tried to sit up again, but it made him dizzy. "We have to find her. Has anyone talked to Otis? He might know something."

"Slow down—you're not well," Faust said.

Suddenly, a voice broke in on Ethan's walkie-talkie. "There's been an accident near Silver Lake on the loop road. They're gonna need an ambulance," it said.

"I'll stay in touch," Ethan said, heading for the bedroom door.

"Let me know how it goes," Faust said.

Jon watched Ethan stride out of the room, then returned his gaze to Faust. "I'm not well Lucas. I've had something going on ever since the Baja trip—headaches, nausea, and ringing in my ears."

"You were knocked unconscious at the border, right?"

"Yeah, but when I was examined by the neurologist he saw a couple of blue spots on my retinas. I didn't think anything of it until you saw them on Elliot's. I've been in denial ever since. I'm afraid I've got Elliot's disease," Jon said.

"You do, Jon. I looked at your retinas when you were out

of it, and I saw the same blue spots. Your case isn't as advanced as his. You've been functioning at a pretty high level, and you haven't had any seizures yet. Your optic nerves aren't blurred, so you don't have significant papilledema, at least not yet."

"Denial works wonders. Plus, I've been on a pretty good adrenaline rush since I pulled Mona out of Las Vegas. It looks like it caught up with me, though."

He fell back onto the pillow.

"So, when do you think you were infected with the virus?" Faust asked.

"Had to have been when I was unconscious in the San Diego customs area. Stringfellow must have been behind it."

"Mona's ex-boss? But why him? He's DEA."

"Somehow, he's connected with this Area 51 military faction that Otis told us about," Jon said.

"And now we know that Kreeger and Pathgene are part of this same cabal," Faust said.

Jon nodded, rolled onto his right side, and looked directly at Lucas Faust, who had pulled up a chair and was sitting next to the bed.

"But, Lucas, what's the bloody motive? Why were we infected? If they really wanted to do away with us, you'd think they would have done something more direct. And now they have Mona!"

He grabbed at the bed sheets, as if trying to tear them into pieces.

"I don't know why, Jon. But you've gotta calm down. You're going to flame out."

Suddenly, the phone by the bed rang and Faust picked it up.

"It's for you. It's your lab tech. I briefed her a few hours ago."

Jon grabbed the phone.

"Diane," he said, almost out of breath.

"Jon, Dr. Faust told me everything. We've just finished synthesizing the viral antidote from the Johnstone isolate," she said in a soft, deliberate voice. "Chris and I are putting the final touches on it and are driving up after that. We'll be there in the morning."

"That's great news!"

"Get some sleep, and we'll see you soon. And remember, stay positive."

He hung up. Lucas brought him a cup of hot chocolate. They discussed the logistics of administering the antidote, and then Lucas left him to rest. He was still exhausted and desperately needed to sleep. His head hurt and his ears rang. He tossed and turned worrying about Mona. He missed her and wondered where she was and if she was with David Kreeger. She could take care of herself, at least for the time being, but he needed to find her, and soon—if he was up to it, and if the antivirus preparation did its job. The antidote was his only hope. The antivirus approach had been successful in certain animal models, but to the best of his knowledge, it really hadn't been tried in humans, at least not yet. If anyone could get it to work he could. It had to work. It would work. He had to find Mona. He had to stop Kreeger.

§

Jon felt himself being assaulted by a loud, high-pitched, shrill. He cringed in pain, put his hands over his ears and sat up. Still hearing the sound, he inched up and out of bed toward a large picture window. Lucas was in the yard blowing a thin silver dog whistle, and his three Siberian huskies were responding accordingly.

Chris and Diane showed up shortly after. With Lucas's help, they tranquilized Jon with Valium and administered the antivirus preparation via a continuous intravenous drip in the guest bedroom. Diane, Chris, and Faust immediately hit it off, and launched into a discussion concerning the progress they had made in isolating and characterizing the regulator elements from the master orchestrator gene. Jon tried to follow along as Diane cued up an updated frog egg video but wasn't up to really reviewing the material until Diane and Chris left and returned to L.A.

The sun had already set when Jon began to page through the lab notebook they had left behind, a cup of hot chocolate in his other hand. Although the experiments were complicated and difficult, his team was getting closer to finding and isolating the piece of DNA that was capable of slowing down the uncontrolled master orchestrator gene. When found, this regulator element would be able to curb and shut down the relentless, cancerous progression in injected frog eggs; and with the right manipulation, this regulator sequence could have prevented the cancerous progression in the young boys kidnapped and implanted with the aquatic DNA program. They had made some progress but were still short of their goal. They would just have to keep on trying.

Jon's thoughts turned to David Kreeger, and he wondered what Kreeger really wanted with him. Why had he harassed him for his transgenic mouse model? Why had he tried to break into his lab? Why had he tried to stop him and Mona on the Westgard Pass? And why had he infected him with the re-engineered viruses? Did Kreeger really have a handle on deciphering the master orchestrator gene? Maybe he was trying to find out what Jon knew.

Jon awoke the next morning on Christmas day feeling refreshed. Throughout the day he noticed that his headache waxed and waned, and he wondered whether the antiviral effect had truly taken hold. Jon had also learned from Lucas that Abner Woods and Abe Lowenstein had found magnetite in the cells lining Johnstone's inner ear, which explained his own hypersensitivity to high-frequency sounds as well as the incessant ringing. Jon also wondered if the frequency and intensity of his dreams were somehow related to the effects of the virus.

After a quiet morning and several cups of green herbal tea, Jon, with Faust acting as coach, utilized a deep-breathing technique in which he visualized the magnetite crystals dissolving out of his tissues and then being eliminated from his body. It was a powerful experience and one that elevated his mood, sustaining his feelings of wellness. It even counteracted his persistent sadness over the loss of Mona. His attitude turned more positive. He felt in his gut that he would see her again. He even had enough energy to check in with his mother, Cathleen, Bob, and the boys, assuring them that he was okay and letting them know that their Christmas presents would be late. They each wished him "Merry Christmas," and Cathleen told him that Chelsea was fine. He told them he would be home soon and looked forward to taking his nephews to the zoo.

§

After a light lunch of rice and miso soup, Jon felt energized enough to take a shower and explore his immediate surroundings.

He descended from his bedroom suite on the top floor to the expansive living area below down a spiral staircase that encircled an interior stone chimney. He then ventured over to the thermal-paned picture window and looked down on a creek, which ran under the house and cascaded over a series of snow-covered rocks to a pond below. On a wall near the window hung a framed picture of Mono Lake and a quote from the Greek poet Pindar that read "The noblest of elements is water." The spatial harmony resonated so strongly around him that Jon was certain it had a regenerative effect on his fragmented mind.

In a back room with a pot-bellied stove and a sleeping husky by its side, Bach's "Air in G" played quietly. Amidst the serenity, Jon found Lucas busy at his computer trying to decipher and translate the hieroglyphic-like portions of Artemus Twitchell's diary.

"What do you have so far?" Jon asked.

"This entry is preceded with a set of longitude-latitude

points. He must have been carrying a global positioning device," he answered pointing to the top of one of the pages.

"Where does it map to?"

"In the Bristlecone Pine Forest near where you found him. Remember me telling you about the New Age types that were flocking there."

"Right, the ranger told you."

"Well, he told me more. It turns out that they're UFO enthusiasts."

"UFO enthusiasts, what's that all about?"

"They've been reporting increased sightings in the Forest and have claimed that there's a debris field up there."

"Debris from a UFO crash?" Jon asked.

"I've heard that pieces of metallic foil with cryptic, hieroglyphic-like inscriptions were retrieved. No craft, no little green men. After hearing what Otis had to say, I'm wondering if this Air Force group planted the artifacts to keep the UFO myth alive."

"And to keep craft like the Ebony Fox out of the public domain," Jon interjected.

"Right, more distractions to keep the so-called crazies occupied, and less attention on themselves," Faust added.

"Maybe Artemus with his Egyptology background was trying to decipher them," Jon said.

"Weird coincidence, I agree, but as I told you before, weird things happen in these parts. Here's what I've got so far. The passages are written in a hybrid format, with classical, Egyptian hieroglyphic characters mixed in with pseudo, hieroglyphic-like characters."

"Can you make anything out of them?" Jon asked.

"A few passages are classical and able to be deciphered. This one says: *The secret of life is that there is no secret of life.*"

Jon laughed. "Sounds like something Artemus would have espoused."

"The hybrid text is more much difficult," Faust said, turning to the next page. "I can make out a few words, which, curiously, recur over and over again. *Life, death,* the number *two,* and the mathematical symbol *pi* are the most obvious. I'll keep working on it though."

"It's all very strange. Mona and I saw a UFO-like craft in that same area. After listening to Otis's story, I'm wondering if it was the Ebony Fox."

"Don't know, Jon. I do know one thing—you're looking much better. How are you feeling?"

"I think I've turned the corner," he said with a smile.

§

Although feeling restless, Jon spent the remainder of Christmas Day browsing in Faust's personal library, where he found a complete collection of Jack London's works, including an original, signed first edition of *Call of the Wild,* printed in 1903. Later in the day and before dinner, he had gathered enough energy to play in the snow with Faust's huskies. After a vegetarian dinner, Jon retired early. He was still dreaming about huskies, dog sleds, and the Klondike when the sound of a familiar voice awakened him.

"Mornin', Doc. Happy holidays," the voice said.

Jon opened his eyes and sat up. It was Otis.

"I hear you're feelin' better, Doc. It's almost time to check out of the Faust Wellness Clinic. We've got a track on Miss Mona and have some business to attend to," he said.

"We?" Jon asked.

A tall, thin man wearing a deerstalker hat and holding a long-stemmed pipe entered the room.

"Wendell Thackerey, at your service, my dear Dr. Drake," he said.

CHAPTER—24

After one more day with Lucas Faust in June Lake, Jon joined Wendell Thackery and Otis Sweeney in Beatty, Nevada. Now he sat by the fire with them in the rear sitting room of the Sherlock Holmes Inn.

"I'm definitely feeling much better," Jon said.

"I'll vote for that," Otis smiled.

"So, let's get down to business." Thackery was impatient. He unrolled a large vellum map and laid it on top of the mahogany table in front of them. "This is our final destination." He pointed to a marked spot in the Nellis Air Force Base "Restricted Zone."

"I don't like the word *final*," Jon said.

"A mere figure of speech, Doctor." Thackery let a slight chuckle escape.

"How are we going to get there undetected?" Jon's voice was tense.

"A relevant question." Thackery quickly pulled out a large transparency and overlaid it onto the map. "We go this way. Except for the last half mile, it's all underground." He pointed to several pairs of intersecting lines.

"Underground?"

Orchestrator 221

"We get to the rendezvous point by going through two abandoned mines that are connected by a limestone cave."

"A limestone cave in Nevada?" Jon was astonished.

"It's one of nature's little oddities, the southern extension of the Carson sink, to be exact," Wendell said.

"You guys really have this figured out."

"Since we were thrown off the Ebony Fox project, we've been, shall we say, keeping busy, Doc," Otis said.

"So you've actually been watching the compound?"

"Up close and personal," Wendell said.

"That's right, Doc. Wendell's not only worked out the course and been inside the security perimeter, he's also been eavesdropping."

Wendell set a tape recorder on the desk and pushed the play button. After a few seconds' delay, the voice that broke through was unmistakable.

"Get your fucking hands off me. I can do it myself," Mona shouted.

Jon almost jumped out of his chair. He stared at the recorder, almost longingly, as Wendell turned it off.

"She's in the infirmary," he said.

"So, she's okay, then?" Jon asked.

"As best I can tell," Wendell answered.

"She sounds like the Mona I know," Otis chuckled.

"You're magic, Wendell. How do you know all this?"

"We've got someone on the inside whose incentives, shall we say, are aligned with our own, and whom I've been able to provide with a set of ultrasophisticated listening devices. The unexpected capture of Miss Larsen gives us an excellent opportunity to work together and accelerate our timetable," he said.

Jon got up and stretched. "What are you guys really trying to accomplish?" he asked.

"We are trying to uncover and expose, Dr. Drake, a power-thirsty rogue black cell within the U.S. military, which is intimately connected with both the DEA-drug cartel axis and the biotech sector of corporate America. We had some clues while we were on the job, but after we were summarily dismissed, our suspicions were confirmed. Their recent malevolent misuse of genetic engineering is a particularly wicked twist. Professor Moriarty, himself, would have been pleased with such a dark tale," Thackery said.

"Weren't they located in Area 51?" Jon said, sitting back down.

"They were originally there when Otis and I were working on the project. But they've recently relocated their nasty little enterprise into the Forty Mile Canyon area of the old Nevada test site, and are using an abandoned building as a hangar. It is deceptively primitive-looking. Their living quarters, the infirmary, and the lab facilities are underground," Wendell said, pointing to the map.

"Do they have nuclear weapons?" Jon asked.

"Unknown, but entirely possible, and also my worst fear. This elitist, self-righteous group is capable of anything. They are an arrogant lot and out of control. They must be stopped," Thackery said, clenching his fist. "They will be stopped."

"I'm in," Jon chanted, leaning forward in the red velvet chair, thinking of the boys who were subjected to inhumane treatment and of Mona, who was underground and in need of rescue.

"Our plan is to fly the Ebony Fox out of the facility to a safe haven, and if we are unable to do that, we will destroy the craft."

Jon paused and thought about the consequences of their bold actions, wondering if they could accomplish their goals and what would happen if they didn't. Finally, his impatience took over. "What are we waiting for?" he said.

"Agreed. Enough speculation for now. We must be on our way," Thackery said, looking at his watch.

He picked up a khaki knapsack, took out three yellow helmets with attached metal headlamps, and doled them out.

"These should illuminate our way quite nicely. Follow me."

He put on his own hard hat and walked toward the dark corridor, which housed the long array of candle-lit dioramas depicting the adventures of Sherlock Holmes.

When he reached the hallway's midpoint, he bent over, pulled on a metal ring in the floor, and opened a large trap door, where a set of wooden stairs led into the darkness below.

"Like the villain, John Clay in the 'Red Headed League,' I have tunneled not into the Coburg branch of the London City and Suburban Bank but rather into the now defunct Rhyolite Princess Mine," he said, stepping down into the abyss. "Light your lamps, and we'll be on our way."

§

Jon strapped his backpack to his chest and followed Wendell's headfirst lead by slowly wiggling and sliding on his back through the confines of the narrow limestone passageway. Otis was behind him grunting. Jon looked up at the rock directly above his face and felt the radiant heat of the carbide arc lamp on his nose and forehead.

"It's pretty tight in here, Wendell." He hugged the backpack, trying to fight back the claustrophobia.

"I'll go along with that, Doc. How much longer?" Otis asked.

"Not long. Sorry for the inconvenience, but we must continue to be resourceful. I hadn't planned on the cave being blocked at the second mine entrance. There was some local seismic activity several days ago. My hunch is that it moved the already loosened rocks. We shouldn't be in this much longer," he said wiggling his body back and forth and breathing deeply.

"An earthquake," Jon said.

"Just a small one, Doctor, nothing to be alarmed about."

Jon felt his stomach migrate to his throat as he twisted under the massive rock.

To his relief, it was only five minutes before they were sitting in a large domed cavern, which resembled an indoor amphitheater. The multiple stalagmites were arranged in linear arrays, as if by design, resembling churchgoers standing in an underground cathedral. Wendell studied the map.

"If my calculation is right, the passage to the rear will lead to a more proximal location in the mine shaft, and we should be able to exit there. I shall confirm and return with the news," he said, pointing in the direction of the rear passageway.

Jon and Otis huddled together on one side of the underground cave under an overhang of stalactites awaiting Thackery's return.

"What's driving you two so hard?" Jon said, rubbing his shoulder.

"Hurt pride, Doc, and the truth."

"So I'm guessing that you were thrown off the project because of some bogus charge."

"That's right. Patterson had us set up, and we were terminated. We were asking too many questions."

"Then what?"

Jon looked up and illuminated the stalactites with his headlamp. As he moved his head back and forth, the shadows on the limestone ceiling flitted like dancing men.

"We were interviewed by an investigative newspaper reporter from Vegas. Then the government debunked the interviews and started to harass us. After that, neither Wendell nor I could get a decent job in our respective professions, so we both had to change our lifestyles," he said, kicking some rocks with his feet. "It was worse for Wendell because he blames Patterson and his operation for the death of his wife."

"What happened to her?"

"It was on one of the nights that they detained us on the base. She went looking for him, was turned away at the guard checkpoint, and then sped off in a frenzied state. She lost control of the car, spun off the road, and wrapped her car around a telephone pole."

"You can see it in his eyes," Jon said. "Revenge is a powerful emotion."

"That's right Doc. They blackballed us both pretty bad and took away our livelihoods. I pride myself as an ace pilot, and Wendell's a world-class physicist. We both took a hard fall and haven't been the same ever since."

"Man, if Stringfellow's in there with Kreeger, I'm really worried about Mona." He put his hands over his face and rested his forehead on his knees.

"Doc, it wasn't your fault she was caught. Besides, she can take care of herself. You heard the tape. She sounded good."

Jon lifted his head and looked Otis in the eye. "I hope you're right."

He hurled a rock across the ledge.

"And then there was Elliot, who didn't fare as well. What a waste of a life," Jon said.

He threw another rock, this time harder.

"So, Otis, you still think Kreeger orchestrated the theft of Elliot's body from Washoe General?"

"I'm sure of it. Wendell and I followed the hearse to a dirt road outside Bishop where a black military helicopter was waiting for them. After they transferred the body into the chopper, it took off and headed directly southeast. That vector connects directly to the Forty Mile Canyon site. Take it from an old pilot. You know Kreeger's sitting pretty in there, thinking he can suppress the physical evidence that resulted in Elliot's death."

"Not for long!" Jon snapped. He clenched his fist.

"Stay cool, Doc, we'll have our chance."

"And the evidence you have so far is that the Ebony Fox is being used by this group for drug running, and the profits are being used to finance Kreeger's and Patterson's genetic projects?"

Otis nodded.

"Jesus, what an unholy alliance. Stringfellow's involvement makes sense now. He's on the take, just like Mona predicted. Who would have ever thought?" Jon said.

"Doc, since we're on the subject, what were those dead aqua-boys all about? Were they meant to be some kind of biologic weapon, before they went sour and got cancer?"

"I think that the military faction was trying to engineer some type of super-warrior that could swim long underwater distances. The tactical advantages are obvious."

"Kind of like a deep water, super–Navy Seal, huh."

"Right and I'm sure there were other prototypes to follow, like high-altitude super-pilots. With a fully functioning master orchestrator gene, one can customize almost anything."

Otis nodded some more, stood up, and looked behind them, where Wendell was making his way back to them from the back passageway.

"My calculation was correct." There was a certain excitement in his voice. "There's an alternative connector to the mine shaft about a quarter of a mile to the rear. Let's get moving. We've got a schedule to keep."

An hour later, at three A.M., the three of them, their faces now clad in black ski masks, stood next to a pair of metal tracks and several derailed, heavily rusted mining carts.

"The exit is above us," Wendell said.

He pointed to a set of wooden stairs, which abruptly ascended to an attic-like opening above them.

"What's the plan?" Jon asked.

"Listen carefully," Wendell replied, pulling a detailed diagram out of his pocket. "The facility is one mile from our exit point and is under a rock escarpment on the far end of a dry lake. We are well inside the outer security perimeter, which means that we do not have to contend with electrified fences, guard dogs, or motion detectors."

"Then how do we get into the facility?" Jon asked.

"I have an access code to one of the side entrances, which should do the trick. It leads directly into the northwest stairwell."

He then reached into his black nylon pack and took out several objects and handed them out to Jon and Otis.

"Tasers, should you need them, and tinted goggles for light enhancement," Wendell explained.

"Doc, once we get into the facility, you have twenty minutes to get Mona to the Fox. Four-twenty A.M. to be precise. Here's where she is, and here's where we'll be," Otis said.

He laid out the 3-D detailed floor plan of the facility in front of them and pointed to the two locations.

"She's in the infirmary, directly down three flights of stairs on Level D, second door on the left, second bed in. We're here on the balcony of Level A waiting for you," he said.

Jon picked up the plan and memorized it.

"Why twenty minutes?" he asked.

"When it's not out in the field, the Fox is routinely serviced every a.m. at four-ten. They bring it up from its hiding place in a large well under the floor. It will take us ten minutes to hijack it. We'll be hovering right here at the Level A overlook, waiting for you," Otis repeated, pointing to the diagram.

"The reason it's a tight schedule, Doctor, is because of the security sweep intervals. We must enter at four A.M. for you to encounter the least resistance getting to the infirmary. I hope the same is true when you're inside the sick bay, but I can't guarantee it," Wendell said.

Otis rolled up a second copy of the diagram and placed it in Jon's hand. "Up we go."

§

The three men emerged from the defunct mine entrance. The light of the full moon reflected off the metallic surfaces of their headlamps as they surveyed the route ahead of them. It was bone cold, and a light wind was blowing. They came across the corpse of a dead coyote, which was sprawled on its stomach as if it had collapsed while running. Jon looked around for roaming dogs but saw none. He noticed that there were no flesh wounds on the corpse, nor were there signs of a struggle. Wondering what the animal had succumbed to, he continued to walk until the building they were to infiltrate came into view. It stood in the bed of the dry lake and was tucked under a prominent rock overhang.

"How do they fly the Fox in and out of there?" Jon whispered.

"Very carefully, Doc," Otis said.

"Come on, come on. We must keep moving," Wendell said, looking up at the moon and sniffing the cold night air.

They had descended into the wash and followed it to the northeast when they came upon a scattering of shacks abutting the bank of the dry arroyo. They passed by the dilapidated, moonlit buildings, and Jon thought he could see furniture in the front room of the nearest shack. As he strained to get a better view, he jumped to the left of the footpath.

"There're people in there," he said in a loud whisper.

"No need for alarm, Doctor. Simulated doomsday towns are only harmless remnants of our nuclear past," Thackerey said.

Jon squinted and was able to make out the faceless mannequins seated around the table in frozen poses. He swallowed hard and kept walking.

They reached the side entrance of the main building at precisely four. Wendell punched in the six-digit access code and, without challenge, the three of them entered the stairwell at the northwest corner of the hangar complex.

Jon gave a quick salute and proceeded down the stairs while Wendell and Otis opened the door to Level A.

"Good luck, Doc. See you in twenty," Otis whispered. "We'll be holding seats for you on the balcony."

Working his way down the steep cinder-block stairwell with Otis's grin imprinted in his memory, Jon tried to mentally prepare for the danger ahead with each step. He encountered no resistance on his way down the three flights of stairs to the Level D entrance, but held tight to the taser in his right hand as he peered through the door's window. Seeing no movement, he inched the door open, stepped inside, and started down the corridor. When he heard the sound of approaching voices, he retraced his steps and ducked into the first open room on the left. He closed the door behind him. Illuminating the dark space with his headlamp, he found himself standing in a large storage closet containing a variety of medical supplies neatly organized on labeled shelves.

As the voices came closer, he turned off the headlamp and crouched beneath the door's window. When the voices became muffled, he peeked out the window to see two figures, one in a military uniform and the other in a white lab coat standing in an open elevator across the hallway, several yards to the left. When the doors closed, Jon watched the letters on the display above the elevator light up in succession from D to C and then stop at B. He checked his watch. 4:07. He had to act. Mustering all of his courage, he exited the room, walked down the hall with taser in hand, and entered the infirmary by pushing the windowless door inward.

The room was smaller than he expected, with only four beds, three of which were empty. The other was surrounded by a white curtain. A lone Air Force guard dozed in a chair at the end of the second bed. Upon seeing Jon enter, he stood up and reached for his holster. Before he could draw the gun, Jon stunned him with the taser. As the uniformed man crumpled to the floor, Jon hurried to the second bed and opened the curtains. Mona was sitting up in bed with a startled look. She wore an ankle cast on her right leg and was dressed in a green hospital gown. Her left hand was handcuffed to the bed rail. Except for her hair being ruffled, she looked remarkably intact.

"Jesus, Jon, what took you so long to get here? I've been rotting in this place."

Jon grinned. "We're taking the next flight out. Otis and Wendell are jacking the Fox, and we've got ten minutes to meet them on the upper level. Where are the keys?" he asked, looking at the cuffs.

"On a retractable key chain locked to his belt loop. You're gonna have to drag the asshole over here to unlock these," she said, tugging on the handcuffs.

Jon lifted the man up from behind, dragged him over, and draped him over the bed while Mona located the key and unlocked the manacles. As they fell to the floor with a clang, she rolled out of the bed and grabbed the soldier's gun from his holster. When the man groaned and started to move, she hit him over the head with the butt of the gun. He fell to the floor in a heap.

"Don't ever try and mess with me again, flyboy."

She got out of bed and picked up a pair of crutches, which were leaning against the wall. "Let's go."

"We're gonna have to try to take the elevator, I don't think we'll make it on the stairs with you on crutches."

"I'm game."

Jon peeked out from the hallway door and signaled for them to proceed to the elevator, whose display still indicated that it was on the B level. "I don't think anybody's used it since I went into the sick bay. Let's hope it's empty."

He pushed the call button and waited to the side with Mona, their weapons drawn. A lifetime seemed to pass before the elevator finally descended to the D Level and the door opened. No passengers. They boarded the elevator. A sigh of relief.

"A Level. With any luck, it's where they'll be waiting for us." He held down the button in the hope that it would override any calls to stop on other floors. He checked his watch. It was 4:15. They had passed C when the elevator started to slow down.

"Oh, shit, we're stopping on B," Mona said.

"Get ready," Jon said.

He stepped to one side and Mona to the other, both of them flattening their bodies to the walls. The door opened and a tall man in a white lab coat got on. Before he could react, Mona tripped him with one of her crutches. He fell to the floor, and Jon zapped him with the taser. The door closed, and the elevator remained stationary. Jon jostled the A button.

"Go, go, get a move on. What are you waiting for, New Year's?" Mona said, hitting the tip of her crutch against the wall of the elevator.

After several seconds, it finally proceeded upward to A Level. The door opened. They stepped over the man's body and out onto an empty aluminum platform.

"It won't be long before somebody finds him," Mona said, as the elevator doors closed behind them.

Jon and Mona headed to the edge of the observation deck butted by a metal railing. One hundred feet below was an expansive, dimly lit indoor space the size of a football field. Jon and Mona cautiously leaned over the rail and saw the black metallic flying disc hovering above the well in the floor of the hangar. Also on the floor in front of the disc were two long, parallel rows of flickering fluorescent lights that resembled a runway. He could hear the craft humming at a low frequency.

"That's it. They've got the Fox. They're right on schedule."

A loud click sounded, and an array of high intensity track lights in the ceiling illuminated the hangar's interior. Seconds later, a gap in the far wall appeared and continued to widen as opposite portions of the wall retracted to either side, opening the hangar to the outside.

"So that's the way out," Mona said.

Jon looked back down—the disc was climbing in their direction. "C'mon baby, you can do it." He took a deep breath and waited.

Suddenly, horns began to blare and two powerful searchlights zeroed in on Jon and Mona's position.

"Don't move or you both die. We've got you in our sights," boomed a voice from a loudspeaker.

With Mona and Jon frozen in place, the opening in the far wall began to rumble and started to close. Jon watched in disbelief and wondered if Wendell and Otis would make it out of the facility at all.

"Jesus, get going, you guys," he shouted, his heart pounding.

Unexpectedly, and with great speed and dexterity, the disc banked ninety degrees into a vertical position so that it was now perpendicular to the floor. A split second later, the Ebony Fox zoomed out sideways through the narrow slit into the night and was gone.

CHAPTER—25

Two Air Force guards escorted Jon into a meeting room on C Level and seated him at a polished wooden table in a cushioned leather chair, a guard to either side of him. He was wondering what they were going to do with him, and where they had taken Mona, when a two-star general dressed in fatigues burst into the room behind him.

"Who took the vehicle, and where the hell did they go with it?" he demanded.

The general was close to an interrogation of a more physical sort when a man dressed in an immaculately tailored three-piece gray suit and walking with a slight limp entered the room. Jon could see that his well-groomed and gray-tinged hair nicely complemented his sharply chiseled features. *David Kreeger.*

"General Patterson, please leave us for now. Dr. Drake and I have some important business to attend to," Kreeger said.

He accompanied the disgruntled high-ranking officer out of the room, leaving the Air Force guards behind with Jon.

Still reeling from his unsuccessful escape attempt, Jon desperately tried to get a grip on himself. He remembered the relaxation exercises Lucas had taught him and took several deep breaths. Feeling calm enough to take in his surroundings, he now noticed the left wall had a mural in the form of a time line that depicted important people and events in the history of genetics. As he scanned the panel from left to right, he recognized the portraits of Gregor Mendel, Charles Darwin, and the *Drosophila* geneticist Thomas Hunt Morgan seated at his Caltech lab bench before rows of mason jars containing his experimental fruit flies. Near to Morgan, James Watson and Francis Crick posed with the DNA double helix, and, further to the right, Francis Collins and Craig Venter stood by a phalanx of DNA sequencers in celebration of the recently completed Human Genome Project.

Jon was staring at the far end of the mural when Kreeger reentered the room carrying a briefcase. His gray pallor and gaunt look were even more evident up close. After dismissing the two guards, he approached Jon and touched him on the shoulder.

"There's a place for the two of us on the time line, Jonathan. Think of what we can do together," he said.

The familiar tone threw him off balance. His father had been the last person to call him Jonathan. He felt his shoulder muscles tighten.

"The genome map is a major accomplishment for humankind, especially since DNA was discovered a little over fifty years ago," Kreeger said. "But you and I both know that even with three billion individual bits of DNA sequence in hand, we still have no real idea how the genetic blueprint works cooperatively to choreograph and form a complete disease-free organism."

Kreeger sat down next to Jon and poured himself a glass of water from a sterling silver pitcher. He picked it up, took a sip, and motioned toward him.

"I've followed your stellar career, Jonathan, and still maintain that your creation of cancer-prone transgenic mice stands as a seminal event in cancer biology."

Jon stared silently at the man and watched him move his chair closer.

"I need your help, Jonathan. It's time we compared notes.

By harnessing the power of the master orchestrator gene, we can shape the future of biological science. We can cure cancer. We can regenerate organs. We can eradicate neurodegenerative diseases, heart disease, you name it, we can cure it. We must seize the moment. Think of the contribution we can make to mankind."

Jon said nothing. Kreeger put the goblet back down on the pewter serving tray and stared back at him.

"Would you like some water?" he asked.

"Where's Mona?"

Kreeger sat back in his chair and rocked back and forth.

"I'm glad you asked. I can assure you that she is fine and will continue to be so, provided that you and I continue our productive dialogue. If this proves to be the case, I'm sure a series of private visits can be arranged. In fact, I want you both to join me for dinner tonight in my quarters."

Jon leaned back in his chair and remained silent for several moments. He was relieved that Mona wouldn't be harmed if he cooperated. God knows he wanted to strangle Kreeger for killing his friend. *Just stay cool*, he kept telling himself, *just stay cool*. He thought of Lucas and his calm demeanor.

"I'll take you up on the water."

"Delighted," Kreeger said. He filled the glass to the top and gave it to Jon, who took a long sip. "And the dinner invitation?"

"I'm looking forward to it."

"Delighted, again."

Jon hesitated for a moment, then asked, "What's there to talk about?"

Kreeger put the goblet back down on the polished tabletop.

"We have an operation to perform, young man."

"Operation?"

"A genetically engineered boy, who I thought would be our first long-term success, has developed shortness of breath and is not doing well."

"So, he's developing lung tumors like the others," Jon said.

"Correct, and it may be our only chance to isolate the

236   *Paul K. Pattengale*

regulator elements from the master gene before they degenerate and self-destruct. If we're in any way successful, we've got a fighting chance to reverse the cancerous process in the boy. I hate to see him suffer like that."

Jon was taken aback by Kreeger's show of humanity but still seriously questioned the man's sincerity.

Kreeger stood up, took off his suit coat, and carefully placed it on the back of his chair. While the older man poured himself more water, Jon struggled with his feelings—extreme anger toward his captor yet excitement over the possibility of isolating the regulator from a living person. Maybe it was his own fatigue and overriding fear of being harmed that was playing tricks with his mind, but Kreeger seemed calm, well informed, and completely in control. More than that, his unexpected charisma was impossible to ignore.

"So where do I fit in?" Jon asked, feeling more relaxed.

Kreeger leaned forward and folded his hands.

"You, Jonathan, are unique. First of all, you already have direct experience with the precise microanatomy and pathology of the malformed implant tissues. But more importantly, your laser-capture technique will allow us to pinpoint exactly where the normal cells are mutating and giving rise to abnormal cancerous progeny. It is at that boundary where the master orchestrator gene is hyper-functioning—where the control elements are being overwhelmed and inactivated, and it is from precisely this site that we will isolate and purify the *cancer regulator*. Since the master gene functions so rapidly in these boys, it affords us the unique opportunity to dissect the cancer-causing mechanism at the exact moment of malignant change. Soon we will have the cure."

"So we need to biopsy the boy's skin-lung connecting structure to get the necessary tissue?" Jon asked.

"Precisely—that's our task. I have all the equipment. By localizing this normal-cell/cancer-cell boundary zone, we will directly compare the cancer-preventing genes to the cancer-causing ones. Our goal is obvious. We must isolate the regulator elements capable of shutting down the cancer—the braking mechanism, the stop-switch capable of halting the malignant process. It's the cure we are looking for, and the cure we will find." Kreeger was positively levitating out of his seat. "Think of it, Jonathan, a cure for cancer. Think of the benefits to humankind."

"I see your logic," Jon said, staring deep into Kreeger's eyes, trying to contain his enthusiasm.

§

When Jon awoke to the knock on the door of his room, the military wall clock read 1300 hours. He had slept for seven hours following his initial meeting with Kreeger.

"Come in," he called from the bed. The door opened to Mona standing with crutches beside an armed guard.

"You've got twenty minutes, ma'am. I'll be waiting out here for you," he said.

"I'll bet you will," she said, giving him a dirty look.

After he closed the door, she hopped around the suite, opening and closing drawers and then checking the floor, walls, and ceilings. She said nothing. After she was satisfied that there were no bugging devices, she kissed him, crutches in hand, and then sat down at a small circular table in the middle of his room. He briefed her on what had happened since her capture at the boat dock on Mono Lake.

"I'm so glad that you're feeling better. That was a close call. Your lab really came through for you," she said.

"I just wish that we could have had the antivirus prep for Elliot." He looked away and then back at her. "Now I want to focus on the boy and the cure. I can't bring Elliot back." He swallowed hard, trying to contain his feelings for his childhood friend.

Mona looked impatient. "So, Kreeger kissed your ass, treated you like royalty, called you Jonathan, and otherwise charmed the pants off you. I'll give that conniving son of a bitch a time line or two to think about."

"Lighten up, Mona. He says he wants to save the boy. I can buy into that. Besides, we've got to play along with him. It may be our only chance to get out of here in one piece. He's the big boss in these parts, for sure. He even got the general to back off. There wasn't another word said to me about the Ebony Fox and who jacked it. Did they hassle you about it?"

"Not a word. Kreeger must want something mighty big from you. So, what's so special about this technology that you're patenting, and why does he want it so bad?"

"When I was at U.C.L.A., I developed a technique for localizing genetic mutations using a combination of dye staining and laser capture."

"In English, please," she said.

"I specifically bred mice with errors or mutations in their DNA, and because of that, they had a high incidence of cancer. Then I worked out a dye-injection technique so I could visualize the mutated cells as they were forming the cancers in the affected tissues."

"You could see the mutated cells because they contained the color of the dye?" she asked.

"That's correct."

"And the laser capture piece?"

"That's the cool part. You biopsy the dyed tissues, make a section, overlay it with a membranous film, find the colored, mutating cells under the microscope, and zap them with a laser."

"Doesn't that harm the cells?" Mona asked.

"That's precisely the point. The laser beam breaks open the cancer-prone cell. The DNA and RNA spill out and can be captured on the film. After that, the nucleic acids are purified, and the good and the bad genes in the cells are able to be identified and then compared to one another in a side-by-side analysis. Basically, you can pinpoint the cellular origin of the cancer, then isolate and purify the regulator DNA, and from there you can devise targeted strategies that can cure it once it's already established. And even prevent it from happening in the first place!" Jon said.

"Man, it *is* the cure. No wonder Kreeger wants your technology. So, the patent's still pending, which means that he hasn't been able to put his dirty little paws on it yet."

"Correct."

"Don't underestimate him, Jon. He has the equipment and reagents, but he doesn't know how to put all the pieces together. That's what he needs you for—so he can cure *his own* cancer. Don't ever forget that."

Jon nodded.

"But from what you told me, you and your lab are close to isolating the regulator, while he's still struggling with it."

Jon nodded again.

"That's right. We're farther along than he is, but I still have a long way to go. We're definitely limited by the autopsy material, and I'm convinced that a viable biopsy has definite experimental advantages. In fact, I think we have a much better shot with Kreeger's involvement. In fact, I'm pretty psyched up about it. I've spent my whole professional life waiting for this opportunity. This could be it."

"You're holding some pretty big trump cards. Once you've played your hand, he's not going to need you anymore. Have you thought of that? Have you forgotten about Elliot?" she asked.

"No way. How could I? In fact, I have to repress the urge to go for his throat," he said, motioning with his hands. "I've been tempted to ask about Elliot, but the mere mention of his name will set me off big time. I've got to control my feelings and keep him off balance. I'll go along with him for as long as I can, but we're gonna need an action plan at some point."

There was a hard knock on the door.

"Time's up. I'm outta here," she said, checking her watch.

"Where are you being kept?" Jon asked.

"Same infirmary, same bed."

Before leaving, she leaned over and kissed him again. He felt the moistness of her lips, the softness of her touch.

"Be careful, Jon. Watch your backside."

CHAPTER—26

Two hours later, Jon, dressed in a white lab coat, stood next to David Kreeger in his research suite. He opened his lab notebook and showed it to Jon.

"Here is the sketched-out protocol. I need you to add the details and go over the equipment list. You can work in my office if you like," he said.

Jon followed Kreeger to an open door, which led to a spacious room containing an L-shaped desk, a circular table with four chairs, and a large rosewood bookcase. On the walls was a series of watercolor paintings depicting various waterfront scenes with boats, wharves, nets, and multicolored floats hanging from the outer walls of fishing shacks. He studied them.

"Are they East Coast?" he asked, sitting down at the table.

"My mother was a painter. She spent summers on Martha's Vineyard."

Kreeger was handing Jon several bound notebooks when two lab personnel, one male and the other female, entered the office.

"Dr. Kreeger, the boy is asking for you again," the man said.

"Well, Dr. Drake, I guess it's time you met our young patient. Follow me."

241

Jon accompanied Kreeger and the two lab assistants to a small alcove at the far end of the lab suite, where a bronze-faced boy with long, straight black hair lay face up in a hospital bed. IVs were planted firmly in both arms. An EKG monitor beeped in the background. Jon could see that the boy had a regular but rapid rhythm with a pulse rate of 116. The boy looked at them and pulled up the charcoal-colored Air Force blankets under his chin with his scaly hands, his breathing obviously shallow and labored.

"I'm cold," the boy complained.

Jon approached the bed and tucked the blanket around the boy's shoulders. He gazed up at Jon and smiled faintly.

"Ephraim, this is Dr. Drake. He's helping me. What can we do for you?" Kreeger asked, speaking softly.

"Dr. Kreeger, the general promised me I could go home after the water-training exercises," he said, tears in his eyes.

"You've developed some medical problems that we didn't expect. That's why you're still here. I told you about the operation that's going to make you well. Dr. Drake is helping me make you better. After that, we'll talk about going home." Kreeger sounded empathic and anxious at the same time.

As they exited the enclosure, Jon saw the boy's dark, searching eyes tracking his every movement. Jon looked back and nodded, trying to reassure the boy with his eyes that he would be okay and resisting the urge to go over and touch him.

After returning to Kreeger's office, Jon attempted to cross-check the equipment list and then to write out the experimental details of the laser-capture procedure. But as hard as he tried, he couldn't block out the boy's pained image or suppress his memories of the Gonzalez boys. Finally, he forced himself to focus. Kreeger rejoined him at 1700 hours.

"How does it look?" Kreeger asked.

"I think we can manage with the equipment you've assembled. The hardest part is the procedure itself. I've written down the steps, but doing it successfully is something else again. There are some real tricks to it," Jon said.

"I'm counting on you to teach it to me, Jonathan. Now go, get some rest, and freshen up. I'll see you and Ms. Larsen in my quarters," he said.

§

After rechecking that there were no bugging devices in Jon's room, Mona sat down next to him on the bed. She lifted her left foot and twisted it back and forth.

"How does it look without the cast? It wasn't really broken, they said. It was only a bad bruise and a moderate sprain. I think they were just trying to keep me down."

"Maybe the color's a little bit off, but it's otherwise okay. How does it feel?" Jon asked.

"Strong enough to escape with," she said.

"I've been so fixated on the cure, and now on Ephraim, I haven't even thought about escaping. I need to conserve all my energy and concentrate on the operation. That's why I want us to relax and have a civilized dinner with him tonight."

She straightened up and pressed her palms onto the bed.

"I don't care what he says and how he carries himself, Kreeger's the mastermind behind the human experiments. I've learned more."

"More?" Jon asked.

"You were right. The magnetite virus wasn't designed for killing."

"What was it designed for then?"

"Mind control," she answered. "In a magnetic field, an affected person can theoretically be commanded at will. It's an old CIA theory that never worked. But with a targeted magnetite virus and a superimposed external magnetic field, it's becomes more scientifically feasible. In fact, it was a great way for Kreeger and his buddies to get you, Johnstone, and Adams to sign your patent rights away to them. But they botched the experiment—big time!"

"I never … who told you this?" Jon asked.

"Otis and Wendell's inside connection made contact with me. He's the deputy security chief. His name is Jacob Savino. He worked with them on the Ebony Fox project. He's on our side."

Jon thought for a moment.

"If what you say is true, the virus didn't work as planned on Elliot and Johnstone. They must have gotten a nasty batch of virus."

"That's what Savino said. Apparently, the virus was designed to target only the thalamus, but all the lots were bad and they spread to additional locations," she said.

"Jesus, Kreeger's got to be thinking that I'm still infected."

"Who knows what he's thinking or what he will do. He's desperate and capable of anything. Watch out for him. That's the only advice I can give to you," she said. "There's more. Kreeger and Patterson have developed a biologic weapon that attracts insects. It's some kind of insect hormone in the form of an aerosol spray. Wasn't there something like that in Bright Star's blood?" Mona asked.

"There was. It means that the old Indian must have been part of an engineered pheromone experiment that was being field-tested in Baja."

"Poor Bright Star. He didn't deserve that," Mona said.

"It's too much to absorb," Jon said. "So Savino's still in touch with Wendell and Otis? Is that right?"

"Affirmative."

"Then he's our ticket out of here. But, Mona, we've got to play it cool. We can't show our hand," Jon said firmly, gritting his teeth and trying hard to hold back his rage as he visualized Bright Star's insect-ravaged body.

§

At 2000 hours, an Air Force sergeant escorted Jon and Mona

Orchestrator   245

to David Kreeger's private quarters on the B level. They were led into a spacious music-filled room and seated at a dining table adorned with three immaculate place settings and a central arrangement of fiery red poinsettias. An oak wine rack sat on a side table next to a sound system on which the large digital display read *Mozart, Symphony No. 40 in G minor, Kirschel 550.* Photographs of a lush hilltop winery with an adjacent stone mansion overlooking a deep valley hung on the walls.

"You're free to pick any one of my private reserve selections, Jonathan, but I would highly recommend the pinot noir."

Mona fingered one of the red leaves on the centerpiece.

"They're real, Ms. Larsen," Kreeger added.

"Nice holiday touch," she attempted.

"I'm pleased you like it. And I'm honored you chose to join us for our little celebration."

An appetizer of caviar, crackers, and a shot of cold vodka was followed by racks of lamb on a bed of lentils and garlic. Midway through the dinner, Jon finally found himself feeling relaxed and, seeing that Kreeger was in the mood to talk, asked about the DNA experiments. He took another sip of the Highridge pinot and focused his attention on their host as the second Bach cello suite began playing in the background.

"First, we reversed the handedness of the DNA orientation in human stem cells, then specialized them with conditioned media into organ cultures, and eventually implanted them into adult mice. The experiments worked remarkably well, and the animals weren't harmed. We went ahead with the human experiments and found that they functioned in the boys at first but deteriorated to cancer over time," Kreeger said.

"And the mice didn't get cancer?" Jon asked.

"They eventually did, but only when I repeated the experiments in younger mice."

Mona growled and fidgeted in her chair.

"I know you think I'm a monster, Miss Larsen."

"You took the words right out of my mouth," she said looking him straight in the eye.

"Yes, I agree, an unexpected and terrible result. But also an opportunity—the isolation of the cure, the braking mechanism, *the regulator*," Kreeger countered.

Mona continued to glare at Kreeger.

"Aren't there over a hundred different types of cancer?" Mona finally asked.

Kreeger nodded.

"So if that's true, you need a hundred different cures? How are you going to deal with that?"

He smiled.

"A very insightful question, and the same one we asked ourselves. I'm truly impressed with your intuitive skills. You see, Ms. Larsen, deciphering and isolating the regulator element will provide us with a common cure that is universal for *all* cancers, a *master cure* of sorts," Kreeger explained.

"He's right, Mona. When the master orchestrator is operative in a stem cell with a functioning regulator, it's capable of driving *all* cell types, first to divide and then to stop and become quiescent," Jon said.

"Because of that, the braking mechanism is a *master regulator* and will work against *all* types of cancer. It's a huge payoff," Kreeger exclaimed. He lifted his wine glass. "To the *master cure!* It's within our reach!"

§

He lay in a creaky hospital bed, arms and legs restrained, looking for his parents—but only his mother peered at him through the glass window in the door to the room. He called to her, asking where his father was, but she didn't respond. Suddenly, a masked figure in a white coat entered the room carrying a hypodermic syringe with a dripping needle. As the figure moved toward him, Jon tried to scream but couldn't. As he inched closer, the figure spoke to him and pointed toward Jon's mouth.

Orchestrator   247

"Open up and say 'Ah.' This won't hurt—just a little sting under the tongue." The figure motioned with the syringe.

Jon finally was able to scream, this time over and over.

"Stop injecting me. Stop trying to control my mind," he yelled, the sweat beading off his forehead.

Jon awoke to the loud knocking on his door and sat up in bed wondering what had just happened to him. He went to the door and opened it. The time was 0500.

"Dr. Drake, Dr. Kreeger is asking for you *now*."

CHAPTER—27

Jon threw on the scrubs hanging in his closet and hurried to the room adjacent to the operating area. Once there, he prepped the equipment and reagents necessary for the laser-capture technique. He completed a successful, mock run-through of the procedure, then entered the compact, windowless operating room. There he met David Kreeger, who was preparing a clear liquid for injection into the IV bag of the young patient lying on a steel gurney in the middle of the room.

"This combination of drugs should give us the sedation we need to do the procedure without subjecting our young patient to intubation and the risks of general anesthesia," Kreeger said, pulling the liquid into the syringe and then placing it on a table next to the boy.

Several minutes later, he and Jon stood in the scrub area next to the operating room.

"The reason I called you so early was that we couldn't wait any longer. I'm afraid he's going downhill faster than we thought. We need to obtain the tissue before it deteriorates any further. I want a good viable specimen," Kreeger said, scrubbing his hands vigorously with the clear hexidine solution.

248

Orchestrator 249

Jon finished washing up, looked through the glass window, and then focused on the boy. An IV hung to one side of the bed, an index finger monitor registered his pulse rate and percent oxygen saturation, and a green surgical sheet covered his body. The boy was still conscious and alert as Jon walked out of the scrub room, entered the OR, and approached the stretcher. Kreeger was injecting the sedative cocktail into the IV line and had started to infuse it into the boy at a constant rate.

"Ephraim, you're about to go to sleep," he said.

Jon looked down at the boy, who was breathing rapidly and obviously in distress.

"What's up, Ephraim?" Jon asked.

"I'm scared," he said, his voice high-pitched.

"Hang in there. We'll get you through this, I promise," Jon said, giving him the thumbs-up sign.

The boy managed to force a smile and then closed his eyes and drifted off. A male scrub nurse approached Jon and fitted him with a gown and gloves. He then did the same for Kreeger.

"Let's get started. We haven't much time," Kreeger said.

The nurse focused the overhead light on the operative field, which was carefully draped and squared off with aqua-green towels. Drake and Kreeger moved into position around the boy.

"Are we ready?" Kreeger asked, peering up at Jon, who was looking at the digital display of the pulse oximeter attached to the boy's index finger.

"It's a go," he answered. "His oxygen saturation is good at ninety-six percent."

Kreeger started the procedure by picking up a pair of forceps from a stainless steel tray and probing the skin-lung connecting structure on the boy's right side. Seeing that the boy was now adequately sedated and not reacting to external stimuli, he proceeded with the operation and exposed the right skin-lung connecting structure in its entirety.

"It's completely filled with tumor, and it looks like it's growing right in front of us. I've never seen anything like this before,"

Kreeger said, poking the gelatinous masses with the tips of his forceps.

"Let's hope the other structure's not so involved with obvious cancer. If it is, there goes our chance for the cure," Kreeger said, his forehead visibly moist.

"Keep your fingers crossed," Jon said.

After several minutes of exploration on the opposite side, Kreeger determined that the left tubular column was still accessible and intact. Then he dissected and exposed the bulk of the left skin-lung connecting structure using a set of metal retractors, which pulled the adjacent skin to either side of the tissue. He moved closer, inspected the operative field, and then sighed with relief.

"It's still intact, anatomically sound, and well demarcated. We've definitely got something here. Stand by for the dye-injection procedure."

Jon beamed as he handed the syringe to Kreeger.

As Kreeger moved closer with the needle, time seemed to stand still for Jon. He thought of his father and how he had suffered with his cancer and how he could have benefited from what they were about to discover. In fact, all future cancer victims would be winners, Jon thought, as Kreeger injected one cubic centimeter of the green dye into the pillar-like structure. They watched the color diffuse into the tissue and then, several minutes later, saw it localize specifically to a small five-millimeter portion of the column.

"That colored band is the boundary zone where the master gene is malfunctioning and where the cells are transitioning to the cancerous state. That's the area we want. That's where the regulator is still functioning," Jon said, trying to contain his excitement. "Oxygen sat holding at ninety-five percent."

"Roger that, Jonathan," Kreeger responded, his eyes gleaming. He set down the syringe and picked up a fresh scalpel, its cutting edge gleaming in the bright surgical light, which had be repositioned by the scrub nurse.

Orchestrator   251

But when Kreeger clasped the tissue column with the forceps and prepared to incise the colored area of the tissue, the boy unexpectedly twitched and coughed. He released his hold on the tissue and then grasped it again. This time Ephraim threw his thickened, scaly arms out to the side in a staccato-like jerking motion.

"Jesus, I thought he was under," Kreeger yelled.

"He's allergic to the dye," Jon offered.

"Then he needs more sedation! Nurse! Double the drug concentration in the IV bag and increase the infusion rate by twenty-five percent. *We need this biopsy*," Kreeger said, motioning nervously to the assistant.

Jon watched the scrub nurse scurry around and fill another syringe with the amber-colored sedative cocktail that Kreeger had prepared. He injected half of the syringe into the bag and readjusted the infusion setting. He placed the half-filled syringe on the table and then turned the page on the boy's medical chart and recorded the drug amounts. After waiting several minutes for the drugs to take effect, Kreeger poked at the tissue column with his forceps, this time evoking a noticeable but less severe response.

"His oxygen saturation is down to eight-five percent and falling," Jon said, studying the monitor.

"Nurse, he needs to be brought down further!" Kreeger demanded.

"Are you certain, Dr. Kreeger?" the nurse answered.

"Nurse, he needs stronger medications!"

"I'll check with my commanding officer and be back pronto."

After the nurse left the room, Jon focused on the boy.

"Oxygen saturation is eighty percent and his breathing rate is decreasing, Dr. Kreeger, he can't take any more meds. He's headed south! He's not going to make it, at this rate!"

"Jonathan, you don't understand. I need the operative field to be completely motionless. I must have a pure specimen."

"I totally get it. You're putting this child's life at risk to save your own life."

"My life?"

"I know you have leukemia. I know you're dying!"

Kreeger appeared startled, paused for a moment, and addressed Jon face-to-face.

"It's not just *my* life. I know more about you than you may think. It could have been your father's life. How about your life and the lives of your children?"

"I'm concerned about *this child's life!*" Jon yelled.

Jon couldn't stand by any longer. He reached over and pressed the stop button on the infusion pump. He glared at Kreeger.

"Listen to me and listen to me carefully. I won't let you kill this boy. I promised him that we would take care of him. You've already killed too many children. It's got to stop!"

Kreeger, who now had beads of sweat on his face, twisted and turned.

"It's the cure, Jonathan, how can you ignore that? Are you mad?"

"I didn't think that this boy would be irreversibly harmed—worse than that, killed by the procedure. He's failing. How can you ignore that? He's counting on us to save him. Did you see the look on his face before he went to sleep? Are you that callous, that unethical?"

"How can you fault me, Jonathan? I'm failing too. I need what he has. The world needs what he has. I implore you to do the right thing, Jonathan."

"I am."

"Don't jump to conclusions, Jonathan. I don't want this boy to die either. I only want an acceptable biopsy."

"Is that why the chart has been stamped and signed with the *Do Not Resuscitate* order on every bloody page? I don't believe a word you say," Jon said, grabbing and holding up Ephraim's chart. "What do you say to this!"

"I, I … " Kreeger stammered.

He shook his fist at Jon.

"And what about Elliot? How do you explain that!"

"It was a bad lot of virus—it wasn't intentional. My colleagues did it without my permission. I only wanted to share the patent rights with him," Kreeger answered.

"You murdered him and almost murdered me. If only I could have gotten the antidote to Elliot sooner. You're going to pay, Kreeger," Jon said.

Kreeger lunged at Jon with the scalpel blade. Jon snatched up the half-filled syringe of sedative from the table, grabbed Kreeger's outstretched hand by the wrist, and injected its entire contents into the thumb pad of his palm. The scalpel fell to the floor. As Kreeger screamed, Jon moved closer, restrained him with a body lock, and put his hand over his mouth. Kreeger squirmed and fought but began to weaken as the drug started to take effect.

"That's right, Kreeger. I've been thinking about how to really treat this boy. Have you forgotten about conventional chemotherapy? His case is unique—his cells are dividing so fast and so synchronously that a modest dose of a cell-cycle inhibitor like cytoxan should kill the majority of his cancer cells without harming his normal cells. Whatever's left can be eliminated with some follow-up low-dose combination chemotherapy. It shouldn't harm the boy. In fact, it should cure him. Did you forget the Hippocratic oath? Do no harm!" Jon said, loosening his grip on Kreeger's mouth.

"You'll destroy all the important tissues in him. There will be nothing left to work with. He's my last real chance," Kreeger moaned in a low voice, the drugs taking him deeper.

When the nurse reentered the OR, Kreeger was motionless in Jonathan's arms.

"Nurse, Dr. Kreeger has fainted, and I need to get him some help. I stopped the anesthesia drip temporarily. Infuse one gram of Cytoxan into the IV, and follow it with normal saline. Resume the anesthesia drip, but make sure his oxygen level stays above ninety percent. Find another surgeon to sew him up and then take him to the recovery room. He should do fine."

"Roger that, Dr. Drake," the nurse answered, giving him a thumbs-up.

§

Jon slowly wove his way through the C level with David Kreeger lapsing in and out of consciousness and clinging to Jon's shoulder as if his life depended on it. He took the elevator to the D level, walked a short distance, and entered the infirmary to find Mona sitting on a chair with an armed serviceman standing over her. She stood up, indicating that she wasn't being physically restrained any longer.

"What happened to Dr. Kreeger?" the guard asked.

"He fainted during the operation," Jon said, placing him on the bed behind them.

When the guard got close to the outstretched body, Kreeger started to groan.

"I'm calling for help." The soldier removed the walkie-talkie from his belt.

Before he could speak into the receiver, the door opened and a trim middle-aged officer carrying a two-way radio walked into the room.

"Colonel Savino, sir, I'm calling for help. Dr. Kreeger is unconscious and needs assistance."

"It's not necessary, Sergeant, I've already notified General Patterson, and we're dispatching a doctor from A level. Go see if you can hurry him up," the officer replied.

"Yes, sir."

As soon as the man left the room, Savino pulled out a remote and pointed it at the internal surveillance camera, which was hanging from the ceiling. He then took out a piece of paper and a set of keys from his pants pocket.

"That's better. The security camera is cycling through a loop of Ms. Larsen being guarded earlier this morning. We don't have much time, so listen up. These fit a Hummer in the motor bay." He placed a set of keys in Mona's hand. "It's in stall 500. Here's how you get to it from here. You should have a clear path." He pointed to the map and traced the way with his finger.

"It's a standard transmission, nothing fancy. Also, there's a loaded handgun under the right seat. The exit gate will be open. Once you're out of the bay, follow a compass setting of 045 to the north-northeast. You know you're on course if you're headed for a black flat-topped mesa. It's the only one visible from the compound."

"How do we get past the fenced perimeter?" Jon asked.

"Just follow the compass setting, and Sweeney and Thackery will be out there waiting for you."

"Out there?" Mona asked.

"Trust me," he said, handing Jon the map.

"Thanks. You really came through for us," Jon said.

"Don't mention it, Doctor. It's the least I can do. I saw what you did for the boy. He's going to be okay. I'll keep an eye on him. There've been some real bad things happening around here, and it's time they stopped. Here's another example that I told Ms. Larsen about. Take it with you as evidence."

He handed the small white aerosol can to Mona.

"The infamous insect pheromone spray," she said, putting it into her left jean pocket.

Savino nodded as his two-way radio crackled with activity.

"Colonel Savino, a security team's headed for the infirmary. They should be there in two to three minutes."

"Ten-four," he answered. "You two better get a move on. Go through the back door. Follow the map from there. I'll watch you until you're outta the compound. Now go!"

After leaving the infirmary, Jon and Mona raced down a rear corridor to the opposite end of the building where they accessed another stairwell and made their way up to the A level. From there they entered a larger room where several corridors branched off to the sides. Following the map, they hurried down the middle corridor, opened the door at its end, and crept onto the concrete loading dock with its overhang of metal eaves. A fenced compound containing a row of vehicles stood below.

"There it is," Jon said pointing to the Hummer in the stall at the far end nearest the exit gate.

He started down the stairs.

"Hit the deck," Mona said, dropping to the ground.

Jon looked and saw two soldiers walking across the compound.

"Stay low—they're just passing through," she whispered.

From where he was crouching on the outside stairwell, Jon could see a bevy of insects flying around Mona. He looked at the metal overhang and saw a line of mud nests on the underside of the eaves.

"Jesus, what are they? They're crazed," she said.

"They're wasps, and they're attracted to the aerosol in your pocket," he said, watching several large yellow and black insects land on her blue jeans.

"But the attractant is inside the can. It must really be strong stuff. Let's go, those guys are gone."

Before Jon could react, a figure in camouflaged battle fatigues burst through the doorway carrying a forty-five automatic. He first trained the firearm on Mona as she lay on the floor and then on Jon as he straddled the stairs.

"Freeze," Stringfellow said. "You two aren't going anywhere. You've both been trouble from day one. You're finished. It's over, and I'm personally going to see to it. Both of you, face down." He waved the pistol back and forth in their direction.

But when Mona rolled over onto her stomach, the wasps changed direction and flew in front of the colonel, who momentarily stopped and swatted at them. She rolled back over and scissor-kicked him across the legs. As he hit the pavement, Mona jumped up, aerosol in hand, and sprayed its contents directly into Stringfellow's face. He screamed, fired his gun in the air, and tried to cover his eyes. In the time it took for Mona to retrieve his handgun, Stringfellow's face was covered with hundreds of buzzing angry wasps. He tried to brush them off, but more swarmed down from the metal eaves and attacked his eyes and ears, then stung the insides of his nose and mouth. He flailed about like a man on fire and finally rolled off the loading dock onto the ground below with the swarm still following. His body twitched for several seconds and then he was still.

"Good riddance, asshole," Mona said, pocketing the gun.

They ran to the Hummer. Jon jumped into the driver's side and Mona into the passenger seat. He started the engine, put the vehicle into gear, and screeched out of the compound. The compass, which was mounted on the dashboard, swirled around several times in the plastic casing and finally settled on a stable reading. Jon steered the Hummer until it reached the desired setting of north-northeast at approximately forty-five degrees and then downshifted for more power. Mona activated the global positioning device.

"There's the flat-topped mesa in the distance. I'd say it's a good five miles from here. Hope Savino's right about Wendell and Otis," Jon said, tightening his seat belt. "And we're about to get some company."

Two more Hummers were racing out of the compound in a swirl of dust.

"Step on it, Jon, we can go as fast as they can."

As he accelerated through the morning mist of the desert, he saw that it was barren and flat except for scattered clusters of cacti and an occasional darting jackrabbit. He trained his sight on the mesa, which was still several miles ahead. He checked his mirrors again and spotted two helicopters headed in their direction.

"They'll be here in no time. Where the hell are Wendell and Otis!?" Mona said. She held both handguns and continued to look out the windows. "They're attack helicopters, Cobras, I think."

"Shit, we're at the fences," Jon said.

He downshifted and decelerated, trying to decide what to do next. The fence was several hundred yards in front of them and he certainly couldn't go through it, so he veered to the right with the helicopters closing the gap.

"What next?" he asked.

When he got no answer, he looked at Mona, who was practically glued to the window, her mouth open. Turning to look in the same direction, Jon saw the black disc slowly rising above the mesa into the morning sky.

"It's the Ebony Fox," she cried.

Once the craft had reached an altitude of a thousand feet, it flew toward them and then hovered above the fence. Jon looked back to see that the helicopters were now in a stationary holding pattern, but that the two pursuing Hummers were still bearing down on them at full speed. Suddenly, the disc dropped down to ground level, swooped over Jon and Mona's truck, locked onto the top of their vehicle with a magnetic device, and picked them up like an owl plucking its prey. Seconds later, they were flying through the air as if they were on a wild roller coaster ride. The horizon was tilted and the ground blurred.

"I feel like I'm going to be sick, Jon," Mona said, clutching his hand.

He felt the same, but couldn't even speak. As they soared over the perimeter fence, he mustered enough energy to turn off the Hummer's engine.

Minutes later, they were gently set down and released onto a dirt road near its intersection with U.S. Highway 95, ten miles north of Beatty.

The Ebony Fox did a figure eight and then darted off to the south.

Mona let out a yelp and gave Jon a resounding high five. He restarted the engine and turned south onto the main highway.

§

An hour later, they were standing next to the Ebony Fox in a hidden, underground hangar near the ghost town of Rhyolite. The Hummer was tucked under the front side of the craft.

"It's good to have her again. She's a beauty," Otis said touching the landing strut.

"What's the plan?" Jon asked.

"Nothing in the immediate sense. We'll eventually leak it to an investigative reporter in Vegas and then return it to the Air Force in due time," Wendell said.

"And on our own terms, Doc. I'm sure it will be quite a story," Otis said.

"I'm concerned about Ephraim. I had hoped to bring him with us."

"Not to worry, my dear doctor, we've already heard from Savino. The dark cell is imploding as we speak," Wendell said. "You must remember that Kreeger, Stringfellow, and Patterson were not popular figures and that their enemies were numerous. Jacob has assured me that the boy will not be harmed any further—that he is in good hands and recovering from the operation."

"I'm going to need to follow up with his doctors. He's going to need some more chemo before it's over."

"That can easily be arranged," Otis said.

"And Elliot's body?" Jon asked.

"It has been located and will be returned via the Washoe County Medical Examiner to Dr. Faust in June Lake for a proper coroner's autopsy. He assures me there will be ample material evidence gleaned so as to press charges against Kreeger and his henchmen," Wendell said.

Jon pumped his fist.

"And tell Colonel Savino that the antiviral antidote is available to anyone infected with Kreeger's mind-control virus. My lab will supply it as needed," he said.

"I will inform the Colonel," Wendell promised.

"No need to worry anymore, Doc. All is well. And I would

even venture to say that Agent Double Eleven now has a good chance of getting her DEA promotion and transfer," Otis said.

"Maybe we can get you to come back and fly for the Agency, Sweetcakes," she replied.

"I'll give it some thought, ma'am." He tipped his cowboy hat. "Enough of all that. You two deserve some time together to get reacquainted."

CHAPTER—28

A month later, Jonathan Drake was speaking to Abe Lowenstein in his research lab. They were discussing Ephraim Northstar's complete recovery after his response to low-dose combination chemotherapy.

"Remarkable!" Lowenstein said. "You hypothesized that the chemo targeted all the malignant cells because they were speeding in the same synchronized phases of the cell cycle."

"Correct, he has no more evidence of tumor or implanted tissue—his imaging studies are completely normal. According to Lucas Faust, he's back in school and playing with his friends. Lucas is even thinking of adopting him."

"So, the super-fast DNA no longer exists in Ephraim."

Jon nodded.

"Then the master cure can't be gotten from a living person," Lowenstein said.

"You're right. Ephraim was the last to carry it. All the others died. I'm still working with the L.A. autopsy material and trying to piece together the master orchestrator gene. It's a huge challenge. I've finally been able to characterize the regulator elements, but just when I think I've got the correct accelerator-to-regulator ratio, the cells race, sputter out, and die. In some experiments, the cells just won't start up at all. I can't find the optimal conditions—it's like a crap shoot."

"Sounds frustrating."

"It is, but I'm not giving up. I never give up."

As Jon put his lab notebook back onto the bench, Chris burst out of the office. "Dr. Drake, I just patched in Lucas Faust on the teleconferencing monitor. He's got some new information for us."

Minutes later, Drake and Lowenstein, along with Chris and Diane, were huddled around the TV screen in Jon's office.

"Jon, I've found someone you crossed paths with not too long ago. You'll enjoy talking to him again."

"Who's that?"

"He's sitting in the study looking at the diary you left with me. He's the author."

"Artemus! You found Artemus Twitchell! How? Where?"

"After our discussions, I had the Forest Service keep an eye out for him in the Bristlecone Pine area, and they found him wandering near the radio telescopes in the Owens Valley near the Big Pine turnoff during a snowstorm. He was hypothermic, and they hospitalized him in Bishop. While he was there, the docs diagnosed him with a mental fragmentation disorder and treated him for it."

"A mental fragmentation disorder?" Jon asked.

"It is a milder and more easily treatable form of schizophrenia. Apparently, he's had it for a while, and for some unknown reason had stopped taking his medication during the spring term at Deep Springs—hence the leave of absence, and the odd behavior you observed."

"Makes sense now," Jon said.

"He's on some stronger medication and is fine now. In fact, he's hoping to return to Deep Springs for the next term. He's a remarkable fellow. He's been bunking at my place for a few days. Artemus, come and join us," Faust said, motioning to his right.

Orchestrator 263

A studious-looking older man with a neatly trimmed beard and a red cardigan sweater appeared on the monitor with a magnifying glass in one hand and the diary in the other. Jon was sure he heard a jazz saxophone playing softly in the background.

"Artemus, this is Dr. Drake."

"Ah, yes, the good Dr. Faust said we had an encounter near the Westgard Pass and that I mistakenly left my diary with you. I must say my memory is a little fuzzy on the details, but I do remember your face, and being attacked by thugs. You were with a woman, weren't you? In fact, she was a beautiful, athletic woman with superior martial art skills," he said.

"Mona Larsen. We were both worried about you."

"Thanks to my doctors, I'm doing much better now."

"I still remember the history lesson you gave us on ancient Egypt."

"Yes, Egypt is still one of my passions. And the good doctor told me of your quest for the cure, and of the DNA that was retrieved from the autopsied boy. Quite an odyssey, I'd say."

"I was interested in the hieroglyphic-like characters in your diary."

"Curious, aren't they. They were written on some pieces of metallic foil that I discovered in the Bristlecone Pine forest. The translation is only partial due to the complexity of the characters."

He cleared his throat and continued.

"Wherever these glyphs came from, the writers were obsessed with life and death and the ratio of two pi to one. This is extremely interesting because ancient Egypt in its early dynasties was similarly preoccupied."

"And the two-pi-to-one ratio? What does that mean?" Jon asked.

"To the Egyptians, It was the ratio of the circumference of the base to the height of their pyramids. I've reviewed my original notes and have noticed an unusual intermingling of a four-character repeat amongst the life, death, and two-pi-to-one ratio."

"I e-mailed it to you, Jon," Faust interjected.

"Hold on, I'll call it up," Jon said, clicking on his e-mail icon and opening it. Abe, Chris, and Diane looked over his shoulder and studied the characters.

"The four characters resemble geometric figures," Artemus said.

"Correct," Chris said. "And two of them look like hexagons sharing a common side with a juxtaposed pentagon."

"And the other two are hexagons," Diane added.

"So they look like two pairs," Lowenstein said.

"Jesus, do you see it!"

"See what, Jon?" Lucas asked.

"The four bases of DNA, ATCG. Look, these two larger, two-ringed structures must represent the purines—guanine and adenine—and the smaller single-ringed structures lying on their sides are the pyrimidines, cytosine and thymine."

They all stared at each other.

"So lady and gentlemen, if these characters represent DNA, what might the life-death two-pi ratio refer to?" Artemus asked, calmly.

"Hold that thought, Artemus—your question reminds me of our DNA experiments with the master orchestrator gene. There's an accelerator portion and a regulator portion that each function like a life-and-death piece. Other analogies would be start and stop, beginning and end," Jon said, excitedly.

"My, I never thought that biology was so universal," Twitchell remarked.

"So if pi is 3.14, our next experiment on the autopsy material will be to structure a DNA accelerator–to–DNA regulator ratio of 6.28 to 1," Jon said. "Artemus, you may have given us an important lead for our next experiment."

§

Orchestrator 265

Three weeks later, after learning from a newspaper article in the *Los Angeles Times* that the former CEO of Pathgene International was hospitalized with a bleeding disorder secondary to full-blown leukemia, Jon decided to visit David Kreeger in the Stanford University Hospital. It had been several weeks since the public hearings, the plummet of Pathgene's stock, and the subsequent bankruptcy filing.

Mona drove her DEA service vehicle into the hospital drive through, stopping at the entrance.

"Call me on my cell phone when you're done. And remember, no matter what he says, he's still a snake. Be careful."

"Don't worry, I've learned my lesson." He took her face in his hands and kissed her. "I've got a great coach."

Jon went into the hospital and checked in with the charge nurse who directed him to the patient's room. When he entered, Kreeger turned and forced a faint smile. He seemed to be half machine, lost as he was in a tangle of IV tubes, poles, monitors, and cords. As Jon moved closer, Kreeger worked the controls and raised the head of the bed. Despite the gravity of Kreeger's illness and the overall weakened appearance of his body, Jon could see that his eyes were still alert and his mind strong.

"So, Dr. Drake," he said, his characteristic swagger resonating throughout his voice. "As you can see, my condition has worsened. I'm running out of options. I still may be able to buy some time with a bone marrow transplant, maybe even a cure if I'm lucky and hit the jackpot, but, as you know, at my age the odds are stacked against me. Though you may delight in that knowledge."

"I've been working on something that may interest you," Jon said.

Kreeger sat up straight in the bed and took a deep breath in, then out. "Let's hear it."

"I've pieced together the master orchestrator gene from the L.A. autopsy, and my transgenic mice carry the correct ratio of regulator sequences in a functional, activated state. So far, they haven't developed leukemia, and I don't expect them to. I'm in the process of purifying the actual regulator molecules that prevent the leukemia from occurring. This is the breakthrough I've been looking for—and leukemia is just the beginning."

"Can these molecules have a curative effect on refractory, drug-resistant leukemias like …?"

"Yes, like yours, Dr. Kreeger. Other animal experiments asking precisely that question are already in the works, and the preliminary data looks very encouraging. I should know more in a few weeks."

"And if they're cured, what about the human clinical trials to follow? Do you have those in mind yet?" he asked, reaching up a shaking hand as if he might try to grab Jon by the collar.

"I do—and they'll come in time. But you know the red tape involved."

"Damn the red tape! I trust you Jonathan—you're the best. You're brilliant. You have the cure. I'll be your first guinea pig, your first human subject, your first success. Promise me that."

Jon was silent.

"I know you think I don't deserve it." His eyes were sad and searching.

"You don't," Jon answered, then paused for a moment. "But I'll do whatever I can."

"You will?" Kreeger asked, looking surprised.

Jon nodded and stared deep into his eyes.

"I want you alive and kicking when the district attorney charges you with Elliot's murder."

§

One week later, Jon and Mona posed with Paul and Mark in front of the koala exhibit at the L.A. Zoo while Cathleen adjusted the settings on the camera and prepared to take a group picture.

"Okay, everybody closer together," she said, motioning with her left hand. "And … one, two, three … smile."

After several more shots, the group dispersed. Mona

accompanied the boys to the gift shop with a plan to meet afterwards, and Jon and Cathleen sat on a bench near the giraffes. They sat for several minutes before Jon broke the silence.

"I wonder what it would be like if one of those guys got a sore throat," he said, nodding in the direction of an adult who was busily feasting on some low-hanging foliage. "That would be one huge case of pharyngitis, wouldn't it?"

"Now that's something I hadn't considered," she said, forcing a laugh.

"C'mon Cath, lighten up. Just joking. Medicine isn't the only thing I think about. And it helps that I finally took a two-week vacation."

"Well, that's reassuring. I was beginning to wonder."

This time they laughed together.

"It took me a while, but I finally made it to the zoo with you guys. Now I'm a koala expert," he said, holding up the colorful brochure.

"It was worth the wait, Jon. We're all having a great time. And your friend is a real keeper. Keep bringing her back."

"I'm planning on it."

"Jon, something else. We can't attend Elliot's memorial service this weekend. I feel bad, but it's just not going to work for us."

"I understand. It's been a long time. No worries. I'll put in a good word for you," he said, reaching over and giving her a big hug.

"Well, it looks like the boys scored big time," Cathleen said, spotting them as they ran ahead of Mona with stuffed animals in hand.

"Uncle Jon, look," Mark said, holding up a baby koala,

"That's so cool, Mark, and it looks like Mona has the mommy. Or maybe it's the daddy?"

"It's the mommy, of course," she answered, nestling the baby in the arms of the larger bear and cradling them in the crook of her arm. "They're so cute. I've always wanted one for my collection."

"Uncle Jon, let's go see the snakes," Paul said, jumping up and down. He pointed in the direction of the reptile house.

An hour later, Jon and Mona had said their goodbyes and were walking toward the zoo exit in the direction of the parking lot.

"Had enough of my family, yet?" he joked, taking the koala and rubbing it against her nose.

"What are you talking about? They're awesome," she said, pushing back at him, and grabbing at the bear.

"Okay, okay, just checking," he said, teasing her some more and finally handing over the furry beast.

"You really are on vacation, aren't you? I've never seen you so playful and relaxed."

"I've been taking your advice."

"My advice?"

"You once told me that I think way too much about work?"

"Yes, that would be true."

"Well, I'm a changed man. I'm only thinking about you," he said, putting his arm around her.

"That definitely works," she said, moving closer and kissing him on the cheek.

"But only for two weeks," he said with a grin, snatching back the koala and running toward the zoo exit.

EPILOGUE

Elliot's memorial service was a simple affair and consisted of scattering a portion of his ashes in the forest adjacent to Lucas Faust's home in June Lake. Elliot was a nature lover and would have wanted it that way, his mother had written. Afterwards, Jon and Mona walked hand in hand on the Eastern Sierra snow pack trying to dodge Faust's newly adopted son, Ephraim Northstar, who was rolling on the ground in front of them with the three resident huskies in hot pursuit. Jon dived into the pile, throwing snow in all directions. Mona laughed and was soon joined by Otis who was following close behind.

"Doc, you're looking pretty good down there, I'd say."

"I'm feeling pretty good, Otis. What's the word?"

"Doc, something you and Miss Mona might be interested in," he said, pulling Jon to his feet with an outstretched hand. "Wendell and I got the word from a reliable source, someone pretty high up in the Air Force food chain, who confirmed that the UFO debris field in the Bristlecone Pine Forest was planted."

"So the hieroglyphics were fabricated?" Jon asked.

"That's the funny part, Doc. *They weren't.*"

"What does that mean?"

"What I mean, Doc, is that the glyphs were transcribed onto metallic foil and copied directly from the material originally retrieved from the Roswell, New Mexico, UFO debris field. I guess somebody wanted to make the Bristlecone site look authentic."

"That was over sixty years ago, Otis," Jon said.

"Right, Doc. July 1947, to be exact."

"Faust was right. Weird things happen in these parts," Jon said, clasping Mona's hand.

Breinigsville, PA USA
29 April 2010
237089BV00001B/4/P